Broken Bodies

Broken Bodies

Sally Emerson

W F HOWES LTD

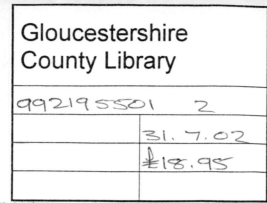

Gloucestershire
County Library

9921955501   2

31. 7. 02

£18.95

This large print edition published in 2002 by
W F Howes Ltd
Units 6/7, Victoria Mills, Fowke Street
Rothley, Leicester LE7 7PJ

1 3 5 7 9 10 8 6 4 2

First published by
Little, Brown and Company 2001

Copyright © Sally Emerson 2001

The right of Sally Emerson to be identified as
the author of this work has been asserted by her
in accordance with the Copyright, Designs and
Patents Act, 1988.

All rights reserved

A CIP catalogue record for this book is available
from the British Library

ISBN 1 84197 512 5

Typeset by Palimpsest Book Production Limited,
Polmont, Stirlingshire
Printed and bound in Great Britain
by Antony Rowe Ltd, Chippenham, Wilts

For Michael

CHAPTER 1

Anne Fitzgerald stood transfixed before a marble man fighting a marble centaur. The centaur had long since lost his head, as had the man, but still they fight on through the centuries, their battle unresolved. It seemed the man might be winning. His right arm, what was left of it, stretched back as if holding a dagger which he was about to thrust into his opponent's heart. But still the centaur reared up, still the soft folds of the man's cloak rippled, still the man remained on the very point of plunging that dagger – long since gone – into the cold stone flesh of his enemy.

'She's been here every day this week,' said one doughy-faced attendant to his colleague, who scratched his hook nose and stared.

A tall young American, Patrick Browning, overheard and glanced over at Anne who was slim, with long red wavy hair and a pale complexion which bordered on sickliness but helped to create a fragile beauty. She took what looked like a sweet out of the pocket of her coat and popped it in her mouth which was oversize and added to the drama of her face. She wore tiny red leather gloves.

1

Patrick Browning ambled across the black marble room, and stood nearby. He was from Connecticut originally, and had gone to college in Boston, then worked for a while on Wall Street before giving it all up, flamboyantly, to be a historian. Since then his life had not been flamboyant in the least, but simply hard work, with very little money. Some of his spare time was spent working as a bouncer in a club. It was not quite the elegant world of the demi-monde he had imagined when he gave up his highly paid Wall Street job. But it suited him well, in particular because it was a long way from home.

'Fabulous,' said Patrick out loud in a voice which was curiously intimate, compared with his broad-shouldered appearance. With his baggy beige corduroy trousers, belt and soft shirt, he was dressed like an English academic.

'What?' she said, turning to him. Her tone was light and slightly amused.

When he smiled, and he smiled now, his smile crashed through his face, knocking everything else out of the way. His dark brown eyes were enormous, like walking into a room covered in brown velvet.

Anne studied him for a moment then crossed her arms and returned to the battle between the centaur and the swordsman. He noted she was quite young, maybe early twenties.

'It's a fabulous piece,' continued Patrick.

'Fabulous piece!' she said, turning back to him.

She looked surprised that he was watching her hands not the sculpted frieze of centaur and warrior. 'Fabulous piece! Is that all you can say?'

'Well no,' said Patrick, 'I could . . .'

She gave the impression of having green eyes but he couldn't make them out properly in the light.

'These are the greatest existing works of Greek culture – look at the skin there – you can *see* the bowels.'

'Yes. Amazing,' said Patrick.

'Amazing!' repeated Anne contemptuously.

This conversation was not going as he would have liked but for some reason he couldn't stop. It was almost as though he was becoming annoyed by the intensity of her interest in the statues, whether because he would have preferred her to be interested in him or because he felt the statues were his own private area, he was not quite sure. He pursed his lips, and his brow felt heavy, overhanging, irritable and his hands large.

He occasionally got into fights when suffering from these particular symptoms.

The two attendants were watching Patrick and Anne with pleasure, both crossing their arms just as both Patrick and Anne were crossing theirs, as if to mock this entertaining show.

'Pity,' said Patrick, 'they should by rights be in Greece.'

'I'm sorry?' said Anne, murderously, tucking hair behind her ears, tilting her tiny chin.

His former girlfriend Kate in New York had

always been good natured, and had even been good natured about his leaving for London two years ago. He still received letters from her. Her good nature was one of the things which had made him beat his fists against the white walls of Kate's upper east side apartment. Good nature did not seem to him an appropriate response to the world. Besides, he didn't want a committed relationship, and she did.

Patrick coughed. To his right, broken sculptures from the Parthenon gestured with handless arms, without heads. Above, spotlights bathed the sculptures in a pink light.

'I said it's a pity. They should by rights be in Greece.'

The horses driving the chariot of the sun god surged up through the marble.

Anne's face tightened. She took a step away from Patrick.

'I said they should be in Greece,' insisted Patrick, 'not in the British Museum. Of course, Lord Elgin should never have removed them from the Parthenon.'

'Oh really?' said Anne.

Her lips are far too big for her face, he thought.

'Lord Elgin,' continued Patrick, 'stole them from Athens in the early 1800s. From the Parthenon.' He wished his throat wasn't so dry. His body felt larger than any of these huge sculptures, and far more cumbersome while she stood there like some butterfly, ethereal, poised, questioning, yet without

4

any apparent awareness of the clumsy business of human, mortal limbs. 'As perhaps you know.'

Anne drew back a red glove and examined her watch. As she did so, her hair fell forward slightly. Her silly glittering hairclips did not hold her landslide of hair well.

'You know about Elgin?' he said. 'He was the British ambassador to the Ottoman Empire – in Constantinople – who took it upon himself to steal these invaluable sculptures.'

The woman's high-heeled boots were close together. Her coat was soft velvet, like a cat's skin.

'*Interesting* you say that,' she said.

There was a distant, condescending note to her voice, which unnerved him.

'I must be getting on,' said the young woman, turning away, the folds of her black coat rippling with a beauty more immediate than the cold folds of the soldiers' cloaks all around them.

Patrick panicked. He had behaved like a boor. He should apologise. He couldn't imagine why he did it, except for her tiny hands. His mind sorted through a variety of words and haphazardly landed on 'Lord Elgin was a jerk'. He uttered these words.

Anne stiffened. She smiled gently, pityingly at Patrick, then walked away.

For a moment he followed, but there was something about the defiance of her shoulders that made him stay back.

5

He settled his thumping heart, which felt as though some pulsating creature was at loose within him, by studying the broken wonders all around him.

Behind him Dionysus reclined, his hands and feet gone, and Iris, messenger of the gods, hurries on, the wind blowing her dress against her stone body, racing through time, but never arriving.

As he walked out a few moments later, through the museum, sunlight strikes down over colossal black scarab beetles, over two pillars soaring up, over stone hawks sitting docile through the centuries, a world of violent shapes. This is magic, he thought, this is a world of magic and transformation. He stayed quite still, awed by the sunlight and splendour, the moment of glory in a city day, and as he stopped he saw that the young woman, the young woman of the centaur and the swordsman, of the gloves and velvet coat, had also stopped to look at the sunlight, before hurrying on, away from him, the long coat swinging behind her.

CHAPTER 2

Anne walks off, through Bloomsbury to the new British Library, a desolate place which nevertheless efficiently retrieves books through the computer system. It is odd, she thinks, how certain areas of London always have a particular weather. This no man's area up to King's Cross is nearly always windy. Even when it is sunny it seems faintly apologetic about it, as if embarrassed by inappropriate behaviour. She glances behind her. She strides on, feeling better by the moment as she gets nearer to the library.

Anne takes a fruit pastille from her pocket and sucks it.

She thrusts her bag into the library cloakroom.

In the library she lost awareness of her body bit by bit. First the feet, then the legs, the rest of the body, until just the hands were left, the hands and the head, all that counted. She liked the feel of the pen in her fingers.

'The Grand Vizier,' she writes, 'told Elgin that his name in Turkish means "evil genius, the Devil".'

All day she works, surrounded by others whose

bodies no longer exist. They turn pages, occasionally rustle paper, make notes, and some tap into laptops.

At around 5pm she takes the underground back to her flat near Tower Bridge.

Later that day, in her bedroom, Anne Fitzgerald undresses, watched by Alexander, her lover. Her little red leather gloves lie on the bed. He has a wife in another part of London. She knows that. The wife knows nothing. Alexander likes his double life. We all like our double lives. Anne too likes being with this man who seems to know nothing about her, who sees only what she shows him so the rest of her can remain intact. Alexander sees the outside of Anne Fitzgerald – the lily-white skin, the darkness between her legs, the way she moves towards him with something steely in her eyes. She goes down on her knees.

'Yes,' he murmurs, holding her head.

But even then, at those moments of pleasure, his other life is continuing in his head. His wife boils a kettle, his child skips in the garden, some bills lie on the hall table, and he thinks how his house up near Bishops Avenue has far too many windows. When he bought the house he felt it was wonderful to be able to see out but forgot others could see in.

As for Anne, as she kneels, she thinks only of her books and the library, her other life, her secret life, sweet and private.

Of course she is aware of her milk-white skin, its

beauty, the way it so closely clings to her shape. But this is to her just dreams, mere clothes which she knows she will change in time. She neither loves nor doesn't love her body, or the attention it receives. What she loves is her mind – her clever, solitary, cavernous mind in which she sometimes loses herself in a labyrinth of delight far more exhilarating than this bumping and slipping of flesh and sweat she's experiencing now as the plump Alexander grabs at her, pushing his ill-fitting flesh towards her. His flesh seems to have been acquired for him by someone who has never met him – the flesh is far too heavy and flabby for his bone structure. The shoulder pads are too wide, the arms too padded and lumpy, even the flesh on his legs seems to be designed for someone with longer, different legs. The fat has rumpled up over his short legs. But his ill-fitting body helps give him an endearing quality and certainly his eyes are merry.

'My angel,' he says.

'My little Buddha,' she says.

Patrick thinks about Anne as he lies in bed, tossing and turning, the sheet rippling over him as the cry of an ambulance reaches him through the cool, still streets of London.

CHAPTER 3

In the British Library Patrick stabbed at the computer which allowed readers to access the book collection. He was trying to get out a book on the Elgins. 'In use' sprang up in front of him. He scratched his nose. His hands splayed out on the computer keys.

'Fuck,' he whispered.

Last night he had worked at deciphering what appeared to be the diaries of Mary Nisbet, who became the Countess of Elgin, which he'd managed to buy up in Edinburgh a couple of weeks ago. They were written in tiny handwriting.

Patrick made sure to lock the diaries away carefully.

Ever since he'd got them he'd felt uncomfortable, as if he were being watched.

Patrick recalled with irritation the auctioneer Robert Frank, who had demanded a huge sum for the diaries in Edinburgh. He'd had inflated lips, a bulbous nose and broken blood vessels over his cheeks.

He'd met Patrick in a dark cafe after speaking on the phone, and refused to tell Patrick where he'd got the diaries.

'I promised not to. It was a condition of getting them,' he told Patrick grandly, and took a swig of a mug of coffee. 'I need to sell them quickly. I got your call just after I bought them – hadn't even taken them into the auction house.' He stared intently at Patrick. 'See – if you buy them now, that'll be it. No questions. No auction.'

Patrick had taken the cardboard box, opened it, and felt a shiver through him as he had undone the blue ribbons and held the old paper, saw the tiny writing.

'This is impossible to read,' said Patrick.

'Difficult,' said Robert Frank, taking a flask of whisky from his back pocket and pouring it in the dregs of the coffee. 'I doubt if it's impossible. I made out some words.'

'Huh,' said Patrick. 'I'll pay half what you ask for.'

'I need more,' said Robert Frank uneasily. He kept looking round. His mobile phone rang and he switched it off.

He could probably see how much Patrick wanted the diaries.

'Oh, take the money,' said Patrick, writing a cheque.

Patrick thought about Robert Frank and the stink of whisky on his breath. When Patrick looked back, he did seem almost afraid. It wasn't just that he wanted to sell the documents quickly, without giving the auction house any of the profits. It was as if Robert Frank thought that what he had in his possession could cause him trouble, and he wanted to be rid of the diaries fast.

Patrick tapped more letters into the computer, but still received the same information, that the book was not available. He glowered. He loathed this library, with its steady temperature, its rows of computers, the empty corridors, the virtual absence of books. The old British Library – especially the Round Reading Room – had had magic. It had been like walking into a great book.

Maybe I should stop all this research for a while, he thought. It's getting to me. Sometimes when I'm working late in my flat I even imagine I can see Mary Nisbet – later married to the abominable Lord Elgin – sitting by me, smiling shyly, with that underlying intelligence at the back of her eyes. Biography is all about ghosts, taming ghosts, understanding ghosts.

Patrick stood up. The people all around him looked at him in part because he was so disturbingly tall. He also had broad shoulders, a curious, sweet smile and immense long eyelashes. The mousy-haired girl in blue turned a page, and frowned, the plump man adjusted his circular glasses and coughed, a woman searched for a mint in her pocket. I can't stand this, he thought.

That night he worked again as a bouncer in a club by the river, near Shad Thames, where he wore a black suit and hung about the door in the cold night air. As a biographer he didn't earn much.

His last book on Turner had been received with respect, not rhapsody. He liked being an American in London, a stranger.

As Patrick walked to the tube on the way home after leaving the club, he felt a hand on his shoulder.

Patrick turned round, expecting to see a tramp. He was in a dark alleyway with tall walls near the river. The area by Tower Bridge was still full of the atmosphere of spices, and ledger books and the edges of the river, the way it broke things down, lapping over the bodies that wash up here, over the pebbles, over the Coca-Cola cans, over the mud which represents long ago time, ground down, soft, nothing really, not a human or an object, somewhere in between, the remains of all these things, the dead and dying.

He was faced with three men. One of them had a thin, sharp face, his skin white and taut, another a soft face, with a fat lower lip. The third approached him, his face wide and flat. For a moment it seemed to Patrick that this must be some kind of joke.

'Can I help you?' he said.

To Patrick, London was not a threatening place. He knew he was able to use his bulk to intimidate. He liked the way most of London is so poised, so accomplished, its buildings slotted together with such confidence, different styles of the past elegantly locked together. All those black statues hanging about at street corners, in squares; in the rain they glistened and towered over running figures as if to say *we* can never get too wet, or suffer, the rain just tumbles over our cold stone bodies whereas you, how cold and mortal you are in your thin raincoat and delicate, pathetic white skin.

Some part of him thinks 'Good, a fight, this is what I can do, this is simple, straightforward, this is easier than dealing with the haughty girl or with Mary Nisbet,' and his whole body gathers up, grows bigger. Cars pass but no one stops.

As a bouncer, he knew how to hold himself and the man who'd put his hand on Patrick's shoulder took a step back.

He thought of the purple river up in Edinburgh, where he'd bought the diaries, and the violence of the orange sunset drenching the sky.

Patrick felt his body become steel, waiting for what might happen. The three men seemed a long way below. One, with the taut skin, took out a knife from his pocket and stared at it.

'I think you must be making a mistake,' said Patrick easily. 'I have no money.'

In Edinburgh the dark clouds sank down, clamping out the orange sky.

'We don't want your money,' said the man with the sharp, taut face.

'We'll have his money anyway,' said the soft-faced one.

In some ways, he thought, I should give them my money. I have no credit cards, just about £100 cash. So what? But I have just earned that. Why should I give it to these squat thugs, and besides, he could sense his body wanting a fight, wanting violence, longing to swing a fist at the ugly little faces, to fling them away. And even his own pain, he didn't mind that. Except the knife. He didn't like the knife.

'Get back to America,' said the sharp-faced man. 'Fuck off.'

As they all moved nearer him, he was aware of a man over the other side of the road walking faster to be free of the responsibility, he was aware of the empty houses around him, and he was aware of the way the whole weight of his body seemed to be sinking into the fist he is clenching now.

'Get him,' said one of the men.

With a quick movement Patrick hit the sharp faced man on the chin while grabbing the wrist which held the knife, and twisting the wrist so it made a snapping noise. As the knife clattered to the ground the man yelped and fell to his knees, and Patrick kicked him in the jaw while swooping. to get the knife. As the other two came nervously towards him, he held out the knife and smiled.

'I'd hate to kill either of you in self-defence. I'd feel really bad.' He kept smiling, then took a step forward. '*Maybe* I'd feel really bad.'

And then it seemed, quite simply, that the darkness swallowed them up, engulfed them as they stepped quickly off into a sidestreet while the guy on his knees looked up afraid while Patrick turned his back and walked away, whistling, putting the knife in his pocket, liking the knowledge of the silver steel so close to him, aware they might spring at him, every sense alive and waiting, listening to the hum of the cars, aware of the height of the buildings, the hardness of the pavement beneath his feet.

He strode on.

But when he got back, he was exhausted and sat on the bed with his head in his hands.

The phone rang.

It was Victoria, his married lover, her voice like silk.

'You okay?'

'Sure.'

'I just suddenly got a bad feeling about you.'

'I was attacked by some thugs.'

'Some thugs?'

'You're sure your husband doesn't know about us?'

'Sure.'

'Expect it was some disgruntled guy from some club. Didn't let him in. Or insulted him in some way. That happens.'

'But you're okay?'

'Oh yes. I'm okay.'

But it took a while to sleep. His anger was a problem. It was always there, following him around, leaning casually beside him, sharing a drink. For whole chunks of his life the anger had gone but now it was back, nudging against him, grinning, chatting inanely.

Whoever had been attempting to intimidate him

must be a fool. The thugs had been inept. The attack, far from making him run back to the US, had made London seem brighter, even more interesting.

CHAPTER 4

Mary Nisbet,
Archerfield,
Scotland,
October 13, 1798

I wish I thought of him more.

The cold fat crows sit on the grass outside our house. I do not know if I should marry Lord Elgin. He is a fine, clever man, but eleven years older than I am.

There is something about him. He dreams of glory and immortality. I can see it in his eyes; the way he talks of becoming the ambassador to Constantinople. It seems vain and foolish stuff. There are plagues, primitive people, and the journey there will take two months.

Here in Scotland, I am loved by my mother and father. I love my walks through Aberlady Bay, with the swirling birds and my books.

I fear he may want my money too. My parents say he is an aristocrat: handsome, adventurous. Maybe it is true and we will be happy together.

On my walk today the footprints of the coots lay neatly in the sand.

I am afraid and keep shivering. The winds bang against the windows.

CHAPTER 5

Anne Fitzgerald stood on the balcony of her flat and watched two seagulls scudding through the sky while down below a black tug dragged its cargo of containers, a snail dragging through the grey water, leaving its shiny trail behind. There was a light behind her skin, behind her eyes.

To her left she could see Tower Bridge and the Tower of London, while to her right the Thames swept away to the east. Beneath her the water lapped against the old brick warehouse building. She kicked gently at the bottom rail of the balcony.

She came back into the flat, with its exposed brickwork and a sense of being part of the Thames as the four huge windows opened out on to the long balcony.

On the wall were valuable paintings belonging to Alexander and constantly changing as he bought and sold. In the room there was also a marble hand, a stone head from Cambodia, a vase from Egypt, a small gold statue of a boy. He dealt chiefly in antiquities.

Alexander sat in his favourite armchair, his lip protruding like a grumpy child's.

'You love me a lot, don't you?' he said, and she looked at him intently, thinking he must be joking, but then she realised he wasn't and thought again what a cheat love was, that people believe you are most passionate when you are least, that they love you most when you don't love them, that they only see their own emotions reflected in the other person.

'Perhaps I should leave my wife and we could marry,' Alexander said heavily.

'No, darling, I wouldn't want that,' she said. 'This works well.'

'But I only see you a few times a week,' he said. 'And besides, you never confide in me. I want to know about your work, about Mary Elgin. You know how interested I am in the Elgin marbles.'

'You do love me?' he said.

She picked a pencil off the floor.

'Say you love me,' he said, with dull eyes and thick wet lips.

'You know I can't say that.'

Anne had seen pictures of his family, and had no desire to break that up. Alexander had always had at least one mistress so she didn't feel she was in any way damaging the family, merely keeping up the status quo. Her sense of isolation meant she did not wish to intrude into anyone else's existence; quite the opposite. Besides, Alexander was increasingly shifty about his work. She sometimes suspected his dealing was not completely straight but he always denied ever receiving stolen goods.

In some ways, she knew she should just leave Alexander. She had been here three years. A two or three times a week visit from him was fine with her. Since the death of Paolo, whom she'd lived with in Bangkok, Anne had tried to keep herself calm and intact. She was looking for equilibrium not passion. After Paolo's death everything had changed, their magic house in Bangkok had looked different, strange, a film set after the film had been made. The plants in the garden throbbed viciously and the sun ripped down. When she needed love or passion, she looked back at her past with Paolo.

Alexander was standing close to Anne now, and she feels, with irritation, a vague stirring of desire as his lips touched her neck. It's not just the river that keeps me here, she thought, as his hand slips between her legs.

His hands hurt her arms as he held her down, and afterwards she was angry with him, and as she walked away, he took her arm again and pushed her down on the floor. Alexander's lips were hot on her lips. Sometimes when he made love to her she felt full of fractures, longings, things she didn't understand.

'Open your legs,' whispered Alexander.

CHAPTER 6

Mary Nisbet,
Archerfield,
December 15, 1798

Of course I admire him: his wit, his intelligence, a certain dry persistence which made it impossible for me not to accept him.

He tells me tales of the gardens of Pera in Constantinople, of the Bosphorus, the seraglio. He hopes to win me over. He will be ambassador; I shall be the ambassadress.

But I shall miss the cold fresh wind here, and the curlews calling out. Above all, I shall miss my parents, my friends, the gaiety of balls and parties. I am not sure being a grand ambassadress will suit me at all.

There are rumours of his many affairs.

CHAPTER 7

Patrick strode across the courtyard of the British Library, which was dominated by the statue of Blake's Newton, compasses stretched out to pursue knowledge.

As he walked he felt someone was following him but when he turned there was just a shaven-headed young man loafing along with his head down.

Above the red courtyard the gothic towers of St Pancras station rose up nostalgically like a fairy-tale castle.

That morning he'd had a difficult conversation with his lover, Victoria Napier, who was older than he, richer than he, and more bored than he. She'd wanted to have lunch but he'd said he had to work.

'You're always working. I wish you weren't so secretive and obsessive about your work. I'd like to see more of you,' she'd said down the phone, in her honeyed, expensive voice.

'That's supposed to be my line,' Patrick had said. 'You're the married one.'

'I never thought I'd be jealous of a *dead* woman,' she said. 'And one called *Mary* too,' she drawled. 'What's wrong with a living woman? Why is it you can't get really involved with a living woman? You idealise. You only want the unobtainable.'

Patrick ended the conversation with a promise of a drink later on then lolloped to his desk.

As he worked he considered how curious it was to study poor Mary Nisbet, Mary Elgin, and to find a life lost to view, no longer completely available to be studied, so much of it missing, unrecorded, like the missing parts of the statues – a missing shoulder, an arm gone, a part of the torso no longer there. It was possible to look at the fragments remaining – in the letters, the memories, the historical scraps, the dates, the records of the trial, and, now, the diaries – and to think, who was she? We're given so much – whole evenings of her life, her moods, the quality of her affection for her parents – but not allowed to know it all.

He went up to the Issues Desk and collected the book he'd been studying for the last couple of days. The assistant smiled at Patrick the way girls always smiled at Patrick, as though he'd just said something very entertaining. He took the book over to his desk in the great cruiser of a room and settled to work.

The man beside him wore a yellow T-shirt, like a poisonous beetle, and kept staring at Patrick's books.

Patrick supposed one day soon there would be a letter from New York saying his former girlfriend Kate was getting married to some wholesome young man with a fine future.

He thought about what Victoria had said. It wasn't true that he avoided relationships with living women; he had had innumerable relationships.

Why, he even occasionally missed Kate and sometimes he thought about her, always entering a room, her feet in white towelling slippers, wearing a cotton nightdress, her knees round and child-like, her fair hair messy, that odd lost expression in her eyes. Wealthy, lazy, she would push her hair from her face and peer at him. Slightly short sighted, Kate had often looked puzzled.

She used to tug at her nightdress to cover her knees.

'You've got lovely knees,' he'd say. 'Don't cover them up.'

'They're absurd!' she'd declared, taking a step towards him.

'Absurd knees,' she'd said, and moved to sit on his lap.

'Lovely knees,' he'd murmured, as she kissed him behind his ears.

Kate's flesh had been hot and solid and sweet, tasting of flowers. She came with a sweet cry, whereas he roared out loud, seeming always to shock Kate, who had never invited him to stay the night at her parents' home, a mansion with acres and horses, presumably for fear of such a

25

roar disturbing her demure churchgoing parents. Or maybe there were other reasons.

Kate had met his parents.

His father, a beautiful-looking man with sad eyes, suffered from depressions. He hated his job as a manager of a bank and spent all his free time playing the clarinet. His father's other problem, along with his depressions, was his capacity for falling in love with women. Patrick too loved women, their softness, their giggles, their reasonableness.

Patrick's mother had poured much of her love into Patrick and he could see now her plump freckly hands in the dusty golden light of the summer. The love in her pale grey-green eyes was sometimes too much, and at times he had felt like a bumble bee caught beneath an upturned glass, buzzing and struggling. 'You've done well again,' she would say, smiling, her lips full of lipstick.

Of course, he had been keen to leave home. It was all so familiar and the familiarity drowned him. The Georgian-style redbrick, the friends he had known since grade school. His parents, having the same meals on the same days, night after night; good meals, beautifully cooked, but still dull. There were all his toys piled up in the attic, in cupboards, and over all the ordinariness, the bleak, strange splendour of the seasons bringing their restlessness under the doors, through the gap in the windows, carrying him away from the wide skies to the cramped physical surroundings of London which somehow released his mind.

He loved his parents very much but there could be something throttling about his mother, for all her beauty and glamour. It was possible that had made him nervous of intense relationships. His mother adored him but often he had felt watched by her, like some adored hamster in a cage watched by her young ones; face against the bars. When he returned from school she used to go through his bag, placing his exercise books on to the floor, his papers, his pens, filling his pens with ink, sharpening his pencils, congratulating him on his good manners, often hugging him at the sheer joy in his success.

He didn't tell them about the fights he got into. Occasionally his parents found out about a fight. Once a group of irate parents asked the head to look into a fight in which three of their boys were injured. It had turned out that all three at once had attacked him in the yard. It was the apparent effortlessness with which the tall, fast and extremely strong boy had fought back, something which all the other pupils reported to the head when questioned. 'He didn't seem particularly to want to hurt them,' one boy observed. 'But I don't think he minded that he did. Patrick does get angry.'

His parents were a little silent with him for a week or two after the news of the fight, but then things returned to normal. But he had still needed to escape their warm embrace. In the house in Connecticut, he had been the hot centre of it, the pivot of all their hopes. He could see his mother now, sweeping towards him, dark and beautiful and smothering. It was what he feared most, to be smothered.

Patrick strode over to the library catalogue, which was all on computer now, rows and rows of them, to order another book he needed, a history of the Elgin clan. But the machine informed him the book was in use. He tried another book, about Lord Elgin's house, Broomhall, and received the same response, then another, then another, and for a moment he wanted to hurl the machine over the other side of the silent room.

Patrick approached one of the assistants behind the counter to ask about the books.

'Excuse me,' he said.

The assistant, who had a small, boyish face, gave an earnest frown which melted at the sight of Patrick's handsome face, and she was soon persuaded to tell Patrick which seat had the books he needed.

It was when he was a few yards away that he realised who was sitting at desk 222.

She was sitting with her elbows on the table, absolutely intent, her hands pulling back her auburn hair, as if trying to rid her head of anything but thought. The black velvet coat was draped over the back of her chair and he found himself scanning her hair for sparkly little hairslides.

She wasn't as majestic as she'd been at the British Museum, where she had seemed to be emulating the grandeur of the statues all around her, and also trying to repel anyone from approaching her.

Her profile was very Virginia Woolf, he thought – pale, a little severe, striking – and her little purple cardigan was slightly too small for her, and didn't reach quite to her wrists. Although she was beautiful, it wasn't a robust beauty, as if she could easily have become too thin, too delicate, too pale, with her russet hair and pale skin which was so fine it looked as though it could tear easily.

On her desk was a Mont Blanc black fountain pen, which surprised him; she didn't look wealthy.

He tapped her on her shoulder, and she started. 'Oh!' she cried out.

'Shhh. Sorry,' he said softly.

Her forehead corrugated into a frown and her hands clutched on to the front edge of the desk as if to save herself from falling.

'Sorry,' he said again, eyeing jealously the books she had piled up on her desk.

'What is it?' she whispered harshly, but there was a glimmer of a smile.

'We met before,' he murmured. 'At the British Museum.'

'I know,' she said. 'What do you want?' Her voice sounded heavy, almost as though she were weighing it down on purpose.

The man beside her, who had stringy yellow hair, a button nose and a square-edged forehead, stared at them both. Patrick observed he was studying a well-thumbed book on German sexual fantasies in the Third Reich, and stared back. The man coughed and continued his studies.

'I wondered how long you'd be wanting those books,' said Patrick in as low a voice as he could manage.

She gave a tepid smile. 'Days,' she said, sternly, her mouth still grappling with a desire to smile, and then she turned back to her work.

Patrick was perturbed by his desire to soothe himself by stroking her black velvet coat as if it really were a cat.

'I particularly needed the one about Elgin's house,' he said. 'Badly.'

'I'm doing some work on Broomhall at the moment,' she murmured, without looking round. 'But as soon as I've finished, you're welcome to them.'

'I need them now,' he said.

She turned, gave him a ravishing smile, and as she smiled he noticed her eyes were in fact green flecked with brown.

'You are not being reasonable,' he said. He was used to getting his own way.

'Did I say I was?' she said.

He turned away angrily.

'Bye now,' she said, and put her elbows back on the table, her head back in her hands, and her shoulders high up, a fortress against stray individuals such as himself.

Patrick left the library, striding through the

cavernous hall and out into Euston Road, then walked up through Bloomsbury, faster and faster, surprised at how angry he felt. In his mind he saw Elgin and Mary.

'You once told me my plan to go to Constantinople was foolish and vain, that I should not want to be ambassador to some plague-infested, barbaric city,' says Elgin to Mary, towering over her in the cabin as she blinks palely up at him. 'It's no use complaining now.'

'I haven't complained,' says Mary nervously. 'Not at all. I'm just seasick, darling.' She wipes her mouth.

'Good, that's good,' he says, and strokes her hair, bending down to kiss it.

Patrick strode on, irritated by what he sees, furious to see it all, angry with Elgin for making Mary suffer, wishing he could march in and tell her to go back, go back, go back, but that's what is so hard about being a historian, you can't interfere. At least a politician can interfere and a fiction writer can transform, but all a historian should do is record and interpret.

Nothing prepared you for anything, he'd discovered, no books, no poetry, nothing; everything real came as a surprise, completely unexpected, however many times he had read about it first. But still the writer, someone like him, tried to explain it to others – oh no, it's like this, the writer would say, and maybe none of it helped anyone, not really. He did not know why he was so angry.

31

The next morning, Patrick made sure he arrived early at the library, but the books were reserved as before. There she was, at work even earlier.

The following day, the same thing happened.

That evening he and Victoria made love, fighting together in the half-light, her limbs round and strange.

He didn't mention the young woman to Victoria.

Victoria and Patrick had met at a publishing party, and she had told him she loved American men. It turned out she used to watch a large number of cowboy movies in her childhood and from then on had decided all American men were tall and tough and desirable.

Once she brought a copy of the film *High Noon* to the hotel bedroom and they had to watch it while making love. She was in floods of tears when Grace Kelly returned to support her husband.

He wasn't in love with Victoria, it was just that their bodies seemed to get along together well, his so big, and hers slim and taut and bronze with red fingertips. Victoria was older than he was, elegant, with smooth black hair sleek as a seal and little white teeth, baby teeth which had never been replaced by adult molars. He had marks from her teeth on his left shoulder. Her house in Holland Park smelt of the lilies she kept in every room. He'd been seeing her intermittently for over a year and during that time it had seemed her black hair had become even blacker, her figure even tighter and her faint lines fainter.

'Maybe you and I could go to New York together,' said Victoria, turning away as they lay on the hot creased sheets in his flat.

'I think my husband might get fired,' she said. 'I couldn't bear that. All this time, all this work. He wanted to be at the top of his profession.'
    'Why? Why would he?'
    'Oh, they think he was involved in falsifying some documents for a story and the editor got the blame. It would make nonsense of so much of my life if Charles were fired. My sister would be so *smug* about it.'

Patrick rearranged his coffee mugs in a neat line. Each had about an inch of cold coffee remaining.
    When he was working the flat didn't seem small but huge, crowded with parties and gossip and people. It was perhaps why sometimes he didn't feel he needed Victoria, didn't need anyone. He had plenty of company when he was alone.
    Patrick wrote notes in longhand, in brown ink, round, careful writing, surprisingly childish, on pads of lined paper. Patrick closed his eyes. He could see Mary Nisbet, sitting at a table, in her home called Archerfield near Edinburgh, over-looking the park all around, with a pen in her hand, writing her early diaries in the tiny hand

33

he was now struggling to decipher. Some parts she wrote in code. He told himself it was well worth the work; she'd hardly have taken such trouble to write like this if she had nothing to hide.

CHAPTER 8

Mary Nisbet,
Archerfield,
December 20, 1798

I walked to Aberlady Bay again. The seagulls bobbed over the waves. A circle of curlews lifted off into the air, flying and turning in the cold sun. Beyond the shimmer of the wet sand, the sea was dark.

I do not wish to leave my home. I have been happy here, with my dear mother and father though I do admire and respect Elgin.

I love my village and the house Archerfield stands nearby, through gates, the large, square, granite house surrounded by parkland with only the sea to one side. The trees protect the house from the salt wind.

I have heard Elgin had a relationship with a Madame Ferchenbeck in Berlin.

CHAPTER 9

Outside, the traffic rumbled the tall house in which Patrick stood, oversize, restless, sweat prickling his body. He walked to the window and his steps made the room shake. His hands rested on the window ledge. Patches of sky blazed bright, Persian blue between the fluffy clouds which drifted jubilantly above London. It was there, this piercing beauty; sometimes it was impossible to see it, but it was there, in the drift and sway of a cloud or a branch or the way the girl with the red gloves walked, as if gathering the whole world's sweetness in the movement.

Later, Patrick hurried towards the library. Outside, the British flag waved convivially on the tall flagpole.

He opened an old book on the Elgins which smelt of yellowing pages, of trapped time. The painting of Mary three quarters of the way through showed a beauty – black curly hair and large limpid eyes with thoughtful lips and pearly skin. There was something lost about her expression, even in the early pictures, but nothing to suggest the horror she was to go through.

One man tore out a sheet of paper and the rip made Patrick start, as he sat studying. Another man tapped into his computer with fingers thickened by mittens and had shoulders which shook with laughter as he read.

It was then that Patrick noticed the girl with the red gloves at a nearby desk. As she wrote her notes in pencil, she tapped on the desk with her other hand. Beneath the haughty manner, there was a kind of nervousness and a responsiveness as she read; one moment there was an expression of annoyance, then a little sag of sorrow, then the tiny crease of a smile.

Patrick tried to concentrate on Mary Nisbet. He could see her walking over the beach near her pink granite house. What could possibly be dangerous about some old diaries, and why had Robert Frank been so nervous?

The man next door coughed and Patrick started.

Patrick was aware of someone standing over him.

He looked up.

'Excuse me,' said the girl, 'but you have the book I was working with. As you don't appear to be looking at it, might I use it for a while?'

'I'm sorry . . . I was miles away.'

The man working at the next desk scowled at Patrick and Anne.

She leant down, her hair rippling forward.

He imagined Mary's hands as she took her gloves off after her walk.

'How long will you be using it?' the girl asked in a soft tone with a calm, calculated manner. Her skin was the colour of double cream, white cream, something you could put your finger in and feel the whiteness and softness, and her lips are almost too red, as if she's just been eating raspberries.

The man in the black mittens was watching her rapaciously, as if he'd like to feel her back with what was left of his fingers when the mittens have finished with them.

Her small white hands rested on Patrick's desk. She smelt of apricots. With her aquiline nose, brushed with just a

few freckles, and her wide mouth, she was even lovelier close to.

'I'm so sorry,' he said. 'But would you like a coffee?'

She checked her watch. 'Not now. Another time,' she said, staring at the book.

It seemed the girl might well snatch the book but then her sense of propriety took over and she stalked over to the other side of the room and sat at her desk.

When Patrick looked up again, she had gone.

The next day, when he got to the library the moment it opened, he found she had the book, and was studying it quietly, complacently. Patrick sat next to her. She yawned.

'Early for you, isn't it?' he whispered.

She leant towards him, with a lavish smile.

'Sorry,' she said. She turned her attention back

to studying her book, as she curled a strand of hair round her finger.

That night, he worked as a bodyguard for an Arab couple.

He spent the evening outside a room at the Connaught, watching the lift come up and down, while hearing the fierce cries of a couple making love inside.

Patrick wandered into a bookshop in Charing Cross Road. The shop was crowded with desolate shoppers. He examined the shiny photograph of the author on the back of a biography of Napoleon's Josephine: the woman from the library looked out at him slightly reproachfully, with that hidden smile, as though it were intrusive of the reader to wish to buy the book. The author's name was Anne Fitzgerald.

At the club the next evening he was angry and difficult about letting people in. One man said: 'Don't you know who I am?'

Patrick had frowned and said, 'A jerk?' It turned out he was some minor footballer.

Another blond-haired guy claimed to know the owner.

'Fine,' Patrick said, 'Give him a call and if it's okay with him, you can come in.'

'Can you give me his number?' said the blond-haired guy.

'No, if you're his friend, you must know it.'

39

Patrick felt he didn't want to let anyone in, but another doorman told him to go easier.

'What's up with you tonight?'

He stood at the door of the club for the last couple of hours, and it was quieter now, the early morning streets bare and dark, the rain glistening over them, the night still. He moved into the club, which was smoky and thudding with music. Standing there earlier, at the front of the club, in his black leather jacket, his broad shoulders, he had wanted to smash the face of one weasel-faced young man who had barged into him.

The manager bought him a drink. 'You okay?' he asked.

A girl came to sit next to Patrick, and the strap of her dress slipped off as she spoke to him.

When he left the club she was waiting for him and he took her back to his flat. He knew he shouldn't but the anger and unease had been building up inside him, and the desire too. He seemed too aware of everything, uncomfortably aware.

The next night, he called on a girlfriend he saw every few weeks, Sarah, who had wide apart eyes and fair hair. She blearily let him in. With his large frame, and endearingly uneasy manner, he was used to women liking him.

'Come to bed,' she said sleepily, and after making love they lay in each other's arms. She had a sweet, gentle little snore. But he couldn't sleep and left around three in the morning, and paced the streets.

CHAPTER 10

Anne's friend Elizabeth had returned to her home in Highbury, North London, from a hospital appointment and thrown down her straw bag. She was having treatment for breast cancer and she needed Anne's help. Elizabeth stood at the mirror, brushed her hair then smeared some lipstick on to her pale lips. She was in her early thirties, clever, with a liking for polo-necked sweaters, skirts which were too long, and for sensible shoes. Her light brown hair was short, with a ragged fringe, and she had eyes the colour of bluebells. They had met at Edinburgh University when Elizabeth had been Anne's tutor.

'How are you?' said Anne.

'Not great,' Elizabeth said. 'Still being abused by that jerk Alexander?'

'I'm the one abusing him,' said Anne, laughing, as she made Elizabeth some tea.

'You should get out,' said Elizabeth, standing at the door overlooking her small overgrown garden. In the summer it was full of honeysuckle, roses, hollyhocks and delphiniums. Outside, Elizabeth's daughter Lily was trying out a handstand. 'You've let yourself be trapped.'

'Oh – I just can't find the exit sign,' said Anne.

'Oh, come on. There are exit signs all over. You – you . . .' She frowned. 'I don't know. You have such charm but you can put on this shiny surface so things bounce off you, or seem to. You don't want to move into the next phase of your life. How's the Elgin book going?'

'Well.'

Anne tidied back her hair from her face with her two sparkly hairslides.

Later that evening, Anne went upstairs to read a story to Lily, who was studying her belly button.

'I hate belly buttons which go out, don't you?' said Lily. 'Sometimes,' continued Lily, still examining her belly button, 'I get angry with my mother because she can't do things.'

'It's just the treatment,' said Anne softly. 'It's not very nice. As though there's a battle inside her.'

'I see. A battle,' said Lily.

She lived with Elizabeth and Lily (Elizabeth's partner had long since left them) for a while on her return from Bangkok. Perhaps because she'd been brought up in Hong Kong, she was comfortable in the East. Her father had had to leave the diplomatic service after being been disgraced on corruption charges. Shortly after her father's disgrace, her seventeen-year-old brother had left home, leaving a note to say he no longer trusted his father or anyone else. Her time in Scotland, at university, had seemed a kind of half life, with dimmed lights, whereas in the East there was colour and intensity and vitality. After her brother's disappearance, and the family's return to England, life had been grey and quiet, as if the volume were turned down. She kept waiting for the volume to come back, the brightness to be turned up, her real life to begin again. Once she met the Italian journalist Paolo and lived in Bangkok, it had all started up again. She thought about him all the time, the way he brushed his teeth until his mouth foamed, his propensity for making gnomic utterances such as 'I suppose I am a romantic. I believe in the improbable', delivered with a glitter in his deep brown eyes.

In a way now, in her work with the Elgin Marbles, she had found something expressing the intensity of the East and the coolness of the West, a kind of equilibrium, the passion of the flesh and the coolness of marble, the two sides of her she wished now to combine.

It would have been good to have been as happy as she'd been that year in Bangkok all her life; to applaud the sun for blazing, and the shadows for coming, long and slow, and stealing away the day, leaving another warm regretful night with the cicadas singing out with operatic abandon as though determined to express whatever sorrow or bliss lay at the very centre of things.

Lily would listen to Anne intently, hugging her knees.

'Tell me about Paolo. And the turtle. And the pond. And how you loved him. Do you think you'll die an old maid because of your great love for him? You don't mind my asking, do you?'

Anne smiled.

'My mother says you're too caught up in the past – with Paolo,' said Lily. 'She says you only have today to live in.'

'Oh does she?'

'She thinks you should try to forget him. I think it's good to be caught up in the past. It gives you stories,' said Lily.

In Bangkok, Anne explained once more to Lily, her boyfriend Paolo had had an old house with a huge pond outside where a 100-year-old turtle pondered existence. Anne would often wander out through their terrace lit by scattered candles, over the bridge to where the turtle liked to lurk. And she would lean over the bridge and talk to it.

All around the lovely old house towered tall modern blocks of flats but at night it was easy to imagine that none of them existed.

She would watch Paolo in his office he'd built to one side of the house. Paolo worked all the time. But he worked in such a wild manner it was hard to remember it was work he attacked with such exhilaration, singing to himself, running his fingers through his long hair, walking back and forth in his office, hands behind his back.

He went from one enthusiasm to another. He had

been a capitalist in Tokyo, an expert in guerrilla warfare in Cambodia, a follower of fortunetellers in Bangkok, and now a Buddhist in preparation for his next assignment in India, 'the last place left on earth with a culture'. His other main obsession at that time was being indulgently, exuberantly, ecstatically in love with her.

'How wonderful,' whispered Lily.

Anne told Lily about the little poems and sayings he used to leave on her pillow in the morning when he got up before her to work:

'A word can lie . . . but it takes words to tell the truth, too. And just as a lying word can be mistaken for truth, so the truth can seem to be a lie.'

'We survive by forgetting.'

'Never underestimate the Herculean effort people put into being predictable.'

'Reality is the waste product of experience.'

'Good represents the reality of which God is the dream.'

Paolo and Anne had slept in a seventeenth-century carved rosewood bed which had belonged to a well-to-do Thai lady, bought over a year ago when Paolo was still enamoured of Thai culture, before he decided it offered nothing but a few posturing dances for tourists.

'A rosewood bed,' murmured Lily. 'He wanted to marry you. It was so tragic,' she said. Lily scratched her foot. 'Mummy will be in love like that one day soon and get married to someone.'

He asked her to marry him by the river as they

45

watched the boats drift by, trailed with their tinsel of lights.

'By a river. I like that. Someone will ask me to marry them by a river – and I shall probably say no,' said Lily. 'Except then he might throw himself in, and drown.'

Anne had taken a sip of her white wine. There were even lights trailing over the trees by the river . . . 'down the rivers of the windfall light' came into her mind from 'Fern Hill', and she saw herself as a child standing up on the school stage and reciting 'When I was young and easy . . .' and somehow that little girl with the red plaits and green and white uniform was her and this woman here, with Paolo, seemed to lack definition. I need to work, she had thought; with Paolo I would be swamped.

'I don't want to marry yet,' Anne had said to Paolo, taking his hand. 'I'm happy as we are.'

A smiling waiter had come up and bowed and asked Anne and Paolo if they'd like anything else, and she thought, oh yes, there is something but I don't know what it is and nor does Paolo who is always caught between two certainties, always on a journey somewhere.

'If only mummy had someone to love she might be okay,' said Lily. 'She needs a romance, a huge love affair. Do you know someone? Because she's not very well. She does need someone to love her. I do of course. But I can't look after her well enough.'

On the way back from the restaurant Paolo and

Anne sat in silence, and later she went to the bridge and talked to the turtle.

'It gets sad now,' said Lily, cheering up and scratching her foot.

A few days later Paolo was killed in a plane crash.

After he died, Anne just kept swallowing, as if the grief was some oversized piece of food she just couldn't quite get down her throat.

There was a memorial service. She read from his book of quotations.

'Humankind cannot bear very much reality.'

'We survive by forgetting.'

Back in London, she soon met and moved in with Alexander, because it seemed easy.

'Go on,' said Lily.

'No more,' said Anne. 'There isn't any more.'

CHAPTER 11

Victoria's hair was pulled tightly back into a bun and her skin had a waxy quality as she stood in the doorway of Patrick's flat.

'I'm sorry to call round unexpectedly. I thought – I don't know why – you might be with someone,' she said. 'I had a feeling. I was wrong.'

Then she laughed and pulled away. 'This is so ridiculous. I mean you're too big for this flat. A lumberjack in a bird's cage. And I'm too elegant. It just isn't right. I can't fuck you here anymore. And you can't live here. It's a student flat. Something has to change. Our relationship has to change. You should tell me exactly what you're working on. I could help. We could work together.'

As she pulled away he began to feel more interested. She was like some impossibly expensive ornament bought on an impulse and obviously wrong for the room: the expensive handbag, gold earrings, gold bracelet, polished high heels.

'Why are you so very interested in my work all of a sudden?' he said.

'What a choice for a lover! How did I fall for

you?' she said. 'You don't care about me. You don't trust me.'

She ran her fingers over the window ledge. 'It's even dusty! You live like an eighteen-year-old! Do you have another girlfriend? Tell me, do you?'

'Not really,' he said.

'Not really! What about the historian you're so taken with?' she said.

Patrick frowned at her as she stared at him, with her metallic eyes and her tongue which ran over her lips as if ready to devour all of him.

'I didn't know I'd mentioned her.'

'You don't need to – her book's lying by your bed. But you did mention her in fact, said you'd bumped into her at the British Museum.'

'I don't remember that.'

'You don't remember your conversations with me, darling, because they are of no consequence to you,' she said.

She swirled round, in her cyclamen-pink skirt, her tight black silk top.

'You and I – it's probably just sex,' she said. 'We should face it. I'm not in love with you and you're not in love with me. You don't love anyone! But if we are going to go on with this affair we have to have sex in places which are – suitable – I mean when we have sex here your arms and legs virtually burst out of the window. Only,' she went on, 'We have to be careful about meeting at home now in case Charles suspects . . .' She grinned, her lips grabbing her whole face.

Oh – hell, maybe she is wonderful after all, he thought.

'. . . in all the best hotels of the world! We'll start in Paris, George V, then the Danieli in Venice. And each time we'll pretend to have different names – that will be fun!'

Patrick heard the muffled sound of the traffic below, a bus pass by, a taxi pull away.

She picked up a copy of his last book, on Turner, and ran her hands over the cover. She seemed to be touching everything today, running her fingers there, her tongue over her lips, making the room shake slightly as she moved around.

'And look at you, standing there like the Colossus of Rhodes,' she said. 'How can you be so attractive? How is it possible? Really. I mean you're not handsome. You're . . .' her hands were stiff by her side. He moved towards her.

She moved away, again. 'I should go.'

'Oh, I think you should stay,' he said, and took her to his unmade bed where he undressed her and tenderly made love to her. Her mouth tasted sleepy, of the dark corners of the bed, warm and dense, and his tongue pushed down deep inside her and his hands felt between her legs and she moved slightly and moaned.

She lay on his crumpled sheets, smiling slightly, her sleek dark hair a mess now.

She had a bruise to the left of her breast. It was red at the sides, purple at the centre.

'If only you weren't doing the book,' she said.

She yawned and stretched. 'If only we were rich. You see I have money but it's not *liquid* money, and that's what one needs. Liquid money.'

Later, he got up and moved over to the window, his head nearly touching the ceiling, and she put her arms around him. He jumped slightly, as though he'd forgotten she was there. For a moment he thought he saw tears in her eyes, but there weren't. He kissed her wet wine lips, his tongue reaching to the corners.

'You know,' said Victoria, 'today I feel haunted by all the things I haven't had. The children, mostly. Stupid, isn't it?' Her jewellery seemed to lock her up; the tight pearl necklace, the thin gold bracelet. 'Odd how you can go on for years and years and then the grief overcomes you, for no reason at all. That happened this morning. I should get out. I wish you'd come with me.'

Victoria took his hand. 'Now look how huge that hand is.' She took his hand and put one of his fingers in her mouth, looking at him all the time. Her tongue ran over his finger, round and round, then she sucked. Next she took his hand and put it on her breast.

His hand lay above her breast, near the bruise.

'Your hand is always so warm, did you know that? Much warmer than other men's,' she said.

'Has he done this to you?' he said.

'Sometimes,' she said, ignoring his question, 'I think – how lovely – how easy – how fine to be alive – and other times I think – oh my God – I'm rolling downhill, fast, and everything is whizzing past and soon I'll be dead, and it will be all gone, all this.'

'I don't want to hear all this, Victoria,' he said.

She stared at him. 'No, of course you don't,' she said. 'You don't at all, do you?' She paused.

She plumped up the pillow behind her. 'Charles's job is not going that well at the moment,' she said in a high, falsetto voice. He needs a story. It's why he's so . . . nasty. You will tell me about any stories you might have?'

She tickled his arm by gently running her fingers down his skin.

'You know, Patrick, you pretend to be so open and American, but you're not really so transparent, are you?'

'What do you mean?'

She shrugged and glanced away.

'Come to dinner at my house,' she said. 'It would amuse you.'

'Your husband wouldn't like that.'

'He wouldn't know. I'd choose a time he was away.'

Later, they fell asleep and when he woke he saw her coming out of his study, with a curious, ruffled expression on her face.

'What are you doing?'

'I made a call. Didn't want to wake you.'

That night, after she had gone, before he slept, he took up the floorboard and got out some more pages of the diary. He hoped she hadn't seen the

52

pages he'd left on his desk. He knew he would be wise to put the pages in the bank but he couldn't bring himself to let go of the actual manuscript because it made Mary Elgin close to him, as if she were just on the other side of the door.

Patrick wished it was not taking him so long to decipher them but at least while he was working on them he could keep them secret and private and be close to Mary, reading what she wrote in her own words, time disappearing, sharing it with no one else.

CHAPTER 12

Mary Elgin,
Archerfield,
April 3, 1799

I do not know quite what is about this house. I suppose it is just that I have lived here all my life. It is not a beautiful house. It is square and made of granite, a pink granite. It seems almost brave, so firm and square and a little ugly in the cold salt wind.

Elgin laughs at the house, and says we shall live in his beautiful mansion Broomhall. My parents seem impressed by him, perhaps because he is a lord and they are just very wealthy. He towers over me, and smiles pleasantly when I talk, as if everything I say is amusing but not worth listening to.

I have bad dreams. I keep dreaming of the Parthenon in Athens, which Elgin talks about. In my dreams I stumble and fall but no one rescues me.

CHAPTER 13

'Why did you want to come here so much?' Anne asked Alexander. They were standing in front of the west pediment of the Elgin Marbles in the British museum.

'They interest me,' he said.

Alexander was close to her and he kissed the back of her neck, then his hand crept up her sleeve to the soft skin of her arm. Alexander smelt of peppermints.

On the far left reclined a river god.

'I want you to tell me what parts went missing and when, that's all.' His voice was soft, almost cloying.

'What is this about?' she said, jutting up her chin.

She pulled her arm from him.

'On the east pediment over there, even by 1765, two of the heads still in the Carrey drawings had been lost,' she said. 'The only figure there which retains its head intact could be Dionysus or Heracles. But it is heavily weathered – its nose gone, its eyes gouged out by the elements, I suppose.'

'Tell me about the west pediment.'

'Well,' she said, 'both major figures, Athena and Poseidon, were accompanied by divine messengers; Athena had Hermes and Poseidon had Iris. The head of Hermes had disappeared by 1749 and all that Elgin took away was the battered torso, only part of what must have once been an extraordinary statue. Iris there has little rectangular sockets where her wings were once attached. In 1860 it was realised the right thigh and knee fragment was part of the statue and the left knee in 1875 . . .'

As she spoke Alexander went round standing close to each statue, slightly breathless, his face varnished with sweat. He took a white handkerchief from his pocket and wiped his forehead. His black shoes shone and the creases of his trousers were precise. Every now and again his arm slipped round her waist or touched her bottom.

'There is the torso of Athena. Her head, which had been carved from a separate piece of marble, was missing in 1674 but a fragment including part of her helmet is in the Acropolis museum,' she said.

'So, when Elgin was around, the head of Hermes had only fairly recently gone missing?' asked Alexander. 'Is that so? The head of Hermes?'

'I suppose it is. Certainly neither Athena nor Iris had heads in 1674 when Carrey did his drawings. But Hermes did.'

'Maybe it could even have been buried around there somewhere,' he said thoughtfully.

She blinked at him. 'What's on your mind, Alexander?'

He smiled and his skin rumpled into shiny folds.

'This and that,' he said, his voice wrapping her up, making it dark where she stood.

His caresses boxed her in, packaged her. For the last years that had been what she wanted; the cosy cotton wool of his thick flesh which comforted her without challenging her, or intruding into her private thoughts.

He was playing with her fingers as he held her hand, while the two of them stood before the reclining river god, his skin rough, rippling, the muscles bulging, the ribs just visible, the cloak hanging like a waterfall from his thin arm broken at the wrist.

Our bodies, we often despise them, she thought. Certainly her own butterfly body, with its white gossamer skin, its fine bones, its little bumps for a tummy and its long legs, wasn't anything she adored. She carpeted it in skirts, dressed, and hurried through her life. But here in front of her was a worship of the body, of taste and touch, of living in the moment and living through time. These figures contained the wind and the river just as I do, she thought, whenever I stand on the balcony over the Thames, part of this new century but with time travelling through me, back and forth, making me one with Iris as she springs forward with her cut-off legs, her mastectomised right breast, her drapes carved from stone but made of the lightest, finest fabric, the wind and rain itself.

We think we're hemmed in by walls and wives and husbands and children but none of us are. We're the river god, his stone body marked brown with time in places, we're Hermes the winged messenger, and it's good to be alive, to feel air on the skin.

I can do as I please, she thought, and this is what these statues are telling me, about just how very good it is merely to be alive, not to hide from life.

'In the Carrey pictures, Hermes is portrayed looking over his shoulder . . . There's little of him now – just a hunk of stone shaped with muscles and ribs here and there. But when you imagine the head – it would bring it all to life, make it live.'

He stretched up and leant over and touched the headless Hermes, and his body shivered and Anne was aware of the attendants watching him. He stood back.

She felt that sense of longing, but maybe for these figures here in all their vigour, all completely present yet not really there at all, just clumps of stone mined from some Greek quarry.

CHAPTER 14

Patrick's uncle turned up from New York State and insisted on taking Patrick out in Soho. A tall, broad man like his nephew, he had become steadily more cheerful and outgoing since the death of his wife a couple of years back. They arrived at a restaurant after visiting a number of pubs and wine bars. At dinner his uncle folded his hands in front of him on the table, thumbs touching, and began to bounce his chair gently up and down to the troubled consternation of the waiters.

'Now how's your love life?' said his uncle, whose nose was a little red from all the alcohol testing.

'Fine,' said Patrick.

His uncle called over the waiter.

Patrick studied the long, wide menu with all the items written in careful handwriting. The table was starched white, the cutlery silver and glittering and the waiters, in their black and white livery, polite and efficient. Patrick tore off a piece of bread. It had been weeks since he'd had a meal in a good restaurant.

Genteel poverty was not what he'd been looking

for in life, but still. His life in Wall Street hadn't satisfied him, and this life, strangely, in spite of its innumerable problems, did.

'The sea bass looks good,' said Patrick.

'I want something very British. Steak and kidney! Just what I want!'

Patrick's uncle had made his money selling spare parts for washing machines and when his wife was alive he never spent anything. But since her death he had deftly managed to expend large sums, to his huge, and surprised, pleasure.

His uncle used to disapprove of his brother, Patrick's father, because of his affairs.

The worst incident in some ways was Patrick's father's affair with the next door neighbour. Mrs Eileen Morgan used to come round pretending she wanted to see Patrick's mother, and when she came round the furniture in the main room seemed to wait attentively, leaning forward even, to hear what would happen next. She had a way of making life dramatic, as Victoria had, with her perfect nails, her high heels.

Mrs Morgan used to stand on the step leading down to the main room like someone on stage in a one-woman show. One hand would play with the top button of her shirt, while her elbow jutted out into the air. Her smiles for Patrick were hot and inclusive, lying over him like blankets. Patrick, even when he was as young as eleven, used to like looking at the down of her skin.

Like Victoria, Mrs Morgan reminded him of a

chocolate that you bit into and for a moment it was all creamy and luscious delights until it became cloying and you wanted to spit it out, but it's too late then, and all day you're left with a sense of disappointment and a certain disquiet. But then you eat the chocolate again because you cannot believe that the disappointment was its fault and not yours.

Patrick had been repelled by his mother and Mrs Morgan, but fascinated too. He had the same attitude to a number of women.

Patrick and his uncle ordered their meal.

'So, Patrick, tell me about your latest girlfriend,' said his uncle, neatly arranging his wine glass and water glass, then pursing his lips in concentration.

Patrick hadn't felt relaxed since meeting the woman in the British Museum.

'Joe,' said Patrick wearily, 'I hate to disappoint you but my girlfriend is a dead woman, Mary Elgin, the woman I'm writing about. She married the seventh Lord Elgin, of the Elgin Marbles, and travelled to Constantinople. But she was disgraced in a trial for adultery in 1808 and when she died was buried in an unmarked grave.'

His uncle's mouth took a downward turn. This was not what he'd anticipated hearing. He pushed his thumbs together. Patrick noticed that his uncle's shirt cuffs were slightly frayed. Maybe his life wasn't quite so perfect without his wife.

'My other girlfriend is older than I am,' continued Patrick. His uncle brightened. 'Very sexy. Pretty.'

'You don't have to talk about this if you don't want to,' said his uncle eagerly. 'It's rude and prying of me even to ask. It's just – I want to know how you are. You were always my favourite nephew you know.'

Patrick smiled.

'Married?' said his uncle.

'Married.'

'I see. Children?'

'No.'

'And is it serious, between you and her?'

Suddenly his uncle didn't seem so drunk.

'No. Just casual.'

'You're sure?'

'Absolutely.'

His uncle carefully took one of the frayed bits of cotton from his shirt cuff but didn't seem to make a connection between the dangled cotton and the fact that his shirt cuffs were disintegrating.

Patrick drank some more wine.

'Just don't mess up your life, that's all. Lives do get messed up by mistake, by sheer carelessness. Don't do that.'

Patrick looked round. 'Great place this.'

'Don't be like your father. Try to be faithful. Try to do the right thing.'

'Of course. I saw what his behaviour did. Why would I do the same?'

Patrick didn't want to live like his father.

He stopped talking. Over the other side of the room he saw the girl from the library. She got up from the table she was sharing with a round-faced older man and wove her way between the tables towards the ladies' room.

Patrick put his napkin on the table and stood up. He strode through the white tables, the dark oak chairs, the elegant men and women, bumping against a waiter as he went. He stopped Anne on her way back to the table.

'Hi,' said Anne.

'Who's the elderly gentleman?' demanded Patrick.

As he said this, he realised he must be drunk. Patrick thought she had pretty ears and wanted to touch them.

'I could ask the same thing,' she said.

'So you did notice me. He's my uncle. Is that yours?'

Even here he could smell her. The smell of apricots.

He was surprised just how small she was. He could pick her up so easily. It annoyed him that he had a great desire to pick her up in his arms and see exactly how heavy she was.

'No,' she said.

'Your husband?'

'Maybe,' she said.

He could feel the sweat clinging on his back.

'I assume you're working on the Elgins from the way you looked as though you'd kill me to get those books. Or am I wrong?' he asked, half begging her to say he was wrong.

The rest of the room withdrew, became a faint,

distant jumble of people, just a crowd scene of glasses and a chandelier and polished wood.

'I note you want the same books,' she said.

He nodded, feeling again heavy, cumbersome, masculine, some heavy-footed dinosaur compared to this delicate girl who was fluttering before him about to fly off out of the window at any moment.

'What are you writing?' she said, smiling, and her lower lip stuck out and he thought how young she was, and how he wanted to touch her lip.

A waiter skimmed by, touching her lightly with his shoulder as he went by, then throwing back a light smile, as though somehow she were part of a game they all knew. Patrick was jealous of the waiter.

His whole body felt very warm and he could see the slight sweat on her upper lip. Ah, he thought! She's made of flesh too, she's not just some quint-essence of calm. Her green velvet jacket, it's too hot for the room. When she put it on earlier, she liked the look of it, but now she regrets it, he thought. He could imagine her skin sweating underneath the velvet, touching the velvet.

'Well?' she said. 'What is it? I'd love to know.'

His height made him dominate everyone, and his head bowed a little as he spoke to her, and his shoulders stooped too, as if surrounding her.

He leant forward intimately and she smiled and he said, gently, 'I can't tell you anything.'

'Oh? How rude you are! You take yourself so seriously!'

She motioned him to come close, with fluttering eyes, and then when he did, she turned round with a laugh and hurried back to her table leaving Patrick huge and smouldering.

Her companion watched Patrick closely. He was a plump, tanned man in his forties, the kind who wore gold Rolexes and shirts which were just too white. Patrick nodded his head to him before making his way to the men's room. Afterwards he returned to his table, his heart punching at his ribs in anger.

'Tell me, who was that beautiful young woman you were talking to?' said his uncle's cheery voice.

'A historian,' Patrick said flatly. 'She's trying to compete with me over my book. I fear she's writing a biography of Mary Elgin.'

Patrick watched Anne lean towards her companion and touch his cheek.

'You see, what you have to understand,' said Patrick, 'is that it's infuriating when someone else comes into your area and tries to challenge you.'

'The steak and kidney is great,' said his uncle roundly. 'I see why this place was recommended. So you're afraid of looking foolish in front of all your friends if you fail? All your rich friends in New York maybe? Who cares, Patrick? So what if once you didn't win. You could never bear to lose anything. You got good at pretending you didn't mind, but you really, really minded.'

Patrick pushed his carrots to the side of his plate.

'You still loathe carrots?' said his uncle. 'When

you came to lunch with us you'd always leave them.'

'I do,' said Patrick emphatically, as if challenging his uncle to make him eat them. Then, seeing his uncle's expression of surprise, he smiled.

CHAPTER 15

'Who's that big thug?' asked Alexander, with a faint smile which plumped up his cheeks and narrowed his eyes. His white shirt shone in the half-light of the restaurant and the crisp starched collar seemed to hold up his head. Alexander's voice had a threatening tenderness.

She lit a cigarette and knocked back a glass of red wine. He put out his hand and touched her cheek.

Alexander always needed to touch everything he saw, people and things. He responded to them more on a physical level than an intellectual one. She had seen him tremble in front of the Rodins in Paris, and when he spoke to women he often touched them lightly on the arm first.

Alexander then put his hand over hers, folded it over, as if making cakes, folding the mix, making her hand belong to him. Yet what he liked about her, she knew, was her difference, her independence, which he spent so much time trying to subdue but always failed.

'He works in the library. He's the one who keeps

using one of the books I need,' said Anne. 'Grumpy young sod he is. American. I can't bear people who treat life as though they're chipping away on a coal face when all they're doing is having a nice time pottering round libraries.'

'You think he's working on the same subject?' said Alexander.

'Maybe,' she said, with a shrug, blowing out a little fog of cigarette smoke.

'I see,' said Alexander, his eyes small in his thick-skinned face. His skin was always hot, a much higher temperature than anyone else she'd ever met. His tie had a neat knot. He looked over at where Patrick sat with his uncle, his shoulders up, drinking wine too quickly, the bulk of his shoulders like a wall, too good looking, too tough, an unlikely academic.

'What else do you know about him?' asked Alexander.

'Nothing,' she said.

'Suppose he's writing the same book?' he said.

'I can't reserve historical characters.'

'You can try. Besides, are you sure he's a historian? He doesn't look like one. Maybe he has other motives.'

'What other motives could he have? You're so suspicious,' she said. 'So devious.'

Sometimes, she thought, when he smiles his cheeks swell out as if he has toothache. He reminded her of some overweight thirteenth-century madonna with swollen, wood-carved cheeks.

'I'm a businessman, darling. I deal in things.'

Although Alexander was capable of generosity, sympathy and kindness, his underlying quality was self-interest, and she had known that from the moment they met. It had been three years ago at a piano auction where she had been buying a piano for her goddaughter Lily, and he had been buying one for his son, or so he said. She realised later he was intending to sell it on.

Somehow their meeting, in the rarefied and magical atmosphere of the piano auction, had placed their relationship on a higher level than it probably deserved.

At the auction people in different stages of eccentricity had squeezed around the hall trying out the pianos which lined

the walls and filled the centre of the room. A man plucked the sounds out of the black and white keys, looking as if he were unravelling knitting. Another man, in a black cowboy hat, had thundered down one end of an old grand while a serenely dressed lady carefully tried a few notes on a piano within a rosewood inlaid frame. The notes rang out querulously.

'That one's had mice,' a heavy voice had said as Anne had examined a pretty brown piano which had an estimate of between £150 and £200. 'They've eaten bits of the notes, and their urine has damaged others. Not a good buy.'

'Oh,' said Anne, turning and grinning at the

little man beside her who had sparkly little eyes, an immaculate suit and a round face. Apart from his roundness, he showed little sign of the rampant strangeness displayed by the other people in the room as they twirled long scarves round their necks, caressed the smooth cases of pianos and closed their eyes as they spread their hands out and conjured sound of out these large pieces of furniture. If she'd first met Alexander while surrounded by normal people she would probably have been unsettled by him. Even here, at the piano viewing, there was a worldliness which amused her, certainly compared to the unworldliness of the other customers.

'The one next to it is a good cheap piano. It's new you see. The old ones have too many problems. That black Yamaha's a steal if you get it for under £500.'

'Oh – but isn't it rather plain?' she said. 'Rather dull.'

'Plain? Yes, it's certainly plain,' said Alexander. 'You don't look like the type for dull things,' he continued, as she stood moving from foot to foot, her wrist half laden with silver jewellery from Mexico, her eyes as bright as some jewelled beetle from Madagascar.

He examined the one on the other side of the mouse-eaten one, checking out the insides, caressing the mahogany case, studying the auction catalogue notes on it, before sitting down, closing his eyes and playing rather well.

★ ★ ★

Alexander finished off his red wine. He dabbed at his mouth with his napkin, leaving damp red stains.

'If I were you,' said Alexander, 'I'd find out about that big guy's book.'

Alexander looked around for the waiter. Combining indolence with impatience, Alexander flickered between a desire for control and a Mediterranean sensuality.

'The main course,' said Alexander to the waiter.

'Darling, do you really think that hasn't occurred to me?' she said. 'Sometimes you treat me like a baby.' At first Alexander had entertained her, let her free to think about the subjects of her work, to think about Paolo. She wondered what absurd gnomic utterance Paolo would have made about Alexander. Once Paolo said: 'If you want to know what God thinks of money, you have only to look at those to whom He gives it.'

'I don't like to hear of competition,' he said to Anne.

'You make it sound like business. It's not. It's history,' she said.

'Everything is business,' he said solemnly, and she watched the folds of his face and his turbulent little mouth. 'I want the best for you,' he asserted.

'Oh really?'

'I know you are a superb writer but there's always someone better. At everything. You have to watch out for him, or her. That's all. You should find out more.'

'I just do what I'm good at, that's all.'

'Yes, and I admire you for that. But it's not always enough. Sometimes you have to fight. That guy,' continued Alexander, tearing a piece of bread, 'is quite talented.'

Anne tilted her head and frowned.

'I'm sorry?'

'I said he's quite talented.'

Anne tapped her fingers on the table.

'Ah. So you do know about him?'

'I make it my business to know everything about you.'

'I thought you said he didn't look like a historian.'

'I meant he doesn't look as if he's *just* a historian,' he said.

'You're nosy, Alexander.'

He shrugged. 'When you mentioned someone else was using your books, I made enquiries. At the library, then at the bookshop, then with his publisher. It wasn't difficult.'

'You didn't tell me,' she said, adjusting her cutlery, then lifting her knife and directing the point at him as if it were a gun.

'I want to look after you but I don't want you to know I'm looking after you,' he said.

'Bang!' she said, miming killing him, her knife a gun. 'How sweet you are,' she said curtly, leaning back in her seat. 'How very godlike,' she continued.

'Thank you,' he said expansively as the waiter brought him an overflowing plate of rare steak, baby potatoes, runner beans. 'His name's Patrick

Browning. An American. His last book was on Turner, beautifully written, thoroughly researched. He is determined, not one of your wimpy British historians. Lives in a tiny apartment and supplements his cash working as a bouncer and bodyguard. Has a number of casual affairs and a steadyish one with a married woman. He obviously thought being a historian in England would be romantic, you know, prove you don't care about money, but he had no idea it would be this impoverishing.'

'Thanks,' she said.

'I heard a rumour that he'd bought some diaries up in Edinburgh which contain . . . certain revelations which would interest me.'

'What diaries?'

'Mary Elgin's.'

'That's absurd. There weren't any diaries. She didn't write diaries.'

He shrugged. 'That's not what I hear. Find out,' he said.

'Who told you this?'

'A contact of mine in Edinburgh.'

'Some low-life contact? What could one of your guys care about Mary Elgin's inner life?'

He coughed. 'There is no need to insult me,' he said. 'I want to help you with your book.'

'I find that hard to believe,' she said. He had never shown so much interest before. 'Tell me, who told you about these diaries?'

'I forget,' he said, with a smile.

★   ★   ★

Later that evening they stood in the main room of the flat. 'Come over here,' he said.

She thought of Water Raleigh, in the Tower of London, just nearby, lying in bed, overlooking the river, the raw rain falling. And Elizabeth I, fearing the slice coming down on her neck, touching the rough walls, seeing the light pressing through the bars, planning.

Mary Elgin had moved from one prison, from her relationship with her husband, to another, the shame of the rest of her life.

'I said, come over here,' he continued.

'I'm tired,' she said, standing on one leg with the other leg stretched out behind her.

'You find him attractive, don't you, that big guy?'

'That great thug? No. He looks like a storm cloud. I wouldn't want to fuck a storm cloud.'

Alexander moved closer to her.

He took one of her fingers, and sucked it, watching her. She looked away. He took his left hand and moved her chin back to face him.

He smiled, that soft, easy smile which just curled up a little at the corners.

He put his hands on her shoulders, turned her round and directed her to the centre of the room.

'You look very sexy today,' he said, and he put his hands up her shirt, to her breasts, and his hands were warm. They were always warm, even when he came out of the cold. 'I want to fuck you. Pull up your skirt.'

'Not now.'

'I said, pull up your skirt.'

He put his mouth on hers, covering it all over like a snail.

She pulled up her skirt. He felt the silk of her pants. He ran his lips lightly over her forehead, his hand between her legs, touching the silk. He unzipped his trousers.

How do we all get locked in our various prisons? she thought. When she first moved into his flat she only saw Alexander once a week, but recently he came round more often, and she was unhappy about the frequency of his visits. He was increasingly possessive.

Outside, on the river, a tug went by and its noise stung the air.

She could still see her tall father, his head bent, standing by the window of their flat overlooking Hong Kong harbour. Her father had been an important diplomat, always striding from one place to another, adjusting his tie, carrying his briefcase, an unreal creature from an unreal world, one of the gods.

'He works so hard,' their mother would say.

Their mother, however, was anything but a goddess. Giggly, funny, she went in for wearing enormously high heels from which she would occasionally trip.

From Hong Kong, they visited Bali, Thailand, Australia, their father with a guide book and a frown, their mother with high spirits.

Often their father would go away on business trips alone.

And then one day he told his family what he'd been doing as he stood before a pink sunset, the huge windows behind him. Later, some policeman came and put him in handcuffs and took him away. It was shortly afterwards that Anne's brother disappeared and never came back.

There was something about Alexander which reminded her of her father, a certain shiftiness.

'Take the pants off,' said Alexander

She slipped out of them, and he made her stand further back, then further back, until her back was resting against a drawing of a horse in a Russian winter. He pushed himself inside her. At least Alexander didn't threaten her memories.

'You don't have any secrets from me, do you?' he said afterwards.

'Yes, Alexander, you know perfectly well that I do,' she said, and kissed him on his podgy little nose, before turning lightly away with a laugh.

CHAPTER 16

'Life should be *fun*,' said Victoria, as she kissed Patrick's neck. She'd turned up yet again at his flat, phoning just a few minutes before, with dark shadows under her eyes. There was what looked like some bruising to the left of one eye, which she had tried to cover up with foundation and powder. 'And last night I had to go to a banquet and sit next to one of the living dead. The living dead.'

'Your eye,' said Patrick. 'Is it okay?'

She shrugged. 'Too many late nights.'

'Victoria, look . . .'

'I don't want to talk about it now,' she said brightly. 'Please, not now. Chat to me. Ask me what I've been doing. Don't talk about Charles.'

'Where was the banquet?' he asked.

'Oh, at the Guildhall. Terrible. Really terrible.'

'What plates did you eat off? Were they gold? I heard that at Buckingham Palace banquets they eat off real gold plates.'

'Oh, just some porcelain. I tried to notice for your sake. I know how you appreciate details. Limoges, with blue and red flowers round the rim. I don't like pots and pans – I like paintings.'

Victoria had amassed a fine collection of paintings over the years. She had made the most of her money with her sharp visual taste and interest, and bought and sold with skill and financial acumen. The paintings, she had told Patrick, were all in her name for tax purposes. Charles was a minor aristocrat with a Scottish estate. She was proud of his job, but seemed to despise everything else about him, as if his own background of inherited wealth and natural indolence horribly reflected her own laziness. Her husband's career was important to Victoria; she liked to show her parents, particularly her father, how successful he was, how successful she was. But every time Patrick saw her she seemed just a bit more unhappy.

She could do anything she wanted, whenever she wanted, yet it seemed there was nothing she wanted to do. Her intense interest in him seemed one of the most important parts of her life.

'What did you have to eat?' Patrick asked Victoria. 'And was your husband there?' He was unbuttoning her shirt. 'Go on, tell me,' he insisted when she looked away. Usually she was poised, immaculate, perfectly in control but today she was blurred at the edges.

'I can't remember. Some terrine. Some meat. Something fattening. As much wine as you want. I like that. That I like. The wine. It helps me to sleep. I've been sleeping so badly.'

Mary Elgin had risked her reputation for her lover Robert Ferguson. 'We live but for one another. It is now all in vain to talk of the world . . . we have but one chance,' he wrote to Mary. Some of their love letters were read out in her scandalous trial for her divorce from Elgin. But Victoria was not Mary. She was colder, more calculating.

'I sit there being frivolous,' she said, 'but it wears me out. And then when I got back I got the news that my father had been admitted to hospital. He'd had a stroke.' She shrugged. 'Not that I care.'

She often talked about her father, whom she claimed to loathe, but had his photograph in the drawer by her bed. Once Patrick had found her with the photograph in her hands, staring at it.

'My mother wanted me to visit him today – but I don't want to – I'd rather see you . . . I don't want to see him. He's such a shit – full of anger – all he ever cared about was my clever sister, a lawyer like him. Now he's ill, why should I care?'

'Victoria . . . I . . .'

'And the night before that,' interrupted Victoria, as she ran her fingers over his face, 'I went to a party. Everyone circled round everyone else. There was no warmth. I thought, if Charles loses his job, it will all be pointless, like being about to win snakes and ladders and tumbling down a snake back to the beginning of the board, with nothing to show for anything. I kept thinking of you – how big you are, your shoulders, and the way you blunder into rooms and knock things over. I never thought I'd marry a failure, that Charles would turn out to be a failure. I thought he'd be editor one day, I really did . . .

'I kept working out who I would fuck first if I had a choice. I thought that idea would amuse you,' she said, playing with her thin gold bracelet, looking up at the ceiling, glancing at him every now and again, 'and I made a mental list. It was fun, going round, talking about this and that while thinking all the time whether the man I spoke to was nine or ten on my list – the one with the narrow hands, the one with the fat lips, which would be which.'

'But your father . . .'

Victoria turned away, her swan's neck registering some kind of sadness, and he ran his square hand over it.

'And I thought of what we do together,' Victoria was saying. 'And I felt all shivery. A girlfriend of mine I hadn't seen for a while said I looked different.'

'Victoria.'

'Yes?'

'Go and see your father.'

CHAPTER 17

Mary Elgin,
At sea,
September 6, 1799

Sometimes Elgin seems so savage, and so ill. There are still more rumours of his affairs. Worse than that is his coldness. I stopped the marriage ceremony, because I wanted to tell the bishop my fears. But my mother spoke to me, and the marriage continued.

We are at sea now. How sick I feel. We are on the way to Constantinople via Gibraltar and Naples and the ship is crammed with people, beds and trunks. Only the sight of the seabirds soaring above us keeps me sane. The seagulls cut through the air and seem to enjoy themselves as they dip and plunge into the foam of our wake.

Elgin is remote, as he so often is. It is as if he is on a higher plane than the rest of humanity. I write, pretending I write to my dear mother (which sometimes I do), then I lock up my words. I write merry letters to my mother asking about the village of Dirleton but all the time I wonder what I have let myself do?

Elgin keeps saying he wishes to fill Broomhall,

which still isn't finished, with classical sculpures and monuments he intends to ship back. It was his architect Thomas Harrison who first suggested it. At least monuments do not get seasick.

CHAPTER 18

As Patrick walked through Bloomsbury on the way to the library he had a sudden cold feeling in the back of his neck. He stopped and turned.

A man with white hair quickly crossed the road while one in an anorak hurriedly overtook him. A woman in a beige raincoat looked startled as he glared at her. There were about twenty people who could be following him.

He walked on. He looked round again. The crowd milled around behind him. He noticed a tall young man with a shaven head. Was he the one who'd been behind him when he went to the library that time? The young man crossed the road. It was probably nothing. So many people looked much the same – that rangy, ape-like walk, the long sleeves, the cropped hair. But his sense of unease continued.

The first-floor reception rooms in the Bloomsbury squares had long full-length windows behind which lights glittered as if perpetual parties were taking place. The rain spluttered over the green leaves. There was no one following him, he was sure.

When he reached the library Patrick noticed Anne Fitzgerald at a nearby desk. He knew she'd seen him too; he could sense the tensing of the shoulders.

He stood up and walked in her direction and said hello to Anne, but she gave him a frozen smile. The book she was studying, he noticed, was the history of the Elgins.

'Now do you feel like coffee?' he said.

'No thanks,' she said.

He was not used to such a constant lack of enthusiasm. It made him like her more. She tucked her papers together like someone tucking a child in at night, then gave him an icy look, 'I don't drink coffee.'

'Tea then?' he said, with warmth, standing closely over her.

Anne looked up at him once again, and for a moment he thought she was going to say 'Go away'. Instead, she just said, 'No thanks.'

'Okay – whatever you like,' he snapped.

He strode out of the library, head first, shoulders forward, someone ploughing through the air. By the time he got to the British Museum he was calmer, then once he'd passed marble hawks, winged goddesses, all the swerving, swooping shapes of the mythic past of the Egyptians, the Babylonians, the ancient Chinese, he was completely calm again.

Inside the Duveen Room, the Elgin Marbles danced and seemed almost to move as he stood in the middle, drawing in their power, a kind of certainty that at the centre of life is vigour, the dance, while the great gods still loom over us, amusing themselves.

He addressed the attendant, who sat in a chair, and blinked at him. The attendant had a black moustache.

'You know,' he said to the dull-eyed man, 'that the Athenians used to think these were real people enchanted by magicians?'

'Maybe,' said a voice from behind him, 'they *were* real people enchanted by magicians.'

Patrick swung round. 'Hi!' he said. Anne stood a little distance behind him.

'Well, they could have been real people, in a way, don't you think?' she said, smiling.

She came over to him and put out her hand.

'I hurried after you. I feel as we're both working in the same area, it would be sensible to be friends. I'm sorry I was rude.'

They shook hands. 'Anne Fitzgerald, as you know.'

'Patrick Browning,' he said.

The attendant sniffed and looked away, down at the marble floor.

'Do you know,' Patrick said, 'that as a child I used to think when you died you became a statue. My mother took me to Washington and would say "There's so and so, he died in whenever . . ." pointing to a statue, so it was natural to assume that's what happened to you. Of course I worked it out eventually but still, you know, something makes me think that when I die I'll suddenly be frozen in place, some grand place actually, and have bronze poured all over me.'

'It would be a good idea, in some ways. You'd just sort of rot inside, but by then the bronze would have set,' she replied.

'Not sure that's how it works,' he said, screwing up his nose.

He was aware of the murmur of schoolchildren down the other end of the room. Some had coats shrugged back to below the shoulder, some had coats half hanging to the left or right, some dragging rucksacks, some clutching lunchboxes. They contrasted with a group of Japanese tourists who all looked neat.

'Do you have a deadline?' said Patrick.

'By the spring.'

He coughed. His throat felt dry.

'And you?' she said, smiling pleasantly.

'Soon.'

'For publication when?'

'I'm not sure,' he said.

'Ah, so if you're late we may publish around the same time,' she said.

'That's right,' he said. On her feet were grey suede boots, and her body seemed to spring up from the boots, up along her maroon velvet trousers to her purple shirt and black jacket. She held her red gloves in her hands.

'Have you come across any interesting new information?' she asked, staring at him. 'I hear there are some diaries around.'

'Really?' he said lightly. 'No, I haven't.'

'My information must be wrong,' she said. She touched him on the arm. 'Don't be so glum! Maybe the two books will help create interest! Like two restaurants in the same street, each doing better because of the existence of the other.'

'Absolutely,' he said, though he knew that was not what the effect would be, as no doubt she did.

It was hot in here, he decided, and his clothes clung to him while on the wall the white figures seemed so free and unconstricted. There was a coolness to her too, a coolness of intellect.

A voice rang out, 'Anne!' and she turned at once and something shivered over her face which looked a little like fear. But then she smiled. 'Alexander!' she said as he strolled towards them. He wore an expensive suit. From his circular face he smiled expansively but his eyes remained cold, somewhere else.

'Darling,' he said, kissing Anne on both cheeks.

'How did you know I was here?' she said.

There was a short pause, a heartbeat.

'I guessed!' he said. He turned to Patrick. He put out his hand to Patrick. 'How do you do? Aren't you the man from the restaurant?'

'That's right,' said Patrick. 'Patrick Browning.'

'I hear you're writing about the Elgins.'

'Mary Elgin.'

'And are you attacking Elgin for taking the marbles?'

'Absolutely.'

'How original. Everyone attacks Lord Elgin for taking the marbles,' said Alexander. '*Byron* attacked Lord Elgin. I'm Greek and I don't care,' continued Alexander. 'Why should you? They're beautiful.' He turned. 'Anne is right. It's the stories that matter. The history. The old stones are there in the British Museum.'

'It was imperialistic of Elgin to take the marbles,' said Patrick.

'Well Britain was imperialist in those days. So what?' said Anne in that cool, intelligent voice. 'The British Museum is a multicultural museum. A great museum. If you hand back everything to where it came from, every country would end up displaying only its own antiquities. A schoolchild wouldn't be able to see the past of any area but his or her own.' There was a slight flush to her face. 'Maybe Elgin shouldn't have taken them, maybe he did it for bad reasons, but still,' she said softly. Alexander was watching her intently, and the glow of sweat above her upper lips. Patrick wanted to shove him aside. 'They are magnificently displayed in one of the greatest museums in the world.'

'Exactly,' said Alexander.

'The fact that you're Greek and you don't care merely means that you don't care, not that all Greeks don't care. Most mind very much . . .' said Patrick, wanting to hit the round man with the fat lascivious hands in the face so he'd spin round and round like a top.

'Do you speak Greek?' asked Alexander, taking a step towards him. 'Anne speaks Greek. She's very clever. My advice is not to mess with things you don't understand.' Alexander put his hand on Anne's arm. 'I don't wish to alarm you but this isn't merely an academic's subject.' Alexander squinted at him.

'I can assure you, you don't alarm me in the least,' said Patrick, smiling. He noted that Alexander seemed a little afraid of him, in spite of his bluster.

'Come on,' said Alexander to Anne. With his arm round her waist he walked with her to the door, but at the door she shook off his arm, then turned and smiled at Patrick.

CHAPTER 19

'Why be so rude?' Anne said to Alexander in the taxi home. She lit up a cigarette. '*You* say that!' said Alexander. 'You gave a tirade!'

'You told me to be nice to him. I'm nice to him. You storm in and grab me and start arguing. You're so sinister. You behave like something out of *The Godfather*.'

'And you couldn't resist joining in, could you? Once there's an argument you can't resist slicing it up with that intellect of yours. Besides, you weren't nice to him because of what I said. That's not why you were there. I know you,' he said. 'You like him. Besides, a little difficulty, a little stress, will make him like you more. He may confide in you.'

'Darling, I don't like him. He happens to be a rival. We're both working in the same field, we're competitors. Besides, he seems too edgy, always on the edge of a fight. Why would I like him?' she said.

'Well, he likes you,' said Alexander.

'Maybe,' said Anne, breathing in her cigarette. 'Maybe not.' She tapped her ash into the ashtray.

He took her arm. She stared at his hand on her arm.

'I'd much rather you weren't quite so . . . disrespectful,' he said.

'Take your hand away,' she said.

He gripped it harder.

She took her cigarette and pressed it into his hand. His hand slapped her hard across the face and she reeled back, holding it, winded but half laughing.

'Well, you shouldn't treat me like your possession,' she said. 'I don't like it.'

When she'd lived in Hong Kong as a child she had been jostled in the markets, and grabbed sometimes, and had seen blood oozing from the hunks of meat, and some of it had smelt bad. In the river she'd once seen a body floating by in the awful days after her brother's disappearance.

He sat back in his seat and tipped back his head. His tie was loose, and he looked as though he were melting. He sucked the skin where she had burnt him.

She wound down the window and let the air blow in her face. At times Alexander would be sweet and kind, helping her clean the house, admiring what she cooked. But he would change from being quaintly ordinary, watching television with his food on a tray, and wearing a cardigan, to screaming in Greek down the phone about his dealing in paintings and antiques.

'You followed the giant, didn't you?' insisted Alexander.

'I was in the British Museum anyway and so was he. Have you been spying on me?'

She put the black flip-seat down and put her feet on it, crossed over.

'I may go up to Edinburgh in a couple of days,' she said.

'Good. People trust you, confide in you.'

'While you look like something out of the Mafia.'

'You want to go without me?'

'Yes,' she said. 'You don't go in for high-minded academic research. What is it? I can't understand your excitement. What is it you want?'

She could hear his quiet breathing. He put his hand on her knee, and she found the hand reassuring. She placed hers over his.

'I sometimes wonder if you care about me at all,' he said, sorry for himself now.

'You can be such a baby,' she said.

CHAPTER 20

Mary Elgin,
Gibraltar,
September 23, 1799

Not too long now before we get to Constantinople. I feel a little better. On the way here we came quite close to the coast of Africa; a barren burnt up country.

Last night we had dinner with General O'Hara who lives in a grand style in an immense house. Never let anyone talk to me again of rooms that are only 40 feet long! His table was broader than any other I have ever seen. But I was rather taken in, expecting some meat in the second course, instead of which there was only tarts etc but not one bit of meat. I shall be wiser tomorrow.

The weather is most intolerably hot. They say it is one of the hottest places in the world.

Such a garden as there is to this house, I never saw. Great large orange trees and myrtles, they quite shelter one from the sun.

CHAPTER 21

On the train to Edinburgh Anne drummed her fingers as she watched the green fields disappear and transform into small grey towns, then return to green fields again.

Every now and again, to her irritation, she found herself thinking of the thuggish Patrick Browning and felt a discomforting aching of the skin. She'd bought a copy of his book on Turner. It was brilliant, with real energy, and the photograph of him stared out and she found herself gazing at it for some time. She had hidden it before Alexander came home.

It was a strange kind of rivalry. The sense that Patrick was aware of what she was doing and she aware of what he was doing gave her a sense of being pursued, as though she were never quite alone, even on this train here. But maybe it was Mary who was with her.

It was to Edinburgh Mary came as a young woman, to society balls and parties, and here she used to meet her lover Robert in a hotel along Princes Street, then called the Fortune and Blackwells Hotel. It was a dark, old city, even then, in Mary's time, with its strange castle, its sudden pink skies, the sense of it being high somehow, above Scotland, above England, a place spun out of dreams.

Anne's room at The Balmoral was beautiful; she wondered where Patrick stayed when he was in Edinburgh, and thought of a white sheet lying over his sleeping body. She was surprised by these thoughts and tried to put them out of her mind. She thought of Paolo.

That afternoon, Anne wrapped her scarf round her and slipped out through the cold streets to Grassmarket, where she called in on an antiquarian bookshop. The assistant, his desk on a raised platform, wore a tweed jacket, and had an anxious face, surprised bushy hair and gleaming spectacles.

'Excuse me,' she said.

'Er, yes. Er, yes. What can I do for you?' he said, his caterpillar eyebrows jumping up and down. He fondled a book to him like a teddy bear that he feared someone might snatch.

'I'm looking for anything you may have on Mary Nisbet, the Countess of Elgin. Mary Elgin,' she said, in her high, clear voice.

'Ah!' he said, eyebrows shooting up again. She felt like darting over, leaping up and catching them before he lost them. She tried not to smile.

'Countess of Elgin,' he said, clutching his book even closer to his chest.

The old books and manuscripts lined up in piles on both sides.

'No! No, I don't have anything on the Countess

95

of Elgin. Nothing! Such a shame.' He lowered his leather bound book and peered forward.

'Thank you,' she said. 'Oh – a tall American hasn't been in here, has he? Asking the same kind of questions?'

The bookseller's eyebrows plunged together.

'Tall,' repeated Anne. 'Handsome I suppose. With a big jaw and a big nose. Dark hair. More like a lifeguard than an academic. Very memorable.'

The bookseller's mouth saddened a little at the edges.

'Ah!' he said, as if the mere thought of this tall big-jawed American was threatening. 'No! But I'm often not here! I get a lot of colds. I could ask my partner Frederick. He's away in Holland at a conference.'

'I don't . . . I don't suppose you have a number for him I could phone?'

'A number in Holland? For Frederick?' said the bookseller, in a shocked tone, as if she'd asked for some bizarre sexual service.

He tossed his bushy head back, then looked at her again, a little fiercely, then gave a nervous smile and shuffled up the stairs to his desk and rummaged around the papers to find the number, which he wrote down carefully on one of his sheets of writing paper, in brown ink, his handwriting meticulous and perfect.

'I did hear a rumour that some diaries of Mary Elgin had turned up. But you hear all kinds of rumours in this job.'

'Who told you?'

He frowned. 'I really, really don't remember.'

Back at the hotel, she rang the number but was put through to voice mail. She rang off.

The next morning, she went to work in the Scottish Records Office, studying the accounts of Mary's scandalous divorce trial.

At manuscript sales Anne would fondle even the old mortgage documents. The records of Mary and Robert Ferguson's divorce proceedings, all in neat brown writing, called out to her.

This time of computers and e-mail won't have the same power to move historians of the future, she thought. The crisp little letters of the computer give so little, make everything uniform, reasonable.

She bent over her work, her shoulders up.

On her way back to the hotel, she had a sense of someone behind her again. But when she turned round, there were innumerable people milling around on either side of Princes Street, tourists and workers.

Maybe Mary pursues me just as I pursue her.

I am spending too much time alone and growing strange, she thought, hurrying on through the crisp air.

Anne walked up to the National Gallery of Scotland and stared for a while at the portrait of Mary Elgin by Francoise Baron Gerard, with her dark curly hair, soft eyebrows and deep brown eyes matched by the dark velvet of her gown. It was a picture of someone pretending to be something they are not, and staring out from the confines of a white ruff and rich constricting dress, with a huge gem hanging between her ample breasts.

Anne stood there for a while, and Mary looked back at her intently. We are alike, we two.

The portrait of her mother, Mrs Hamilton Nisbet, was more romantic, but then it was by Gainsborough. Here was someone happy, with mysterious trees behind her, a pale-plum dress sweeping silkily around her and her greying hair piled up on her head and flowing over her shoulders. Her feet were dainty.

She had been loved, that woman; she looked whole.

It is that which drives us all forward, she thought, the desire to be whole.

And maybe it is love, maybe, waiting there, round a corner, at the back of a young man's eyes, love in the sunset, in the kiss, which makes someone whole. That's what we look for, the moment when everything grows still and some hidden director nods and says yes, that's it, that's absolutely it.

The rest of the day she called on bookshops all over Edinburgh and left her name and details, asking them to call if anything at all turned up about the Elgins.

In one bookshop, the Oak Bookshop, Anne asked the owner, as she had asked person after person in the other antiquarian and secondhand book-shops, whether they knew of the American Patrick Browning and whether they had any information about the Elgins. Patrick had left his name in most of them. It infuriated her to learn how thorough he'd been.

The woman at the Oak Bookshop was sitting on a high stool and had blue, alert eyes. When Anne asked about Patrick Browning she checked in a little red book, putting on her reading glasses as she did so.

She searched through her notebook for a while, licking her finger to turn the pages, then stopped. 'Here we are. Patrick Browning. That is all I can tell you.'

'That's wonderful,' said Anne, glancing at the Bloomsbury address written in black felt capitals. 'Very kind of you.' The books with their torn and faded covers lined up in their martial rows. The bookshop's owner had a fine pointed nose and gentle rivulets of wrinkles running everywhere. 'Trelawny,' said Anne. 'Do you have any books on Trelawny?'

'Let me go and look,' said the woman, speeding up to the other end of the shop.

In the short space that she was gone, Anne quickly changed Patrick's street number and postcode with the bookshop owner's black felt pen and put back the pen before the woman reappeared, carrying a flaky maroon copy of Trelawny's *Recollections of Shelley and Byron*, which Anne duly bought, at an inflated price, and left her own name and number in case there was any news of Mary Elgin.

She again called the number that Jimmy, the nervous bookseller, had given her, and this time got through at once to his partner Frederick in Holland.

'Jimmy mentioned you'd been in and would phone me,' said his breezy voice. 'Told me you were beautiful. With rivers of red hair and eyes like emeralds.'

'Poetic but hyperbolic, I'm afraid,' said Anne.

'Well anyway, whatever you look like, what is it?'

'Do you know anything about new papers on Mary Elgin?'

'Will you have lunch with Jimmy next time you're in Edinburgh? I've never heard him lovestruck before. Didn't know he had it in him.'

'Absolutely.'

'All I can say is ask at the auction house, Adam and Turner.'

'So there is something?'

'Ask them,' he said.

Anne hurried to the auction house off a sidestreet and spoke to the man behind the counter, a leathery sort of man of medium height with a crumpled figure and creased features. He looked at her from over his glasses. The room was panelled in wood and there were piles of books leaning against the walls, some with their covers falling off, some with embossed spines. There were a few boxes scattered around, one full of early *Beano* comics and another of paperbacks. Lying on the top she saw Shirley Conran's *Futurewoman* and one entitled *English Cookery*. The room smelt slightly of damp and the yellowing pages of books.

'Excuse me, is there someone who deals with old manuscripts?' she said.

'Yes. I deal with them,' said the leathery man.

'Could you help me? My name is Anne Fitzgerald, and I'm an historian. Could you possibly tell me if you've sold anything by Mary Elgin? I'm working on something about her.'

'No,' he said abruptly.

She was taken aback by his tone.

'You remember everything ever sold here, do you?' she asked, taking a fruit pastille from the bag in her pocket.

'Yes, I do,' he said as he glared at her from over his glasses.

A quiet girl with pale hair stood close by, examining some paperwork. She gave Anne a quick conspiratorial smile, clearly having put up with the man's rudeness for too long.

'Robert Frank used to deal with old manuscripts,' said the girl.

Anne sucked at her pastille.

The man scowled at the girl. His jaw jutted out and his hand smoothed out a piece of paper on his desk, like a lion pawing the ground in rage. The capillary veins on his face were broken, making it red, a roadmap of motorways.

'Would it be possible for me to have his number?' asked Anne.

The leathery man's face creased even more.

'We don't give out the addresses of our staff.'

'Former staff,' said the girl. 'He left.'

'Ah,' said Anne, watching the girl's face for signs of further information.

The man glared again, and sweat appeared on his forehead. He stroked the piece of paper in front of him.

'Did a tall American called Patrick Browning come here?'

'We can't possibly remember all the people who come here,' the man said. 'And anyway we keep our clients' privacy.'

'When was it Robert Frank left?' asked Anne.

'Recently,' said the girl.

'Jean – stop it,' snapped the man.

The girl shrugged and went on with the paper-work.

'He might have some crucial information about Mary

Elgin,' said Anne. 'I'm writing a biography of her.'

'I told you. We can't help you,' barked the man, and dismissed her by staring down at the paper he'd been straightening so fiercely, which she noticed to her amusement was in fact a leaflet for pizzas.

Jean shrugged at Anne, and nodded her head in the direction of the door.

A few minutes later Jean stepped out, shivering.

'My boss has gone for coffee down in the back

kitchen,' Jean told Anne, looking back nervously into the auction house. 'Robert Frank was sacked for serious misconduct. He was selling things he shouldn't before they'd been properly examined and priced and taking the money for himself. It isn't something we want to broadcast, you understand. I imagine this could be one of them. A tall American did come in. I'm sure he was called Patrick Browning; I remember thinking it was a lovely name,' she said, slightly dreamily.

So Alexander might be right about Patrick, after all.

'Where does Robert Frank live?' asked Anne. 'In Edinburgh?'

'He's gone abroad, to Spain I think, to drink himself to death there. That's why he sold things.' She shivered. The girl wasn't wearing a coat, just a cardigan, and a tweed skirt to below her knee. 'He confided in me about the sale – I think he felt guilty. But he wouldn't tell me who he'd bought the diaries from except it was an old man. He'd promised not to. Other people have come round asking questions but I've told them nothing. But I'm fed up with this job. I'm going to leave. I just don't care anymore.'

The man swung thunderously through the front door and caught the girl by the arm.

'You're fired if I catch you talking to journalists.'

'I'm not a journalist. I'm an historian,' Anne said.

His voice bellowed over Anne.

'Get out of here. Leave us alone,' he said. 'If you speak to Jean here one more time, she's fired. Is that understood?'

The cold wind on the street smacked into Anne's face as she walked. Maybe I'll just go straight down to London and confront Patrick. But maybe even if he has them there's nothing in them, just inconsequential bits and pieces.
I shall find this old man.

That day, Anne checked out of The Balmoral and travelled out by train, about half an hour from Edinburgh, to North Berwick station and then on by cab to Mary's little village of Dirleton. She intended to return to Edinburgh the next day and try somehow to trace the old man.
She checked into the hotel in the shadow of old Dirleton castle.
'Is there a guest book?' she asked while the receptionist filled in her details.
The receptionist, a young man of almost eerie pallor, looked up. 'Usually people write their comments in it when they're leaving, not when they're arriving.'
He smiled and pushed the book down towards her, his eyes lingering on her white hands. She looked back through over the last months and, of course, there he was, Patrick's name, and a comment. 'Great place.' Great place! she thought crossly. How inadequate a way to describe this.

104

Outside the hotel old Dirleton castle raised its stumpy fingers to the sky.

At least she was here now. She had been too comfortable going through the historical records available. Anne unbuttoned her coat. She hadn't fought enough to find new material. It was wrong to think history, the past, was something static, merely ready for different interpretation. Much of history was wrong, or partial, simply because so much evidence had been lost.

'Is it far to Archerfield?' she asked.

The receptionist frowned.

'No. Not at all. It's derelict, you know.' He pushed over a form for her to sign. He watched her. 'Men were billeted there during the war, that's when it began to go down,' he said. 'A potato gang stayed here once, and one owner took out the marble staircase and the cornices and took them down south. The same guy kept a granary cleaner there. They're big machines.'

'Do you remember a writer coming here recently, Patrick Browning?' asked Anne when she'd signed. She looked around. The office was bare, but comfortable. As she'd entered the hotel she'd seen the elegant main drawing room with its robust wood fire.

'Yes. American, wasn't he? Stayed in the room you're staying in, with the castle just out of the window,' he said, a little wearily. 'Can I help you with your bag?'

The room was beautiful, with curtains covered

105

in peonies and with one double bed, looking out over the castle. So Patrick had slept in this bed. She imagined his huge body lying in it.

The man from reception stood at the window, his long heron's legs leaning back on the heels of his black shoes.

Anne tipped generously. She unpacked, showered in the tiny bathroom, dressed up warmly then walked by the blazing fire of the drawing room and out by the village green, the local church, past a lodge and into a corn field towards the old house where Mary ended her days alone. A circle of curlews lifted off into the air, flying and turning in the cold sun.

Soon she saw the house there, in the distance, much grimmer than she would have imagined, but her heart lurched with pleasure all the same. Few people had written of Mary and of Archerfield. Great houses often had all their magic used up by being endlessly described by others until it was impossible for anyone to see them for themselves.

The pink tinge of the granite was visible, but still the building, with its blind eyes of windows filled in with corrugated iron, was severe.

It seemed intolerable that the house remained while Mary, with all her life, had gone.

Grass sprouted from the roof and two rooks swooped up from a chimney into the blue sky, across which clouds scudded, trying to make a cathedral roof. Around the old house were crops of trees here and there, bare and black. Every now and again a group of black birds skipped across the sky, above the skeleton trees.

Brambles and nettles grew up all around. But a side door had just a thin wooden covering with a triangular corner missing at the top right. Anne wanted to go in but saw a farm labourer working nearby who kept looking at her. A board was propped up against the door saying in red, 'Dangerous Building', then in black underneath, 'No Admittance'.

It seemed the house was hiding something – the way the moss covered the roof and the grass and rust hid the balcony which looked over towards the sea. The grass on the balcony was brittle, wintry, indifferent as, down below, the brambles curled and danced. Supposing there was some secret buried here? Supposing Alexander was right that the diaries held some secret?

I'll go back tonight, she thought, in peace, with no one watching me. I'll know her better then, when I've entered her house.

She returned to the hotel. It was strange to sleep in the same bed Patrick had slept in. At one in the morning she climbed out of bed. First, one layer: thick tights, thermal vest. Next came a pair of black trousers, then a velvet black pair, then a thick pair of boots. She took her torch.

She went back for her gloves, the red leather ones her brother bought for her on her thirteenth birthday all those years ago. The night was glorious

– cold, fresh, with the castle outlined black against the sky, full of stars and the moon, as she hurried along by the low-lying cottages, the cold stinging her face, the air filling her lungs.

All her limbs were close together, her physical restlessness enjoying the movement.

Everyone's asleep in their tidy beds, she thought, maybe murmuring in their dreams, in this tiny village, unchanged, resting through time. There's the church, with its sombre dark yew trees and their stunted tops, like overgrown ornaments. There are no lights anywhere, every eyelid is shut, every curtain drawn. The red telephone box is out of place. The frost clung to the ground on the village green, and she almost slipped on the ice.

An owl hooted. She passed the low-lying lodge, the house Mary added gables to during the last years of her life, and saw the Castle Lodge she had built.

She moved more quickly as she passed the white gates by the lodge into the Archerfield estate. The lodge had gables decorated with bright blue paint, celebratory paint. Mary built some of this – the Castle Inn, the church tower and the wall hugging the castle.

Later I'll climb into my white sheets, be safe, get out of time, out of these intersections, leave physical objects in their time.

But physical objects, houses, statues, bring back time, unlock doors.

When the moon went behind a cloud she switched

on the torch, to light the way ahead. The cornfields were dark on either side. The darkness hunched round her and she heard a rustle – some night-time creature, she thought, tramping on.

She liked the sound of her footsteps and the grey sky with the black trees clawing their way up the sky. The sea, away in the distance, tugged against the beach, smoothing everything out and hurling white foam against rocks.

A fox moved in the corn. Her hands were sweating. The austere old building reared in front of her, so forlorn now, with a splat of water from a pipe making a regular sound, and helping to make the area of greenery around it thicken.

Anne first went round each window, checking if she could push at the corner of any of them, her heart thumping as she pulled at the corrugated metal, at the wooden boards, struggling with the barriers.

She tugged at the piece of wood blocking the doorway, her feet pressing down the brambles, and cut herself. She swore. There was a rustle behind her, just a bird, she thought.

There's only darkness left, old memories, grief. The children, Mary's children, all four of them – Bruce, Mary, Matilda, Lucy – used to play here, but the Earl of Elgin came and took them away, then abandoned them himself, left them with his stern mother.

She hoped his ghost was tormented too. How she disliked him and his vindictive trial, with the team of top lawyers, and his greed to get money from the man who loved Mary.

She wrenched at the wood, determined now. A small corner came away. She pulled more and more, with all her will, and the wood fell away. She switched on her torch and climbed in.

She turned up the brightness of the torch. No staircase, nothing. There was dirt underfoot and the air was still and dank. She thought of trying to dig up some of the floor but when she bent down she found it was covered over with concrete. All these years, and there was nothing here at all.

The smell of dankness made her choke. The dark swirled around her, and time too, encircled her, all the time spent here, the laughter, the children's voices.

She wanted to shout out warnings to Mary, hoping they would reach her through the centuries. But of course we are all locked in our time, in our characters, and cannot hear the ghosts calling us.

Lifting the torch up, the light spread around and she saw fallen wooden beams, broken fragments of brick, a light from a third-floor window.

She looked round. All that volume of darkness which had once held voices. Here Mary lived all these years with her secrets after breaking up with Elgin, marrying Robert Ferguson then living here after his death, still disgraced and cut off from her children.

A bit of flooring here, a bone there.

She stood still, turning her torch round and round, over the cracked walls, the bare stones, the grass, the sense of the outside world taking the place over, fighting to dismantle it, return it to blackness, to nothing, taking away the voices, distributing them into the turning air with the birds.

'Look after my Bruce,' Mary had written, 'for some reason I think he's the weakest of them all.' He died young, never having married, never becoming the next Lord Elgin, violent and crazy, maybe a victim of Elgin's syphilis.

It was here the men came to Mary to serve a petition on her, to take her to court. Her poor mother and father had had to suffer the shame of the scandal; their only daughter an adulteress, and every detail made public.

The darkness in the air. There had been a darkness like this, lingering there, after Paolo died. It had seeped into corners, lain with her in the bed.

She tried to imagine Mary. Maybe it is not possible. The past is somewhere else, down a long corridor.

Suddenly weary, Anne sat on a wooden beam and it cracked – the damp had rotted it and destroyed it. She crouched on the floor for a while. There was rust everywhere, and a few fragments of glass. A few patterns in the stone, places where fireplaces used to be.

Then she heard the sound of someone's footsteps. She slowly stood up.

From the chimney, she heard a rook fly up. The

sound rose up through the drainpipes, through the tiles of the moss-covered tiles as the rooks scattered off into the sky.

Something crackled under her feet and she looked down at the bones of a mouse. Her heart thumped as if the bats and rooks were inside it.

Then she heard his easy, engulfing voice.

'Hello, Anne.'

She caught her breath.

'Find any treasure?' Alexander said, and shone his torch into her face.

'What the hell are you doing here?' she said.

She at once realised she wouldn't be able to return to Edinburgh to try to find out more about the old man. Alexander would insist on coming too, and would try to find out what she knew. And she didn't want him in any part of this.

'That's the question I very much wanted to ask you, darling. Sometimes, you know, I do fear you're not completely straight with me. What exactly are you looking for here?'

His intense interest was odd and inappropriate and she did not trust him.

'Ghosts,' she said.

She found it hard to fall asleep that night, Alexander stirring beside her. Everything seemed vivid.

All the time, she thought, of course what we don't see, what we can't know, is the people studying us, not just from our time, and not just from the past, but from the future.

We watch the past, trawl it for interest, illumination, understanding, but the future watches us too, presses its face against the window, watches as you walk towards your love, as you make that decision, as you plan and deceive and invent.

We exist in all these time frames; we play roles in the lives of the future. Bit parts, perhaps, not as important as Mary Elgin's; maybe we turn up again just as a fading photograph in an album examined by some distant relative, or maybe more.

Mary Elgin: she lives again as Patrick and I research her, and her life is changed by us. It isn't finished by her death. It remains in flux, reviewed, reinterpreted, revived, maybe redeemed. And as I remember Paolo, so he lives.

Elizabeth tells me we only ever have the present, only have today, and I understand that. But sometimes the present seems so thin and frightening, the past so compelling. I want that moment when it all comes together, the past and the present and the future.

CHAPTER 22

Mary Elgin,
Palermo,
Sicily,
October 4, 1799

I have received no letters from my parents yet. I sent a long one today, but when will it reach them?

I keep thinking of stepping out on the iron balcony which leads from my mother's bedroom, and standing out there, watching the green park roll away before me. I try to remember what my mother's voice sounds like.

CHAPTER 23

'Darling,' said Victoria, 'I am so glad you came over.' With her dark hair and red lips and her silk shirt, the colour of plums and bruises, she reminded him of the dark petals of a hollyhock. She seemed to swim over to him where he stood on the doorstep.

The Holland Park area looked sumptuous and settled and green. The wide streets with their elegant white houses suggested that no harm could ever come to anyone. Even the weather seemed warmer here, dulcet, and the houses displayed oil paintings, antique furniture and grand curtains tied back in extravagant swathes of material. Patrick had rung Victoria before coming round, and her voice had sounded nervous.

She took his arm, laughing, and dragged him into the hall with its glittering paintings and mirror. There was white lilac on the hall table for a change and Patrick wondered where she got it this time of year.

Patrick ran his fingers through his overlong hair.

Victoria led him into the drawing room and then abandoned him while she went round tidying up, straightening the objects in the room, the photograph frames, the collection of ink wells, the magazines shimmering out from the coffee table. All the time she smiled and chatted about a party she'd been to a few nights before.

Victoria was thickly made up, with a porcelain make-up, and her two dark eyes made her for a moment a china doll. He thought he could see a bruise on her cheek, under her make-up.

He could feel his Adam's apple huge in his throat. All the paintings seemed to crowd in on him, the flower painting with the wasp on the rhododendrum, the picnic in the garden, the young girl in a dense white frock, and his mouth was dry. The yellow ochre walls were too intense too, pushing towards him, and the mantlepiece too, pushing towards him, piling over him, and it was all too warm, the heating was up to high, and her voice hung hot and sticky in the air.

He could hear a dog barking in the distance. For a moment he wished he were home, in Connecticut, in the neat house. It was straightforward there but here nothing was ever what it seemed. It was as though all the past here got into every thing and everyone and burrowed away, as though the sense of the past could be something wonderful, expressed in the Elgin Marbles, an expression of the power of humanity, or something destructive. Patrick was aware of the destructiveness within himself, otherwise he would never have come to this woman's house that first time, knowing she was married. He'd been drawn to her partly because she was older, and she seemed to contain more time, more complications, than he did.

There was a brooch above her right breast, of two birds entwined together, and it seemed to him they were half throttling each other with their pearls and little rubies.

Victoria's perfume was heavy, much heavier than usual. It occured to him that she may have been drinking.

'I had such an awful day. My father's still in hospital. As you know, I can't stand him but somehow . . .' She shrugged. 'I thought you said you were too busy,' she said, stretching up and putting her arms round his neck and throwing back her head. Her lower body pressed against him, and her mouth as he bent down to kiss it was the dark heart of a flower.

'You haven't been here for so long it seems,' she said, lowering her glance then turning it up towards him. Her hands ran, with pleasure, over his broad shoulders.

His eyes felt fuzzy and a little blurred, as if he couldn't quite focus as she pressed hard against him and her lips kissed his neck.

On the mantlepiece a photograph of her husband stared sadly out from a marquetry frame. He was dressed, absurdly, in his MA gown and hat from his student days and looked in this photograph even more insect-eyed and perturbed, as if he'd just lost something important and was about to look round to try to find it. His hair spread out

117

all around him as if that too was not in his control. But if she weren't married, would Patrick see her? Maybe not. He felt uncomfortable with himself. What was he afraid of? He shouldn't walk through life opening doors and walking into rooms, other people's worlds, then closing the door and locking it when he left, as though the rooms were all just boxes he could look into when he pleased and shut when he didn't.

Here she was on tiptoes, kissing his neck, running her hands over him, her hands in the pockets of his jacket then feeling the softness of his frayed collar where it had rubbed against his neck.

'Mmm,' she murmured.

It was warm in the hall, and his skin stuck to his clothes. He could taste in his mouth the flavour of her skin.

He pulled her down and he was aware of the carpet with its soft roughness, the glass in the mirror above the mantlepiece, the wood on the floor. Her skirt was over her thighs.

'You see,' she said afterwards, 'you and I – we should go away together. Escape him. He asks me to do things I don't want to do.'

'Maybe,' he said.

'To somewhere where we can smell orange blossom and drink wine and have sex all day long. I have plenty of money. Plenty. Enough for us to live on for years. You could write wherever we went – to Malta maybe, or the South of France.'

'But where do you get all this money?' he said, sitting up on his knees, zipping up his jeans, everything suddenly feeling quite sordid as the room came back into focus, the mirror fine again, the walls stern and white, even the lilac looking less impassioned.

The picture of the husband continued to stare bleakly out at him.

He pushed back his black curly hair and she flinched slightly and he thought, maybe she does really love me, she watches my every movement. But I shouldn't be here.

Victoria was standing at the mirror.

'I've been selling some more paintings. Charles doesn't know.' Her black skirt hugged her bottom and her pants were still lying on the floor; white silk pants. He picked them up and felt their softness. 'Well, why should he? He's been so savage recently.'

The quiet-looking Charles gazed down at Patrick.

Victoria looked into Patrick's blue eyes and winced again.

'Let me come away with you, darling,' she said, tidying her hair.

He stood up, uneasy now, wanting to be away. And when she looked at him her face went flat and drained.

'Patrick,' she said.

'Yes?' he said.

'Please help me. I don't know what he's going to do next. Remember what he's done to me already,' she said.

119

'You should go to the police. Shall I do it? Shall I speak to them? Or to him?'

'No, don't darling, it would cause more trouble.'

The smell of lilac was delicate in the still air. He tucked in his shirt as he wandered into the drawing room where a Victorian painting of a spaniel hung at one end of the room facing the large ornate gold mirror, which reflected the whole room, with its carefully chosen air of comfort and splendour. The house was too still today, the drawing room with its ochre walls, the ornate cornices, the reds of the Persian carpets, the chandelier, the coffee table books with their sumptuous covers of wild flowers, Rajastan Palaces. He wanted to get out of London, out of endless interiors, to somewhere with warm sun and breezes. Sometimes he wondered if Victoria made these marks on herself to win sympathy.

'And I can't sleep,' she said.

I don't know what I feel about her, thought Patrick. It changes from moment to moment. It changes too much. If I really cared about her it would not change like this according to how she looked from second to second – the sleeves are rolled up, maybe I adore her; her hair is coiffered too tightly, I don't adore her. Absurd. She doesn't make my heart dip and turn. It is not fair for me to visit her like this. I should break it off. But am I using her or is she using me? That has never been quite clear. Even now she moistens her lips as if desiring another mouthful of my flesh. Her hair wrecked, her mouth with lipstick reapplied looking as though it is bleeding, her red marks on her body, and her eyes watchful and flickering.

She's funny and intelligent though. Too intelligent for the life she is living, and that is her problem. Her picture buying and selling just fills in time, and this house seems far too full of time. Her relationship with her father is a problem too. Is it possible that she taunts Charles into hurting her, just to make something happen?

'I want to get out, Patrick, with you. I want to help you with your work. I want something big in my life, something momentous. I'm being buried here,' she said, moving towards him. The cream curtains hung in swathes of silk. It was another world, someone else's, which was what he liked about it. 'This house. Everyone's so impressed by the fucking house. We bought it when we were in our twenties and now I'm getting older and we're still here and I chose the colours and paintings so well they're in better condition than we are. Charles just gets more perturbed and more empty, as though the whole of life is just a matter of decanting what you started off with.'

'You're beautiful,' he said gently.

'It's not enough, just to be beautiful,' she said.

She moved towards him, unable to take her eyes from his face. Watching him, she undid his belt.

Sometimes, when Victoria was close to him, he could see Mrs Morgan in his mind, the woman who had lived next door to him as a child, and had an affair with his father. He had been fascinated by Mrs Morgan's smile, such a peculiar smile, a sugary ambiguous smile.

Mrs Morgan used to smile down, far away, her lips perfect. She would reach out her long hand and touch his head, then she would smile that smile.

He often thought of Mrs Morgan. Sometimes he felt trapped in that time, as if he were endlessly having to relive the sins and pleasures of his father. He recalled how he'd disliked her husband. He disliked Victoria's husband in much the same way.

'Would you go and get your mother, Patrick?' Mrs Morgan had said one day, stooping down. He remembered this day better than all the rest.

Mrs Morgan had worn a white silky blouse with a golden brooch in the shape of a leaf. That must be a treasure too, Patrick had thought, but wished it had been in the shape of a griffin or something else interesting.

Mrs Morgan had come in and closed the door. He was on the stairs and through the metalwork of the staircase he could see her walk into the centre of the drawing room, on the rug, as though it were her rug, her room. It is as though she owns everything in the whole world, he had thought happily, and hurried up.

'Mum!' he had yelled.

His mother had burst out of the bathroom wearing only a black towel. Her hair was a dark storm all over her head.

'What is it?' his mother had said.

'It's Mrs Morgan! She's here! She's come to see you! She's downstairs. Get dressed. Come quickly. She's waiting.'

'She's waiting,' Patrick had said again, looking up.

He followed his mother into the green family room. The name of the paint was 'caterpillar', his mother had told him, and it was a little like being inside a caterpillar, he had thought.

His mother let the towel drop and she slipped on a light summery dress, and shook out her hair. His mother's feet were bare on the wooden floor.

She put on some lipstick, pursing her lips as she did so and put her hair into a bun.

And then his mother appeared at the top of the stairs, and moved down as graceful as a ghost.

'Why, Mrs Morgan, hello,' his mother had said. Mrs Morgan looked up from a notebook his mother must have left on the coffee table.

'Your husband just came round to discuss the surprise party he wanted to give you,' said Mrs Morgan to his mother. 'That's why you saw him coming to the house.'

'Run off and play now, Patrick,' his mother had said. His mother was finishing clipping her hair up in a bun, but still some tumbled down. The shoulder strap of her flowery dress slipped down too. Her feet were bare on the staircase. She never really seemed quite ready for anything.

123

It was as though everything took her by surprise, even breakfast.

Mrs Morgan smiled down, far away, her lips perfect. She reached out her long hand and touched his head, as if knighting him. Patrick liked the stories about King Arthur and Queen Guinevere. It was annoying though, being little, looking up through your fringe and wearing teddy bear pyjamas.

'I should go. I can see this isn't a good time,' said Mrs Morgan.

Mrs Morgan swung round and walked – back straight, head back – to the big wooden front door. She seemed to select each step before she made it, while his mother moved like water.

His mother flowed over to the door.

The door opened out on to sunlight and bright green grass. It seemed so strange the way the house could be so dark and shadowy while outside the sun shone cheerily.

'Leave the room, Patrick,' said his mother. 'Go to your playroom,' but he hid on the other side of the door. He heard all kinds of things, things about Mrs Morgan, things about his father. It turned out that Mrs Morgan and his father had shared a bed together, which seemed odd, and his mother was very angry about it.

It all seemed very glamorous and exciting but also shocking, somehow, upsetting, as though his life was being taken to pieces, turned into a jigsaw puzzle with missing pieces.

124

It was a scandal, his mother said to Mrs Morgan.

Patrick ran out and the sun fell into the room and Patrick ran into it.

'What are you doing here?' demanded his mother.

Mrs Morgan walked off, an empress, down the crazy paving of the pathway, and Patrick ran after her to wave goodbye. The grass felt good underneath his feet. But then he remembered about the huge ants he'd seen in the back garden yesterday and he came back inside.

He tried to picture his mother's face, as it had been, but it was like something seen underwater, changing, unfocused.

He could see his mother spinning him round, holding his hands and spinning, and crying out, 'Patrick! Patrick!'

But when he came back to the house her face was different, crunched up, and her lips were as wobbly as jelly. He'd put his arms round her.

After that, he thought, his mother and father had grown closer and yet more rigid, as if both were afraid of crossing into that other region again, the region of elegant jewellery and Mrs Morgan (who moved away not long after that day). His mother no longer wore her hair like a dark storm and let her dress straps slip down. She became well organised, precise and never spun him round and round while laughing.

Perhaps it was just that he was growing but, from around the time of the Mrs Morgan incident, the house had seemed much smaller to him.

125

'I've been thinking – I believe we should stop seeing each other,' said Patrick softly.

She looked down as she did up the buttons of her shirt.

'What, darling?' she said.

'I said I think we should stop this.'

She looked up.

'I'd hate that,' she said.

CHAPTER 24

Elizabeth's kitchen was an inferno. She refused to let Anne help her cook Sunday lunch.

'You have to know how to cook,' Elizabeth continued, addressing Lily who hovered at the door. 'It's no good not knowing how to cook. You're growing up. You're eight. You have to know how to cook!'

All over the kitchen were saucepans; copper saucepans, red saucepans, saucepans with ancient burn marks, saucepans with burnt handles.

'All women should know how to cook! It's just a matter of timing! Patience and timing! Supposing something happened to me! You have to be able to cook!'

Some work had been done in the house – new bathrooms put in, old boiler replaced, everything painted, but Elizabeth hadn't been able to bring herself to replace the good-quality old cabinets in the kitchen, and had instead just had them painted white. The cooker was still the old avocado green 1970s one.

The heavy wooden kitchen door was on an

automatic spring and every now and again it sprung shut, but now Lily was standing there, holding it open.

'It's smelly in here,' said Lily.

'Nonsense!' said Elizabeth. 'Okay,' she said, and battled with the catch. 'It is a bit stuffy in here.'

The smoke fumes filled the entire room.

'We're having roast beef and Yorkshire pudding and roast potatoes. After we've eaten I'll tell you exactly how to do it all. Most important is the choosing of the meat.'

A recipe book lay open on the red formica counter top, which was something else she meant to replace in time.

'Can I do anything?' said Anne.

'No. No, I want to show Lily myself,' said Elizabeth. 'Now, Yorkshire pudding isn't easy to make but . . .'

Elizabeth dragged back the door of the fridge and seized milk, then put it on the table, butter, then put it on the table, then closed the fridge door.

'Mummy . . .' said Lily 'I don't mind – I don't mind what we eat.'

'Sunday lunch! It's good to have it. Everyone sits together and talks.'

'Did you do that when you were a child?' asked Lily.

'No. Never,' she said, as she burnt herself. 'Oh God.'

'You know,' said Lily softly, 'you really are a

very good mother. Honestly,' added Lily. 'I see other mothers and I think how much better you are. And I like the way you're at home when I come in.'

'Well, look, Lily . . .'

Elizabeth continued to whisk up the batter for the Yorkshire pudding, sending a fine spray round her as she did so.

'I might not be here forever,' said Elizabeth. 'If I had an accident, for instance, you'd have to look after yourself. Anne's not a good cook.'

It was as if Lily's skin had become too tight for her, and she stood by the fridge with hands clenched tight and her mouth waving up and down, trying not to cry.

'The house wants you to stay here always. I won't feel safe if you're not here,' said Lily to her mother.

Elizabeth stormed over to the cooker, as if to an enemy. She peered into the oven and the heat made her step back suddenly.

'What you do,' said Elizabeth to Lily, as she sawed at the meat, 'is first choose the beef . . .'

'Yes,' said Lily.

'It should have a fresh, slightly moist appearance, and when cut should be bright red with a brownish tinge. Actually, all meat is purple-brown when first cut; oxygen in the air turns it red. Anyway,' she continued as Lily stared at the charred meat, 'you dump the joint in a roasting tin, smear it with butter and put it in the oven for twenty minutes a pound and an extra twenty minutes. That's it,' she said.

There was smudge of butter on Elizabeth's nose.

'I feel exhausted,' said Elizabeth.

When it was ready, they sat down and Anne helped serve out the food.

'This looks really good, Elizabeth. You are clever,' said Anne.

'I don't know why everyone in the world doesn't simply swap countries with someone else,' said Elizabeth. 'All the really happy and successful people do. Look at Pamela Harlech. It was her recipe book. She was American, came to live in England, and the flap to her jacket says she kept up households in Wales and London single handed!'

'Pamela Harriman did it the other way round,' said Anne. 'She was born in England and took up with Americans.'

'Yes,' said Elizabeth. 'And Australians are always striding around Europe and America being wildly successful. You should remember that, Lily. Think about going to another country.'

'I don't know where I'll live,' said Lily, dabbing her mouth with her napkin, the window behind her, sitting straight at the old pine table.

Elizabeth pushed back her hair.

Anne looked down.

'You see . . .' said Lily. 'If I lived in America then I'm neither English nor American am I? I can't be both,' continued Lily. She straightened her napkin.

'You were born in England. You're English,' said Anne.

'You make Yorkshire pudding by sifting a pound of flour and salt into a bowl,' said Elizabeth, 'beating it to a smooth creamy batter with an unbeaten egg, half a pint of milk, then stir in the rest of the milk. You pre-heat the oven to hot, put in two ounces of butter, pour in the batter and bake for about thirty minutes. It's very dull to do. Cooking in general is very, very dull.'

'I quite enjoy it,' said Lily. 'When you and I make biscuits together.'

'It's important to be able to cook but cooking gets very hot and tiring and it burns your hands, and if you have guests it's torture. You cook then have to breeze out and be charming and remember everyone's names while remembering when the peas are ready. And then, when you've gone to all that trouble, the guests just sit there eating it. You want to snatch the food from them and say, "How dare you just sit there and eat that food I've spent so long preparing? It's preposterous. How dare you?"' said Elizabeth.

Lily and Anne laughed.

'You think I'm making it up. You wait . . . don't look worried, darling,' Elizabeth said, putting out her hand to her daughter. 'I'm just a little overwrought.'

'You don't like cooking,' said Lily, blinking hard.

Elizabeth shrugged. 'It's the way it vanishes, as I

say. The desolation of the plates, with bits of food stuck to them.'

'I hope the apple pie's okay,' said Lily.

Elizabeth jumped up, rushed to the oven and brought out the pie, on a pretty dish, only slightly burnt.

'Sometimes,' said Elizabeth, later, over coffee, 'I wish I'd travelled more. I've never been to Athens. I'd like to see the Parthenon. Anne makes it sound so magical.'

'You said that before! We could go!' said Lily.

'I'm just too busy at the moment,' said Elizabeth.

CHAPTER 25

Mary Elgin,
Palermo,
Sicily,
October 5, 1799

We have been invited to stay with Sir William Hamilton and his wife Lady Hamilton, who is the mistress of Lord Nelson.
I fear I should not have married Elgin. Although he is capable of warmth, there is an arrogance and possessiveness about him.

CHAPTER 26

Patrick's publisher had invited him to a party at his modern offices in Kensington. Stewart Edwards, the head of the firm, came towards Patrick, hand outstretched.

'I need to talk to you privately,' said Patrick.

'Do you know,' said Stewart Edwards, 'I hear the delightful Anne Fitzgerald is doing the same book as you. Now isn't that an unfortunate coincidence? She's turned up tonight.'

Stewart Edwards smiled at someone over in the corner. Every few seconds he checked out the room, his head bobbing up and down. He made the most desperate Wall Street traders look as though they were on tranquillizers. He adjusted his narrow tie, and Patrick thought how irritatingly English he was.

'You know, she's a very impressive writer,' said Stewart.

Patrick gave him a tight, murderous smile. The publisher's impatient head tilted to one side and his eyes were narrow.

'The drinks are over there. Red or white?' Stewart asked him.

'I have some significant new information,' said Patrick.

'Great . . .' He touched Patrick on the arm, and moved to greet someone else. 'I look forward to it.'

A girl in a short skirt came over to Patrick and offered to get him a drink, regarding him with an interested, lowered gaze.

'Do you work here?' he asked.

'No. Just thought you needed a drink.'

'Perspicacious.'

The girl had sharply cut jaw-line hair and an air of irony. She grabbed a canapé as it went by.

'Yuk. Used to be good healthy sausages, now it's all raw fish. Raw fish! Red or white?'

A tray came round, and he took one.

'You a journalist?' she said. Patrick was watching Anne being greeted profusely by Stewart Edwards, who seemed more or less on his knees before her, while she remained faintly distant.

'I'm a writer,' said Patrick.

'Surely journalists are writers too? I'm a journalist. You don't write novels do you?'

Anne twisted a curl of hair round her finger, as if wishing to twist Stewart Edwards's neck. But why had she come to this party? He couldn't imagine her turning up at any party, unless of course she knew these were his publishers and wanted to know more details of his book. His agent was here somewhere, no doubt she'd start chatting away indiscreetly.

'No,' he told the girl who was standing close to him, pleasantly close, and tilting her head as if trying to get into the right position to dive down his throat. The level of talk was increasing, and it was beginning to get hot. Anne hadn't seen him yet.

'I'm an historian. Or rather I recently became an historian. I used to be on Wall Street,' he said.

'What does that actually mean?' she asked, almost on tiptoes as she spoke to him, trying to reach his height. 'I always picture someone on the top of some wall. I mean I know it's hectic young men holding up their fingers to signify numbers then getting home all worked up and screwing their girlfriends. But apart from that . . .'

Patrick grinned. His grin was lopsided, up the right side of his face. 'It was a bit like that.'

'You're still hectic though, I sense. You don't seem otherworldly like historians should. Do you still screw your girlfriend?'

'Why yes, but a different one.'

'She's not that woman over there, who keeps watching you?'

'No. She's not a girlfriend. We're rivals doing the same book unfortunately. I'd probably in fact classify her as an enemy.'

The girl scrunched up her face as she observed Anne, who was surrounded by three men making a semicircle round her, although she was facing Patrick.

'Maybe. Not so sure,' said the girl.

Anne walked over towards Patrick.

The girl sighed and scribbled her name on a card. 'My name's Jill. Ring me. I'd like to hear about your book.'

Anne took Patrick by the arm and led him out on to the balcony.

It was cold outside, above the traffic.

Inside was the noise of the party and it all seemed far away. Her eyes were round and a little anxious, and bits of hair strayed out over her face. She kept wiping them away, as if she were swimming through seaweed, as if it were all very difficult.

It struck Patrick how thin she was and young.

'What's in the diaries?' she said.

'What diaries?'

'They're historical documents. They don't belong to you,' she continued. Her woolly cardigan had little bits of fluff escaping from it and her trousers were thin on the thigh. She was no longer this perfectly put together icon, but an anxious little girl. She played with her silver bangles.

The green square was laid out before them, with black patches of trees.

'You're bluffing,' he said.

'You don't trust women, do you?' she said.

She turned away towards the trees, which were illuminated by the street lights. He found himself next to her, his arm suddenly resting on her frail shoulders.

She turned round and he felt her warm tongue in his mouth and she was limp in his arms and he was dazed and the feeling of her body against him made his head swim. Her mouth was dark and certain, and his body was all structure, muscle and bone.

'What are you doing?' said Stewart sharply. They jumped apart, and he saw her face was different, slightly red and smudged with desire. Her mouth. He couldn't take his eyes off her mouth.

'Huh!' said Stewart.

She was shivering again. The night was black but the sky was stencilled with stars. He was still watching her huge mouth.

Anne turned away and leant against the railings.

'You should come in,' said the publisher. 'It's cold.'

'Can you leave us alone?' said Patrick.

'What?'

'Just get lost,' said Patrick as he towered over him.

Stewart's little mouth became even smaller and he turned round, and left them alone on the balcony. They looked at each other, and she grinned, then she threw back her head and laughed.

'I'm sorry,' she said abruptly, no longer laughing. 'I shouldn't have done that. Kissed you.' Her arms crossed over her front, hugging herself, and it seemed suddenly there was a great distance between them full of crossed arms and hands. But he didn't know where the sudden seriousness had come from after all the warmth and gaiety. Her face seemed to tense up, all the features gathered together, become smaller.

He put his arms around her but her body was

stiff and pushed him away and she refused to look at him.

'I shouldn't have done it,' she said steadily. 'It was just that . . . that I wanted you to tell me about the diaries. That's all.' She put her hand up to her hair.

And her eyes looked coolly into his. Close up, her eyes seemed even bigger, black in the shadows, as if the colours were floating layer upon layer, thickest in the depths, clearer on the surface.

She's joking, he thought. She's pretending. But the look went on and her voice was going on telling him that she wasn't interested in him but only in the diaries. But then there seemed to be some alarm, and sweetness, back in her face, and her hand hung on to the balcony rail as if tightrope walking. And all the time all he wanted to do was have her mouth against his, and all the time he could feel the heat from her little sweater and the tenderness, although he was three feet away from her, and wanted to touch her skin again, to feel the way it heated up at his touch, the way it gave way, and her gasp.

'That's not why you kissed me,' he said.

'Yes it is,' she said. Her eyes were wider now, less blurred, and she leaned against the rail, smiling confidently, as if taller again. She laughed.

'Yes. I want you to tell me what's in them.' She stood up straight. 'I shouldn't have done it, I can see.'

'You're lying,' he said.

She gazed straight at him. 'Am I? I know who you got them from. Robert Frank. He shouldn't have sold them to you.' She wanted to see the effect of her words.

He swung away, back into the party and left with the journalist.

He looked up and saw she was watching him from the balcony.

The next morning, Patrick sat studying Mary Elgin's diary, touching the thick yellow paper. The paper was blotchy with time, covered in little brown bruises, her writing in tiny letters, presumably to prevent anyone reading it without great diffculty.

The paper was slightly torn in the places where it had been creased. He read about Lady Hamilton, whom he felt had influenced Mary Elgin, though she disapproved of Emma Hamilton. In some curious way she gave Mary the first clue that a woman could be outrageous, could live life on its own terms and be free. He was working more quickly now, sensing her growing rebelliousness.

After studying the tiny lettering he tied the blue ribbon back around the pages and put them in a cellophane bag, which he placed in a grey fireproof safe under a floorboard.

CHAPTER 27

Mary Elgin,
Palermo,
Sicily,
October 6, 1799

We dined with Lady Hamilton, Sir William and Lord Nelson. It is clear Lady Hamilton rules both men completely, but she did look very handsome at dinner, quite in an undress. I am told if the Queen of Naples wants a favour from Lord Nelson, she simply sends Lady Hamilton diamonds, and the deed is done. She seems to be made completely of white flesh, but she certainly sang well and has good musicians. Nelson could not take his eyes off her, and makes a fool of himself, as does Sir William. My father would consider her a fine figure of a woman.

Nelson looks old, with most of his upper teeth missing, and has no animation whatsoever, unlike Lady Hamilton. He seems to see badly out of one eye and has a film coming over both of them. He explained to Elgin that he has constant pains from his old wound in his head. I have to say, I could not love an ugly old man like that, however many battles he has fought.

I realise now that I must grow a little more worldly. We were invited to a ball by the King and Queen of Naples and Lady Hamilton assured me that I should go in a common morning dress because nobody would think of dressing splendidly for the event. When I arrived, what did I find? What an innocent I had been! Lady Hamilton wore a glorious gold and coloured silk worked gown and diamonds; the Queen and Princesses in fine dresses with pearls and diamonds. Everyone insisted I looked delightful in my plain dress but I returned home to change. Apparently it is a constant trick of Lady H. to make everybody she can go underdressed to events, in order to make herself more dazzling.

Elgin says he intends to bring extraordinary treasures back to England from the East. He likes me to agree with whatever he says.

I think I am very lucky to be here, to be experiencing all this. Of course I love my books and the places they take me – but this – I would never have guessed I should see what I have seen these last days.

Shall I be the same Mary Nisbet when all of this is finished?

CHAPTER 28

Anne's mother called her, with a tremulous voice, and asked her to come round.

'Oh Anne,' she said, as Anne entered, swirling into the room, her long skirt somehow taking up much of the room in the little cottage. Her mother seemed quite alert, and sported a brooch on her blouse, something she hadn't done for years, as she nodded at Anne from the armchair. It was as though, after her husband's disgrace and her son David's disappearance, she had simply repackaged herself as an unthreatening old woman, apart from her high heels which suggested she was not just what she seemed. Her hair had grown grey, as if to help her out with the disguise she had embraced so willingly. She smelt of lavender, something left in a well-aired drawer in a country house and bore little resemblance to the glamorous young mother she had been. Her hair curled softly round her face, and she had a way of gently pushing away her hair that was both inquiring and apologetic.

Her mother had kept up with some of her friends, and her past life was well recorded in the immaculately kept cottage, with the photographs in silver frames, the throw over the side table, the dried roses in a vase, the air of a tidy, well-organised life.

Her mother was sitting up straighter than usual, and the lines which she'd willed so successfully to etch her face seemed to have grown less deep.

For a moment, Anne thought she might have heard something about David whom her mother constantly expected to turn up.

'I had a visitor.'

'Oh, that's nice,' said Anne, taking a seat, leaning forward, waiting to see what her mother would say. On the table in front of her were copies of *Country Life*. It seemed sad that her mother was reading about the life she should have had; the country house, the dignified husband, the gardening, the status which always mattered very much to her because she had never worked and created her own status.

On her mother's shelves were a number of surprising books on Milton, Shelley, history.

'A young American.'

At once Anne knew who had come here. She could almost sense it in the room. Something new, more open, more excitable.

'A charming young man. Asked all about you. I didn't know anyone was writing an article about you. For some US magazine I'd never even heard of.'

Anne's emotions swirled into her lips, which tightened.

So he was here, she thought, coming into my life,

through a back door. He is without principles. She tidied her skirt on her knees.

'Apparently it's called *Historians*,' said her mother. 'He said I was very helpful.'

'I see,' said Anne. She couldn't bring herself to tell her mother that the American had merely been finding out about her, and that no such magazine existed. 'But next time, phone me before seeing anyone, okay?'

'He was just round the corner. I didn't have time to call, and afterwards I felt a little anxious and thought I should phone but then I didn't because I knew you were coming round soon anyway.'

'How did he get your number?'

'He said the publicity department of your publishers had told him all about you, you know, because he was writing an article on you, including the fact that your mother was living in Kensington. Well, I'm in the phone book. He just looked me up.'

Anne nodded. She got up and went to the bathroom and splashed cold water on her face. She took some deep breaths. The towels were always clean, freshly washed, like a hotel, as if always expecting someone to arrive. The ones in the small lavatory were apricot, and matched the apricot soap, a new bar, just put out. Patrick is unprincipled and ruthless to turn up here. And as for me, she thought, looking into the mirror, who is it my mother sees, Patrick sees, Lily sees? Paolo used to say my face was cool as snowdrops. Recently she had felt different, less nervous, more forceful.

A few weeks ago she had been merely tense, and energetic, but her emotions seemed more focused now, perhaps because of Elizabeth's illness.

'So,' said Anne, as she came out of the lavatory, 'what kind of questions did he ask?'

Her mother looked up from the magazine she was glancing at. 'Look at this one,' she said. 'It's in Gloucestershire. With seven acres.'

'What did the American ask?'

Her mother pushed back her hair. 'Oh, I can see you're annoyed I spoke to him. I only said nice things. Some tea?'

'What nice things?'

Her mother looked uncomfortable. 'Oh, I told him we used to live in Hong Kong, and about your father, and about your brother, and how brave you were over it all. And you were, darling, you kept us all together after that. I was thinking about it . . . your brother just went, but you stayed. You never complained. I told him all that. I suppose that was wrong?'

Her mother had perfected the role of the innocent old lady.

'What else?'

The silver vases had recently been polished. Her mother's marriage and engagement ring dug into her finger.

'Are you sure you won't have any tea?'

'No. It's important you tell me everything.'

'Oh really,' said her mother. 'You're getting to be like you used to be, always making everything so dramatic.'

'Dramatic?' said Anne.

'You've seemed so serene for the last years, nothing can touch you, but as a child everything was a drama. You acted all the time. "Suddenly," you'd say, "I was looking out of the window and a huge bird swept by. It tried to carry me off!" There was always something. But then when something really dramatic happened you just coped with it. You were very matter of fact.'

'That's as may be. What else did you tell him?'

'Well, what huge, horrible secrets do you have? I told him you lived in a flat near Tower Bridge, that you'd written a book, that you were determined, that you were brilliant, and always had been, and that you were a good daughter. What's wrong with all that?'

'Nothing. It's fine,' she said.

Her mother's hands lay neatly on her lap.

'His face lit up whenever I spoke about you.'

'Oh, cute. He was just being nosy. I sense he's one of those guys who doesn't want a real relationship. He doesn't trust them.'

'I'm sorry?'

'Nothing.' Anne roamed over to the window, with its little net curtain through which passersby glared.

'My friend Elizabeth is very ill,' said Anne. 'She doesn't think she'll recover, and if she doesn't she wants me to look after Lily.'

'What about Lily's father?'

'He's a drug addict living in Ibiza. For someone as meticulous and practical as Elizabeth, she made

147

a lousy choice of husband. He's not interested in looking after himself, let alone Lily, and all the grandparents are dead or dying or in nursing homes. So there's me.'

Her mother paused, and straightened the photograph of David on the table.

'But your work?'

'I know. Still, it may not happen.'

'It's not your responsibility. You always took too much responsibility for things.'

'Sure. That's why I've been holed up for years with some unsuitable Greek, writing my biographies, is it? Because of my strong sense of responsibility?'

'You'll have your own child one day.'

'Sometimes Lily feels like mine.'

'It's not the same though. Why take it on? It's too much. You're young. You have to fall in love. Get married. Have a child. You have to do things in the right order. It's important. The right order.'

'Sure. Maybe I will have that cup of tea,' said Anne.

Anne and Alexander stood on the balcony looking out at the slate-grey river.

A few boats ploughed through the river, making white furrows. A little tug went by, then a speedboat bouncing over the water, its flag waving.

Anne longed for some sun, for colours to escape their objects. Here there was too much grey and deception. In Greece, there was colour. She thought of the wine and the good food. Here everyone was nervy, suspicious.

She held on to the rail. Alexander's hand was lying on her neck.

'Are you going out tonight?'

'Yes,' he replied. 'I have a business appointment.'

'Where?'

He coughed.

'In Holland Park. About some paintings.'

At least she didn't mind where he went. She hated the idea of being with anyone who might destroy her if he walked out one morning and never came back.

'Is my mother going to be okay?' Lily had said.

'I don't know,' said Anne.

'She wants to go to Athens.'

'She must rest, I'm afraid,' said Anne.

'She wants to see the temple you keep talking about,' said Lily, frowning. 'Why?'

'It's time,' said Anne. 'The marble statues from the Parthenon are time. That's what we all want.'

'But she's not well enough?'

'Not yet,' said Anne.

'She says the British should give back the old stones you like so much to Athens,' said Lily.

'Maybe. When I look at them I think how beautiful they are in the British Musuem, and how glad I am that they are so well looked after, but also how sad they can't all be united back in Athens.'

★   ★   ★

Later, Lily was meticulously painting a stone green and smiled up from her work as Anne entered the kitchen. Lily pushed her hair back, getting green paint over her cheek.

'That's nice,' said Anne.

'When it's dry I'm going to paint a daisy on it!' said Lily.

Anne wiped off the green paint which had splattered over the pine table.

Anne took the green stone and put it on to a piece of newspaper on the windowsill to dry.

Love is in the detail, she had realised; yesterday Anne had watched Elizabeth cutting up carrots to provide vitamin C, then sharpening Lily's pencils, each act a kind of epiphany. Those who pity mothers and others who look after children know nothing, Anne thought, opening the fridge door and wondering what to have for dinner. But all the same Anne wasn't ready, she felt, to look after Lily.

Lily was sitting crosslegged on one of the old sofas in the basement playroom, and she was throwing plastic darts into the dartboard pinned on the wall.

Pale and serious, she hit one after the other into the dartboard while Anne sorted out the washing for Elizabeth, who was resting.

'Sean says I'm odd,' she said. 'He spends his time working out ways to blow up the school and he thinks I'm odd. Really.'

'Blow up the school?' said Anne, dropping a large black sock into a pile.

'He does complex little plans. They're really weird.' The dart went into the centre of the web again.

'And what is he going to blow up the school with?'

'Dynamite, I think. He's rather old fashioned.'

Anne laughed.

Lily threw another dart.

'He does charts with little arrows in particular corridors. All colour coded in reds and blues. He's clever but he doesn't concentrate on his work because of his plans. It's a shame really. Mind you, I like his plans. They're so complicated.'

'Dorothy collects pencil sharpenings,' Lily continued. 'You know – the bits left after you sharpen a pencil.' Lily shook her head. 'Weird.'

'Is school going okay?'

'Fine,' said Lily, and threw another dart. 'Why are you so sad?'

'No reason,' said Anne.

Lily walked out into the garden, to the swing, where she leaned on her tummy and twisted the rope round and round and round until her feet were above the ground, then she let go and spun quicker and quicker and quicker.

She rested, tummy on the swing, as she'd done last year and the year before. She wasn't really grown up yet, she told herself, whatever her mother said.

'I worry what would happen to Lily – if I died,' said Elizabeth.

'That's not going to happen,' said Anne brightly, and a streak of sunlight fell on the wooden floor of the kitchen.

Elizabeth wearily stood up, opened the wooden doors of the kitchen and with a burst of energy from somewhere stepped out into the garden where Lily turned a radiant smile on her mother and, seeing her face fluid with unhappiness, ran to her, and tumbled into her arms and Anne could see Elizabeth's separate pieces inside her all coming together as she hugged her daughter.

When Anne had stayed with Elizabeth and Lily after returning from Bangkok she used to run beside Lily's bike like a trainer as she raced along the pavements of Highbury.

'I might have a shop when I'm older *and* write novels,' Lily had said once, before speeding down a hill. Anne ran after her, hair clenched back in a ponytail.

As she ran she had thought of Lily's knees, the soft down of her arm, the curious revelry of her turned-up nose, the way her skin rose up and caressed the area around her ear – and the ins and outs of her ear going back and back, curling and swirling like some ultimate ride.

Lily had begun to make her admire mankind again – the curve of an elbow, the energy in the tilt of a head.

On Lily's wall had been a poster of Queen Elizabeth I. Even as a very young child, Lily would only listen to children's stories featuring royalty. She liked *The Princess and the Pea*, *The Little Prince* and *Cinderella* but refused to listen to *101 Dalmatians*. 'I want to have a *remarkable* life,' Lily had said, just a few days ago, as she sat on the bed talking to Anne before saying goodnight. Lily had looked at her fiercely and said, 'I'm not going to live a conventional life, you know. I shan't do what everyone else does. I shan't be like Mummy or my babysitter. Instead I shall live on a boat with no one around and wear a white dress and everyone will look at me and wonder who I am. And I shall have marvellous adventures in distant places.'

'If there's no one around, who will look at you?' Anne had said, smiling at the way men and women give up their wildness, their world trips, their affairs, to give their children security and then their children pity their conventional lives.

At first, after losing Paolo, Anne chose unsuitable lovers, almost as though she didn't want anyone whom she would love.

Once at night she'd made love to a man in Hyde Park, and had grabbed at the wet leaves and seen a little blackbird watching her as if wondering what was happening to this woman lying on her front with her skirt up, agony on her face, her hands grabbing at the glossy leaves in a kind of ecstasy. And just then a spider had run over her hand; lives interconnecting, tiny legs trailing over the rough skin of her hand, the minute pinpoint of the end of its legs touching her like being brushed with silk. And at that time, which moved her more – the thrust of the man, or that touch, telling her of other worlds, former worlds, future worlds? The man had bitten the back of her neck while both spider and bird vanished into the smothering darkness at the bottom of a laurel bush, and she had felt so alone.

At least Alexander had been better than these casual lovers, and she could keep herself safe. When she felt lonely she'd buy cheap jewellery to cheer herself up, and be comforted by the glitter of her butterfly hairslides, her lizard brooches.

CHAPTER 29

Mary Elgin,
Constantinople,
January 30, 1800

The strange illness that has devoured most of Elgin's nose shows no sign of abating. Elgin takes mercury for his disease.

A young man called Robert Ferguson came to visit us. He lived near Elgin in Scotland and knew him when a child, though Mr Ferguson seems young, about my age.

CHAPTER 30

Late in the evening Patrick was at his desk in his London flat. Propped all around him were postcards of the Parthenon marbles. From a black background charged the head of a horse with bulging, exhausted eyes and open mouth, one of the horses drawing the chariot of Helius, the Sun god, on the east pediment. Beside it, on another postcard, reclined the half-broken body of a river god.

He transcribed the diaries in longhand, with a fountain pen and brown ink, and enjoyed watching the ink roll over the page. Outside, the traffic muttered softly up and down, while the walls tightened round him. The rented flat was furnished with curiously incidental furniture – the desk was 1970s cheap varnished teak with a few deep cuts here and there, and inside a drawer were a child's purple crayon scribbles.

You just needed something from the past, thought Patrick, as he worked – a diary, but the actual diary, just as with a few cells, a little DNA, soon it might be possible to recreate the whole person again. With a diary, with the slope of handwriting, the words chosen, the feel of the paper, it was possible to imagine the person there, bowed over the page.

Handwriting, he thought, magical signs on bare paper, each word a story in itself, a way into the personality of the writer, brown or black or blue or pencil marks to fall through into another person's mind. The helter-skelter of personality; tight letters, cramped together, fearing to let space enter and blast the writer apart; elegant curving letters suggesting the privilege of control and grace. Handwriting different in different moods – hurried and untidy and blotchy when life got grim, neater and more wholesome when things were going well. All the moods and different frequencies of existence were experienced in the inky movements of a person's hands. Mary's writing was cramped, Lilliputian, but every now and again she forgot herself and a few words were larger, easier to make out.

The phone rang.

He was still torn betweeen a desire to finish transcribing them all – to find out all Mary's secrets – and the knowledge that once he had finished his work this extra ordinary time would be over.

The wooden floor was carpeted in skyscrapers of books and papers: books bought secondhand, new paperback editions, old paperback editions, books used at university, library books, photocopies of books, books with coffee stains, books with pages

157

turned down, books with annotations, some with furred edges where they had been touched over and over. The room smelt of secondhand bookshops, which was what Patrick felt time itself must smell of: that musty, complicated, forgiving odour.

'Hi,' said a girl's voice, 'it's Anne.'

Ah, he thought, so she's not that grave, untouchable, after all.

'Why, Anne, I . . .'

'Let's meet,' she drawled, 'shall we?'

'Sure,' he said in an unsuitably startled voice, sitting bolt upright, gazing in astonishment at his vast trainers at the end of his feet.

'Now. I want to meet now.'

Ah, he thought, so she is just ordinary.

'I'd love to but . . .'

'It's one o'clock in the morning. Is that the problem? Too late for you? Well,' said the girl's voice, 'I'm in the bar at the Savoy and wondered if you'd like to meet up with me. I feel rather lonely.'

'This is Anne?' he enquired.

'That's right.'

'Sure,' he said, still gazing at his scuffed and oversize trainers.

He dressed in a suit and tie, shiny brown shoes the colour of conkers, huge shoes. His mother used constantly to lament his rate of growth. He straightened his tie a little, and sprayed on some aftershave. Why was she calling him now, at this time? Her voice sounded odd. Perhaps she was upset. The thought of her being upset, to his surprise, disturbed him. He was not used to being very much affected by the emotions of other people.

Patrick hurried down the steps of the house, closing the front door behind him gently, then strode off through the dark London streets.

He walked into the Savoy, past doormen whose coats had shiny buttons and by receptionists whose eyes were watchful under the chandeliers.

His mouth felt dry. Damn.

'Can I help you, sir?' asked one of the staff, in a funereal suit and with a face like a cadaver. Patrick shook his head.

He got to the bar and ordered a drink, and waited, and waited. He yawned. A joke, he supposed. Perhaps to get back at him for using the same books. Absurd. Ridiculous. But it didn't sound like her. The voice sounded foreign, not English. Why then believe it's her? We believe what we want to believe. Besides, he thought, sitting up straight, this isn't too bad, being here.

He watched each female as she entered the bar and rearranged her features so she resembled the austere Anne Fitzgerald. Miniaturise that nose, add a rich shade of auburn to that hair, move the eyes further apart, take away the redness in those cheeks.

After the third vodka, he left, looking round the hotel as he walked out.

The area around the Savoy had homeless people in most doorways; tucked up in sleeping bags, in newspapers, in blankets, surrounded by straggling possessions. He walked down to the river and stared out, at the black water, with all its promises. The bridges straddled the river, arch after arch, decorated with lights; lights against the blackness.

He heard the sound of men coming up behind him. He moved off. Not again. He did not feel in the mood for a fight, especially as the drink he'd consumed that night made his body feel like some loosely sewn sack of straw. Maybe I'll run. He instructed his legs to walk faster, but somehow they didn't. The footsteps were right behind him now. He swallowed, and turned. Four men faced him, all with woollen hats pulled more or less completely over their faces and they all surged towards him at once. One of them had a gun, which stuck into Patrick's side.

'Go home to the US, would you, boy?' said one grating voice. 'This time nobody's playing.'

'You get the message?' said another, kicking him in the leg.

'Sure. Have we met before?'

'Just fuck off. Get out of England now. Go fucking home, hear us? We don't want to have to do this again.'

One of the men without the gun punched him, and another hit him with the gun on the side of his head.

Pain slopped through his head like water into a sandcastle.

Patrick went down on his knees. He tried to get

up, feeling dazed. His first thought was, if I hadn't had those vodkas my reactions would have been quicker.

The looseness of his limbs meant that his fall didn't hurt that much, and he somehow had managed to protect his head well from the blows, but as he was hit for the third time, then kicked, fury overcame him and he managed to struggle up and grab one of the men and aim an effective blow into the man's face, and the man lurched back with a yell of pain.

Just then a cab came by and the driver shouted: 'Leave him alone. Watch out – the police!'

The thugs shot off in different directions like lumbering bears.

When Patrick managed to get up to his feet he leant against a wall, trying to get his breath. It was cold, a light layer of frost lying on the street. His head hurt.

The cab reversed down the road.

'Come on, mate – hospital or home?'

'Home, thank you,' he said. He sank back with relief into the soft taxi-seat. 'I'm glad you came by.'

'Ruffians like that should be locked up – there are too many about, and not a policeman in sight,' said the driver.

Outside his flat, Patrick climbed gingerly out.

'You take it easy, mate,' said the driver.

Patrick smiled, thanked the man again, and gave him a big tip.

Patrick found his walk up the threadbare carpet to his flat intolerably long. It seemed as if terrible weights had been tied to his legs and his head was throbbing.

On the second landing he paused for a few moments. This old house was full of creaks and moods and shadows. It stood with others in a row, facing similar houses over the other side, as if about to partake in a formal dance, or a fight.

On the top landing he stopped and stared. His front door was wide open, and the lock had been broken.

The sitting room didn't alarm him. It was untidy, certainly, but he had left it like that – a red coffee mug sitting on the television set, an overfull waste-paper basket as if an overflowing volcano.

Still holding his head, Patrick walked into his study.

One drawer was open; the lock had been broken. As he walked over to his desk the colour left his face. His papers were strewn about over the floor.

He searched the back of the drawer. The early diaries he'd locked in the drawer after working on that day had gone. He'd failed to put them back in the safe under the floorboards. He assumed it was Anne who had stolen them, or someone working for her. Fortunately, the bulk of the diaries remained where he'd hidden them.

Patrick couldn't sleep but lay awake in a rage, watching dawn seep up into the London sky until the moment that the morning cracked open like an egg, then he managed to sleep and when he woke his head was not so bad. He didn't look good though. Unshaven, eyes heavy, mouth made of clay, skin sallow, hair standing up in places like a rare duck's plumage.

Patrick showered, put on deodorant, brushed his teeth, then rang Anne. The answer phone was on. 'Call me immediately' was his message.

He meandered to the British Museum, his headache returning. Then he caught a bus to the British Library and stalked through the endless rooms looking for her.

Outside, the wind was bustling through the trees, and the clouds lay low in a gunmetal sky. The plane trees stood back, wearing their camouflage bark, sentries.

With growing anger, he crossed EC1, past Hatton Garden, through little pools of history. And then finally, in a cab now, he came to the river, wide and glorious, which always surprised him. One minute he'd be lost in towering buildings and then, there, suddenly, was this dazzling waterway carrying another, darker kind of time in it.

The river slid through London, a great snake changing its colours by the minute, green then grey, and at the bottom of the river he could sense the bones and gold rings and tyres, layers and layers of time, every kind of secret.

A speed boat bounced over the water, flag waving, while builders' cranes stood at the side of the water, prehistoric creatures preying on London.

Two seagulls flew, enormous, over the river, eagles of the river.

The cab drew up outside Anne's warehouse building. Patrick stepped out, rang the bell. Today the wind blew sharply even along this narrow passageway with its metal walkways above.

There was no reply. He stood down below looking up and a couple of young chefs in white uniforms passed him, talking in lisping voices as if stewing their words to a tasty softness. A man in black leather and shaved head pushed past him, leaving the building, and Patrick slipped in. He scratched his nose. Fuck, he thought. Fuck. The stupid painting in the hallway glared at him from its purple and crimson blotches. As he walked to the lift he felt like some great ape dragging his feet, aware of his whole heavy body and his anger. Surprised everyone doesn't scream and run away, he thought, only there was no one in the hall, only the obnoxious painting set against the bare brick wall. He slammed the palm of his hand against the button for the lift. The diaries which had been taken were delicate, made of fine old paper, yellowy, fragile.

He entered the lift and pressed the button for her fourth-floor flat. Already, as he stood in the stainless steel lift, he felt slightly less angry. Tower Bridge was a gateway into south London, and here maybe different rules applied. In Bloomsbury stealing letters sounded outrageous, but here it was different. This was, after all, still a curiously hidden place, of old warehouses, old criminals, a place of gold and spices and smuggling, of old and new entrepreneurs.

The lift opened, and the door to Anne's flat was open too and he walked in.

'Anne!' he yelled.

The plain brick walls displayed various paintings. There was one landscape that took his breath away, which portrayed the end of the afternoon by the sea, with birds floating low, and he could almost hear the sounds becoming more muffled as if the day were being quietly wrapped up.

The bookshelves stood stiffly against the wall, with their shiny coloured covers. At intervals on the shelves were various artifacts – a primitive grey stone face of a woman, with mouth slightly apart, eyes two slits, a large clay frog with odd markings, a small gold statue of a boy. But there were no photographs. For someone who dealt in the past, it was curious that Anne, unlike her mother, had no records of her own past on display.

'Anne!' Patrick shouted, standing firmly in the middle of the room, legs apart, the Colossus of Rhodes. 'Come out. Come out!'

He heard someone moving in the other room.

'I want those papers!' Patrick yelled.

Alexander filled up the doorway of the room with what looked like a paperknife held by one plump hand and resting on the palm of the other.

'Are you looking for something?' he said.

165

'Anne,' said Patrick. 'She took some of my papers.'

'Terrible kleptomaniac, Anne. It's no wonder that Elgin interests her.'

'I should like her to return my papers,' said Patrick, and Alexander's lips twitched with amusement at Patrick's formal, rounded tone. 'She's the only one who could want them this much.'

'She's not here, I'm afraid,' said Alexander, looking down at the silvery paperknife in his hand. He wore Moroccan-style slippers, and a white shirt over black trousers, as if informing Patrick how very much more a man of the world he was. His hair shone a little under the light and it was heavily flecked with grey. 'So I can't help you.'

'Do you know about these documents?' asked Patrick.

'Should I?'

'Have you seen them?'

'No, I haven't seen them. What do they look like?'

'Very beautiful. Fragile. Yellowing. Tied with a blue ribbon.'

'Charming,' said Alexander.

Patrick was aware, out of the window behind him, of the London skyline sprouting innumerable shapes of domes and turrets, from the dainty towers of the Tower of London to the curve of St Paul's, and the harsh angles of satanic city buildings. But these warehouse buildings were so bare.

Alexander smoothed down his hair with his free hand, and for a moment Patrick thought, he's nervous of me. Even my feet seem too big for this place. Patrick took a step forward on the wooden floor. Halogen lights gleamed down.

'Where is she?' said Patrick.

'Do you want a drink? You seem a little . . . unsettled?'

'I am angry. She stole some documents.'

'You're sure about that?'

'Yes. Of course.'

'Ah,' said Alexander, and Patrick thought how very brown this man was, brown and gleaming, freshly polished. His gold ring glinted and his white shirt looked new, exceptionally white, bright white. 'And can you tell me what exactly is in these documents?'

Alexander's head was courteously to one side. Behind him Patrick could see the bed, with women's clothes thrown on it, a shirt, a dress.

'I'd have thought she'd have shown you,' said Patrick.

'Really? You don't know her well.'

Alexander's nails were well manicured and even they shone. Both men stood where they were, as if they had been positioned there by some invisible hand. Patrick swayed slightly. Alexander's little fist tightened on the knife. Even in restaurants, when Patrick quietly asked for a table, waiters were nervous of him because they interpreted his height as aggression and impatience.

'Tell me,' said Patrick, 'did you ask her to get them from me?'

Alexander laughed.

'Shall we sit down?' he said, looking down at the knife, as if surprised to find it in his hand. He put it on top of some books on the bookshelf.

'No thank you,' said Patrick.

'I just wondered . . . there's something of some consequence in these documents, is there? Something about the Elgin Marbles?' said Alexander, going to the kitchen area and pouring himself a gin and tonic. 'You want one?'

Patrick shook his head. His anger was mixed with weariness. He could see Anne reaching out and taking the diaries, placing them in her bag.

'No. They have charm, that's all. A sense of the past.' He looked into Alexander's face above the glass from which he sipped the clear liquid, and saw an intensity which suggested he perhaps did not already know the exact contents of the diaries.

'Have you had me followed?' said Patrick.

'No.'

'And did you make her take the documents?'

'No, again, dear boy,' said Alexander. 'As I say, she just refuses to share things with me, unfortunately.'

'I was beaten up. Was that to do with you? Or her?'

'It happens,' said Alexander, with a shrug of his round shoulders. 'You live in London now, not some two-bit Connecticut town.'

'Ah, you know a lot about me. They told me to go back to America.'

'You're just too big,' said Alexander, crinkling up his eyes in an approximation of a smile. 'Makes you a target. You should be short and round like me.'

He put down his glass. 'You sure you won't have one? Do tell me what's in the diaries,' said Alexander. In the distance Patrick heard the whine of a police car. 'I'd be so interested.'

'As I say, your girlfriend will no doubt tell you,' said Patrick.

Alexander shook his head.

'She will do what she proposes to do. If she never comes home again, it wouldn't surprise me.'

'And you wouldn't go and get her?'

'Oh yes,' he said, with a smile tugging somewhere in his ballooning face. 'I'd certainly try.'

Alexander stooped down and brushed something invisible off a magazine cover.

'You're very inquisitive, aren't you?'

Patrick's lips narrowed and he took a step towards Alexander.

Alexander was watching him with a cautious expression. How small Alexander's hands were compared to the rest of him.

'If I were you, I just wouldn't bother with it. I liked your Turner book. It had flashes of real genius. It had *promise*.'

A seagull squawked out in the sky beyond the balcony.

169

'Are you threatening me?' said Patrick.

'No. Would you like to be threatened? Then you'd have an excuse to hit me and you'd love that. I assure you, I'm scared of you. I'm not a brave man in the least.'

'I want my property back,' said Patrick.

'She's been away a few days,' said Alexander flatly. 'She was in a mood to get out.'

Patrick turned.

'And don't worry,' said Alexander. 'She doesn't love me. I wish she did. Close the door as you go out. Please.'

CHAPTER 31

Mary Elgin,
Constantinople,
September 4, 1800

When he came to stay Robert Ferguson talked about the sculptures on the Parthenon. He said that every form was altered by action or being at rest. The two sides of one figure's back varied, one stretched from the shoulder blade being pulled forward, and the other was compressed from the shoulder blade being pushed close to the spine as he rested on his elbow. He described it as 'all life and movement, very particular, very human, and yet, because of its position there, towering above the city, much more than human; man made God, and God made man.'

I am sure that my husband's desire to get the statues from the Parthenon is a desire to win back beauty in his life. When I first met him, he was a handsome man, tall, dignified. Now he suffers from rheumatism, headaches, constant pains, and his face is deformed, the nose quite rotted away.

CHAPTER 32

Elizabeth was curled up on the dirty pink sofa like a broken bird, her limbs too thin but her face more arresting because of that. The eyes were huge, because of the thinness of the rest of her.

'I'd always wanted big eyes,' Elizabeth had said, rearranging some strands of hair in the mirror.

'When I grow up, I shall only act in films like this,' Lily explained firmly to her mother while watching a television programme with a dragon and a beautiful maiden with windblown hair and high cheekbones. 'I shall be her, of course, or characters like her. I shan't act in all those other ordinary films or *series*.'

Elizabeth smiled. Curious, thought Anne, how the personality somehow doesn't get any smaller even when the body does. Her personality is just as gentle and sane and intelligent and without vanity, in her muted clothes. It was Elizabeth's flexible good humour which had helped to keep Anne stable these last years.

Elizabeth was continuing her teaching at a London college and hadn't let them know she was sick. She was tidying the mantelpiece of the pizza circulars, the minicab cards and curling-edged tokens torn out of newspapers but never used.

Elizabeth looked at her thin face in the mirror.

Anne adjusted the sleeves of her cardigan, which felt itchy against her skin.

Anne tidied the table.

'You know what's the most horrible thing about this illness. It makes you feel so *little*. You know, how unimportant you are if such a little thing, a little lump, can kill you.'

'It's not going to.'

'I wish I'd travelled more. I really do. Lived more. I've always been so *sensible*.'

These last weeks had been rough. The most devastating part was watching Elizabeth's slow decline. The chemotherapy was affecting her badly. If Anne allowed herself to feel it all, it was unbearable, like having needles inserted in you whenever you weren't looking. There were so many painful vignettes: Lily standing, hands on her hips, saying, 'I don't *like* your cancer', and scowling at Elizabeth's right breast as if to frighten it into submission. There were Elizabeth's slow motion movements as she tried to cook. It wasn't the illness itself, or even the fact of Elizabeth's possible death; it was the growing gap between Elizabeth's energy and her aspirations that was so poignant. She still wanted to play catch with Lily in the garden but couldn't jump to catch the ball. Even a few months ago she would have been able to leap up.

It was horrible the way the house was growing bigger and more unwieldy around Elizabeth day by day.

'I've got so many books here I've never read,' Elizabeth had said, staring at the books on the pitch pine shelves then sitting down on the sofa, as if she were part of it. It was as though, as she grew thinner and weaker, she was dissolving into the house.

As a child, Anne had thought that when you died you simply disappeared, and this seemed to be happening to Elizabeth.

Lily's continual high spirits were bewildering, but moving too. Other children would have had tantrums from the stress of dealing with the atmosphere in the house but Lily was determinedly holding herself together. On quite a few occasions she had noticed Lily about to give way, but she always hauled herself back.

'But I want you to race in the mother's race! Last time you won!' she had said, her lips trembling, her features blurred.

'I don't know, darling . . .' her mother had said softly.

'Oh, but you won last time,' she said, without her voice even shaking. 'What does it matter whether you do it again or not?' She had taken her mother's hand.

Anne and Elizabeth were sitting beside each other on the sofa in the long through reception room, with the William Morris willow wallpaper and the two black fireplaces with overmantels. Elizabeth had always been so reasonable and sensible, always with the right date and right argument. Her maroon shirt was loose at the neck where she had lost weight; it gave her a startled look.

CHAPTER 33

'Oh by the way,' said Alexander, pulling Anne on to his knee, 'that guy was here.'

'What guy?'

'The one you like.'

He stroked her cheek.

'He insisted you'd stolen the diaries I told you he had. I love your eyes. They're Russian eyes. I'm sure you have Russian blood in you.'

'Well I don't.'

'How do I know what you do when I'm not around? You haven't told me what you found out in Edinburgh. You don't tell me anything,' he said. 'And if you didn't take them, who did? I'd like to know.' He took a packet of small cigars from his pocket and lit one.

It struck her as odd the way the room always looked the same, whatever went wrong there. The books lined up neatly on the shelves, the linen-shaded vases stood decoratively around, the paintings remained unchanged, callously un changed she thought, the waves in the sea scene endlessly about to crash, the sky in the painting endlessly dark, oblivious of everything. A coffee mug appeared on a table in the room every now and again, a meal was put on the coffee table in front of the television then taken away, but on the whole the room remained utterly unsympathetic to anything but changes in light. It was as though the room was part of a great agenda, that of fluctuations of time and weather, and a small agenda, fluctuations of cutlery and crockery, while ignoring the human agenda of rows and sex and catastrophes. Perhaps that's why people sometimes threw and broke mugs when angry, she thought, in a desperate attempt to make their surroundings join in.

Alexander stood chopping up tomatoes. He scooped the tom atoes off the wooden block into a bowl. He looked strange, standing there amid the stainless steel, he was such a timeless figure, a plump Dionysus.

She watched him from the sofa, eating fruit pastilles. They had been her brother's favourite sweets too.

I could enjoy this flat, with its white walls and sense of time and space. It doesn't have to be a battle.

But too often Alexander's lips looked swollen and sulky like the rest of his face.

The juice covered his hands. She stayed with him because sex was good with him, it was as simple as that. Paolo told her once that sex was a 'mad and savage monster' and she'd been impressed, but a few days ago she'd found the remark attributed to Sophocles. She could see Paolo now, with her, looking out as one of the servants went round outside lighting the candles around the pond so that the whole garden glinted with water and light, with emerald leaves and orchids.

When her last book was published everything stopped for a while, and she smiled and signed copies and received praise, but still she was guarded, watching out, just in case a stab wound arrived when she least expected it.

She kicked off her shoes. It doesn't have to be like this, an obstacle course.

I could let Patrick do better than me, let his book be better. So what? What would it matter?

My ambition drives me forward, but I must make sure it doesn't drive me too far away from the pleasure of simply being alive.

She watched Alexander's back at the sink. There was a certain softness at the shoulders.

Anne thought of the knives in the kitchen cupboards, in the blocks, and the butter billowing in the dish, tables separating people, candles burning.

I shall go and see Patrick, explain he has made a mistake. I needn't see everyone as my enemy, my competitor, why maybe we could even work on the book together, be friends. Life could be pleasant instead of a battlefield. I can allow myself to be happy.

Alexander was mixing a salad dressing with olive oil, pepper, salt. She put her bare feet down on the white rug and stood up.

He turned round and raised his small thin eyebrows very high, quizzically.

'I don't want people coming here tonight,' she said.

'They're business associates,' he said.

'It must be curious,' she said, taking a book from a shelf, 'making your money from just shuffling things from one place to another.'

'It's called dealing.' When Alexander smiled his eyes disappeared.

One of Alexander's friends that evening was Anthony, whom Anne quite liked. He had short hair and thick eyebrows, and a way of tucking his shirt tightly into his trousers with one hand as he talked, while waving the other one around. Taki was a quieter, more dangerous character, with a round face and small moustache, a cigarette wedged in his lips. Both greeted her warmly.

The meat lay in front of them, red and with blood coming out, on to the wooden board.

Alexander bashed the steak a little more.

The men leant back on the sofas, their legs stretched out, their drinks in their hands.

She picked up a sharp knife then put it down. The overhead halogen lights sparkled down. She stood close to Alexander as he hammered again at the red meat. There was sweat above his upper lip. The triangle at the top of his shirt showed the hairs of his chest, too many hairs, too thick. He had blood on his hands and turned towards her with a smile, and put two fingers, both covered in blood, into her mouth, still smiling. For a moment she froze, looking straight into his eyes.

She swung away and went out on to the balcony.

After a moment or two Anthony left the sofa, came out and joined her.

'Alexander tells me you're working on a book on the Elgin Marbles,' he said in a convivial tone.

'No, on the contrary, I'm writing about Mary Nisbet, or Mary Elgin as she was called, wife of Lord Elgin.'

'But she was his wife throughout the period in which so many of the statues and panels and so much of the frieze were removed. She was very much around.'

'You're well informed,' she said.

'You know, you shouldn't be sidetracked into *people* overmuch. It's the sculptures that matter – the movement, the genius,' he said. 'People will pay a lot of money for that . . .'

His hands held on to the balcony rail.

'You're still caught up by people,' he said. 'You should go beyond that.'

Anne looked behind, into the lighted room, with the men's shiny faces.

'I was thinking quite the opposite,' she said.

Her mother had come here some months back and had stood in the centre of the room, clenching her handbag, standing with her shoulders close together, just moving her head around as if it were on a spring. She gave the impression of wishing to disappear

180

into her handbag. Her mother had frowned at the exposed brickwork by the kitchen, and her lips had condensed into a small, quite pretty bow.

When Anne was a child they had once travelled through Malaysia, in the jungle, and nothing had scared her mother, and now the big, open-plan flat scared her.

'It's very unusual,' her mother had said, eyeing the exposed brickwork as if it were about to make a lunge at her.

Everything about her mother had moved close to everything else, her arms drew together, her legs, her mouth, even her eyebrows seemed to battle to meet in the middle.

At least it had been brave of her mother to venture out from the cosy familiarity of Kensington to the wildness of the Tower Bridge area.

'I suppose it's inspiring,' said her mother. 'The view of the Tower. Thirteen years Raleigh spent there. Really, it was too much.'

Every now and again a piece of information or thought would wander up into her mother's face and make her alive again.

Anthony blew out the cigarette smoke from his mouth and it drifted away.

Anne leant against the rails. Her earrings hurt and she took them off then threw one, hard, into the water.

'Things,' she said.

He frowned.

181

She threw away the other.

'Why?'

She shivered. 'They hurt my ears.'

'They were pretty.'

She squinted at him. 'Just things.'

Anne walked back into the room, and to where Alexander was finishing preparing the meal as he talked to his friends. She poured herself a vodka and cranberry juice, and turned up the CD player which was playing the rap music which Alexander liked.

Mary was trapped by Elgin, thought Anne as she lay in bed that night, as I am trapped by Alexander. But in the end she escaped and her affair with Robert Ferguson scandalised society, and led to divorce, which was virtually unheard of. What was it in her past which made her able to break with Elgin, and with society's expectations? Was it some earlier rebellion? Some moment of rebellion which separated her from Elgin long before? Or was it just there, in her character, all along?

The next evening, Anne travelled to Patrick's flat off Tavistock Square. The house he lived in was formal, Georgian, five storeys high, with a black door, grey net curtains and a jagged crack like lightning up the front of the house. A short-haired squinty-eyed man stumbled out as she was about to ring the bell so she stepped quickly into the hall with a smile. The man tried to open his eyes to look at her, but gave up, and lurched off, head first, legs way behind.

She felt a little nervous, then reminded herself to be dignified, above it all. In her mind she could see Paolo in his high-necked pale blue shirt and matching trousers, with grubby running shoes. He used to run three miles every morning, believing a journalist had to be able to get out of danger quickly. After his run, he used to meditate by the pond where the fish swam huge and secret, giant muscles in the cool water.

The narrow hall, with its black and white diamond floor, had a table piled up with estate agents' magazines. She found herself looking to see if there were letters for Patrick, and as she did so, an elegant, fine-featured woman brushed by her in a red silk jacket and dark hair piled up into the kind of bun favoured by ballerinas. Anne watched the back of her legs, in their perfect, ladderless tights, proceed up the narrow staircase with its threadbare carpet.

The warm orchid smell of the woman's scent filled the hall.

Anne too went on up, and noted that the woman didn't stop at any of the grubby doors, with their wide variety of fingerprint and other marks. The dingy walls were empty of any pictures, and the light bulbs lacked shades. They swung slightly as the woman's footsteps proceeded up and up.

A dusty window looked out on a small garden below, overgrown with brambles. Anne paused as she heard the woman's steps proceed up to the top floor. The thin grey cord carpet did not appear to absorb any sound.

She heard his door close.

'Darling!' she heard the woman say.

She waited outside for a while.

The hallway had a few gashes in the wall and seemed to have been painted at different periods with different neutral shades, which didn't quite match. There was a streak of pale salmon paint going across, then a vertical streak of pale lemon and all the rest was white, slowly disappearing into grey. The carpet was completely threadbare, mouse grey, but mouse grey right at the end of a mouse's life. It was airless and Anne could hardly breathe.

Anne turned and proceeded downstairs, trying not to creak the stairs, although they did creak thunderously, past the dust-veiled window, afraid the woman would come tumbling out of the flat and see Anne there, listening attentively.

Anne went to Hyde Park for a while, and walked in the thick warm light and felt very lonely by the side of the great hotels spread along Park Lane like ocean liners. She sat by the Serpentine in the dark and watched the seagulls bob on the water. She wondered if she would have married Paolo after all, and had children.

Early the next morning, Anne visited the British Museum for comfort. She walked by the stone lions slumbering, the lions roaring, the Nereids dancing, everywhere movement among these stone things. The folds of their clothes whipped around them.

She stood in front of the broken gods on the west pediment, a small, pale figure in a velvet coat.

It's only a small step, a movement of the head, a jolt of the shoulder, into the moods and hopes of Mary Nisbet, to the hunger of Elgin. And what impresses and enthrals about the Elgin Marbles is not how old they are, but how young they are, how the muscles ripple, the ribs show, how they express the power of being human.

Only the loss of their limbs – the loss of an arm, a foot – suggests the passage of time. We don't dissolve into dust; bits of us live. A child a generation later looking over an ocean and resembling you or thinking of you, that's a limb, a head, something broken but still real and part of present time.

Mary Elgin left much behind: the diaries, her letters so safely kept in the Scottish Records Office, a painting in the Scottish National Gallery, scandal, her good works in Dirleton village, the extension to Ivy Cottage and the church there.

She wanted to read the diaries, and wondered who could have taken them. It was all so confusing. Patrick lied about having them, Alexander was clearly extremely interested in them for some reason he wouldn't tell her, and someone had taken them. She assumed it wasn't Alexander or he'd stop being so obsessed by them.

As Anne walked down the wide steps of the museum, sunlight sparkled on the steps. Outside, the London plane trees pressed into the sky.

I would like to talk to her, thought Anne as she jumped on a bus, to tell her things, to warn her of this or that: 'Don't take *that* route, Mary, don't take the long road to Paris rather than the shorter one, because your child will die if you do, your beloved fourth child William will die and you'll never get over it. You'll come to leave Elgin and to love Robert Ferguson who buried your darling William at your request.'

After the death of William, Mary seemed to turn the full volume of her love away from Elgin, and on to Robert Ferguson, though they both very nobly campaigned vigorously for Elgin's release from imprisonment in France by Napoleon and did not start their affair until much later, in London.

Sometimes, when she studied Mary, Anne felt like a cursed ghost haunting her life, a ghost from the future able to know what will happen to her but unable to warn her. She wondered sometimes if what followed her was a sense of the past, or the future, and that maybe, once she was happy, it would go away.

'I saw a photo in a magazine which looked just like your brother,' said Anne's mother excitedly on the phone. 'I called the magazine – *Newsweek* – but they wouldn't help.'

'I'll call,' said Anne wearily. Every few days

her mother called, asking her to ring about this photograph or that film. 'Which week is it?'

'This week. Page fourteen. You can't miss him . . . except he's the one with the black beard.'

'Oh, mother,' said Anne. 'He had fair hair.'

'Yes, then. But people change. Do you know,' said her mother breathlessly, 'I think we'll find him soon. One of my old friends from Hong Kong – Stella Brae, you remember – called round for tea,' said her mother on the phone. 'We had scones. I felt well. I'm beginning to feel a bit better, as if things are going to change.' Her mother paused. 'You should break off with that Greek. I don't like the sound of him one bit. What exactly did you say he does?'

'This and that,' said Anne.

'I prefer that young man who came round. Ever since meeting him I've felt better. It's almost as if . . .'

'What?'

'Oh – I don't know—'

'What?'

'Oh, it's peculiar but I don't think about David so much. Are you coming over today?' asked her mother. 'Please.'

'Of course,' said Anne.

CHAPTER 34

Mary Elgin,
Constantinople,
February 3, 1801

Over Christmas Elgin was very ill with violent rheu-
matism in his head and in dreadful pain. The doctor
MacLean (who has been sick with the palsy) put seven
leeches on his temple which we hoped would revive him
but it made no difference. Except they inflamed his
face. MacLean says he never saw such leeches in his
life, so very violent. They bite more than any he ever
saw in England. It seems very odd they should have
inflamed him so.

The disease to his nose gets worse. As yet the doctors
do not think the bone is touched and hope to try to save
it. I trust the flesh alone is damaged and it may heal.

I have heard people mention syphilis.

I write as tiny as I can.

CHAPTER 35

Patrick adjusted his tie outside Victoria's house and rang the bell. It was going to be his last contact with her. Victoria had come round once without phoning first and he'd sent her away. He'd go to this dinner she so wanted him to attend, and that would be the end of it.

He moved from foot to foot. Somehow things seemed to be turning against him. As someone – Anne he believed – had taken the first few diaries, she might well guess there were more. But he couldn't bring himself to dump Mary's minute, sad writing into the cold metal of a bank safe. After working on more of the diaries, he had replaced the floorboard, the carpet, and pushed a wardrobe over the floorboard.

The weather was close and seemed to be packed around his body. Victoria's white stucco house at the top of Campden Hill Square was just near Holland Park, and in the past when he had walked up to it he felt free, above everything, as if nothing that happened here could have any effect on the rest of his life. He no longer felt that.

The two bay trees on either side of the door

looked recently clipped and soon the door was flung open and a butler stood there, one of the new-style butlers with one earring.

Patrick entered the familiar hall, with the white panelling, the carefully adjusted paintings on the wall, the Pugin wallpaper. The lilies smelt sickly.

The Spanish maid, Maria, hurried across the hall in her black and white uniform and gave Patrick a quick, warm smile. Although Patrick usually came here on Maria's days off, once Maria had come back early and seen Patrick emerge dishevelled from the bedroom. She had grinned at him, and her little feet had done a little dance. After that they'd met a few other times.

One of his laces was undone and he stooped to do it up. He had torn himself out of his study, struggled to get away from the pages he was working on, forced himself to take steps from the living room out on to the stairs.

He could hear the flutter of voices from inside the drawing room he was about to enter.

Patrick stood up from tying his laces, brushed down his suit (it was his bouncer's suit, black, ideally worn with shades and a swagger) and proceeded into the drawing room, which was glowing with the sheen of expensive furniture.

'Patrick!' said Victoria. Her face lifted with delight: the smile, the eyes, the chin. The sharpness of her features disappeared. Her low-cut dress was green and shimmering, that of a snake, a lizard. But there was another bruise, just below her lip.

'Hi,' he said, affecting a politely languid air he didn't feel. What he felt like was a runner at the start of a race, ready to be off, through the hall, out through the door, over the porch, down the marble steps and away, faster and faster, down the pavements of Campden Hill Square, along Holland Park Avenue.

A little pollen from the lilies had rubbed against her cheek and he leant over and wiped it away, without realising what he was doing, and he was aware of the interested, analytical eyes of two of the other guests.

Outside, it was building up to a storm and there was a curious stillness about the room. The yellow satin curtains cascaded down from the tall windows, shimmering, full of shadows and tassels.

What struck him most of all was how old everyone was and he could see from the way Victoria touched her hair that she was nervous too and maybe realised how very different the other guests in the room were from Patrick.

Of course he was aware his discomfort at their presence had much to do with his mood. It was absurd to be disconcerted by some people because they weren't young. But it was because it highlighted the distance between Victoria and himself. She seemed so youthful because she was clever, funny and flexible.

Or maybe she has invited these people on purpose, to test me, in which case I've failed, dismally, and would like to leave.

A painting of a violin player smiled at him above the marble mantelpiece. His clothes clung to him too tightly, as if glued on.

'I'm so sorry Charles couldn't be here this evening but he's on some assignment and won't be back until tomorrow,' Victoria told a voluminous man, who leant back on his heels and talked to the air, while a group gathered round him. His hands rested on his stomach like a caretaker of some French chateau. Victoria whispered that he was a chef.

'Gluttony no longer appears to be considered a deadly sin,' drawled a woman whose bloodhound face was full of folds as if weighed down by her personal history. 'It is an art form now. Or maybe it's instead of sex. Do you think that's it? We've all done everything we could have done sexually, but there's always a new recipe.'

The room was too hot, and all the faces reared up at him, enlarged, too close, the eyes too small. He towered over everyone and he could see the bald circles at the top of men's heads.

He drank his third glass of champagne and noted on the wall by the window a little drawing of a man in pencil, which Victoria had told him was Charles, and it looked very remote and lonely in the frame.

The faces of the women in the room softened a little as Patrick was introduced to them. Their bodies turned towards him.

Victoria introduced Patrick to a wild-eyed man

in his sixties with a drunken wife. 'Ah, Patrick, this is Joseph Fairley.' His grey hair stuck out in all directions as though he'd just been given an electric shock. 'And his wife Jenny. He's a leading antiquarian bookdealer,' continued Victoria, her voice smooth and rich, as if meant only for Patrick. 'I invited him so you could meet him. He wants to ask you something.'

'Books!' said Jenny Fairley. 'We have books everywhere in Brighton. Under the bed, on the bed, in the lavatory, stuffed in cupboards, hidden in boxes. When I get into bed I find books are in there already.

'Joseph doesn't read the books,' his wife said in her queer and feathery voice, 'he just lusts after them. Looks at them, caresses them occasionally, counts them. Has anyone ever told you that you have the most beautiful eyelashes? They're so long.'

Joseph Fairley pushed his wife to one side as he took over the conversation while she stood there, with narrowed eyes, hurling out the occasional comment as if they'd just had a blazing row. In fact, Patrick imagined, this was how they probably lived, how they were used to living, and they both quite enjoyed and accepted their roles. One, a bookish thug, the other, his personal tormentor, constantly expressing her dislike of what he loved best.

'It's my living,' explained Joseph Fairley convivially, as if he couldn't hear his wife's interpolations.

'I heard there was something about Elgin.' Joseph Fairley's eyes were a pinprick of interest. 'I heard from Victoria you've some fascinating insights into Mary Elgin. Wonderful the way women are being rediscovered, isn't it? We used to think it was just the husbands who did things. Now it increasingly turns out the wives were secretly powerful figures.' He moved closer to Patrick.

'I don't know what it is everyone is so interested in. She was involved with the Elgin Marbles. She had an outrageous affair and a sensational divorce which shocked the world. So what? It has all been known for years,' said Patrick.

'Ah. Tell me. Do you think she had any secrets from Elgin? I mean before she started her affair?'

Joseph Fairley stared at him intently, as if trying to send some surgical instrument into Patrick's brain to find out the contents.

'Maybe,' said Patrick, surprised by the fierceness of Fairley's gaze.

Patrick touched the looking glass behind him with the flat of his hand, and liked the feel of the cold glass.

The man's wife took another sip of champagne from the gold-rimmed glass. 'I saw a man shake a young mother today while her toddler watched from the pushchair. And you know why? She was going too slowly along the pavement!'

Victoria came over and directed Joseph Fairley's wife over to the other guests ('You mustn't let these men monopolise you!'). The wife's diamond ring flashed as she was led away. Victoria slipped her hand into Patrick's and he could feel her hand between his fingers, and for a moment his being seemed to be flowing down into her moist palm. Then she let it go.

Joseph Fairley coughed, and moved Patrick a little to one side. 'I have friends up in Edinburgh,' he said in a low voice. 'The word is there are some interesting diaries around. An auctioneer friend of mine hinted at some amazing revelation. A *valuable* one.'

'I haven't heard anything,' said Patrick.

'We should keep in touch. It's great to find someone who shares my interest in Mary.' His brown corduroy suit smelt of tobacco.

'Where's the picture you had over there, Victoria? Of the spaniel?' asked Patrick.

'How observant you are. Oh, I sold it. I found a marvellous new picture dealer, and I sold it to him.' She lowered her voice, and again the voice was smooth and rich.

'I must look after my other guests,' said Victoria.

As more drinks were served Victoria skimmed around the room, occasionally straightening a man's tie, whispering in someone's ear, but every few moments turning to look at Patrick while all the time her dress glimmered, green, and he wondered what was in her mind.

'How is your father, darling?' he heard someone ask her.

'Oh, dying,' she said. 'At last!' But her voice sounded coarse.

The cornices on the ceiling meticulously displayed flowers and plants, white confectionery in an old room.

It was while they were eating that it happened. It was as they ate their duck that Victoria's husband came home unexpectedly.

His entry was one of those moments which go on and on. As Patrick lifted his fork to his mouth, the door opened and there stood the lopsided man, who, in Patrick's mind, was somehow connected with Lord Elgin.

In fact he stood there with an agreeable expression on his cadaverous face. He was not a good-looking man. His forehead looked as though someone had bashed it at an early stage so that it was situated further back than his jaw, which stuck resolutely out. This two-tiered face was unusual, and should, Patrick considered, be softened in some way, perhaps by tumbling vines, he found himself thinking with a fixed smile.

Robert Ferguson must have played this role, the role of the wife's lover who is on reasonable terms with the husband, many times.

'Charles!' said Victoria. She seized her napkin and wiped her mouth. She jumped up. But was this real, he found himself thinking, or did she know Charles would be here. I shouldn't be here, he thought, what am I doing? He wiped his mouth.

All around, the room, with its damson walls and

candles, seemed to draw back in alarm. The other guests seemed to be playing the game of statues, and each was fixed in one position or another. Only the three main players – Patrick and Victoria and Charles – seemed to be moving, alive, and all the movement was in their faces which registered many different things, the first of which, in each case, was probably confusion.

Mrs Morgan had probably enjoyed this kind of thing, the thrill of dissembling and betraying. Maybe his father had. He remembered the excitement of the confrontation between Mrs Morgan and his mother, how charged everything had been, and how red Mrs Morgan's lips had looked, and how he'd wanted to touch her skin which glowed with sweat. Maybe Robert Ferguson had been like this.

'Is there a seat for me?' said Charles.

'Darling! We – I – didn't know you were coming! I thought you were battling with . . .'

'Well I came home,' he said pleasantly. He had a flat, grey voice.

'Take my chair,' she said, 'I'll get a chair from the other room.'

And Charles just took her seat, took her glass, let Victoria go to get a chair. Patrick jumped up and got it for her, and they stood in the hall, with its vivid wallpaper.

'You see what he's like?' she said. 'I hate him. I was trying to help him – help him keep his job. You remember how I asked you about the diaries . . .

I thought there might be something of interest in them for him. But he treats me like this.'

Patrick carried the chair back while she went to the waiters and cook to ask them to set another place. The other guests, who now seemed to have recovered their life, moved so that he could put the chair down.

To his discomfort, Patrick found he'd planted his chair right next to the bookseller.

'I don't believe I know you,' said Charles to Patrick, from down the other end of the table. 'Come and sit here. I'm Charles! I own this house! I'm the host! Ah! Victoria tells me you're the author! Writing about the Elgins!'

Charles was red-faced, already a little drunk.

Patrick came and sat beside Charles, examining his square hands.

Charles's whole body was wrenched towards Patrick, and he had that glassy-eyed expression which people get when they've heard too many people's accounts of their opinions and lives, when they just don't want to know anymore about anybody but have to continue to pretend.

'I don't have time to read books,' said Charles. 'Political stuff I cover, of course, but not personalities, biographies, that kind of thing.'

'I thought politics was personalities,' said Patrick.

'I'm trying to say I go for the more heavyweight books,' said Charles with a kind of desperation. 'I haven't heard of you; have you been writing long?'

Patrick took a sip of his red wine.

He glanced at Victoria and saw the anger in her eyes. She hates him, he thought. She lives with this man she hates, and this is why, little by little, she is becoming an outline. Whatever she is, whatever she was, she is losing it. Anger and hate solidifies people, makes them smaller. And then her eyes met his, Patrick's, and the hate didn't leave them.

His insides gave a twist.

She hates me now, he realised. She hates me too. Because she knows I'm leaving her. She forgot to take the hate out. She forgot to pretend.

At the door she whispered to him. 'You have to help me. It turns out Charles was involved in falsifying those documents. I think he'll get the sack. Such a silly, desperate thing to do. My father heard about it. Some kind friend. That upsets me, that he heard about it. And now, since the news that he's been in trouble, Charles has been more violent.' She put her hand on his arm, and tucked her hair behind her ear girlishly.

'We should go to the police,' he said.

'I want you to deal with it differently.'

'What do you mean?'

'You know people in your work – boxers, debt collectors, bodyguards. Please, Patrick. I'm afraid of him. You've seen how he treats me. The bruises. I can't stand it anymore.'

'What are you trying to say?'

'The kind of people you know – they'll do certain

jobs for money.' There was a harshness in her voice, though she was clearly trying to keep it soft and beguiling.

'What jobs?'

She was watching him intently. Her tongue slipped over her lips. He thought of her tiny white teeth.

'You know. We've both met people like that. I'm afraid of Charles,' she said. 'I don't want him around anymore.'

He could hear the clock tick on the mantelpiece. He wanted to get out, into the clean air. The bruise below her lips was showing up more now. He did feel sorry for her, but he wanted to get out. She moved a little closer to him. He could hardly breathe. His mouth felt dry and his shirt clung to him closely. He felt he was being nailed somewhere he didn't want to be, some insect or butterfly pinned on a piece of board by an avaricious collector.

'Go and see your father, talk to him about everything,' said Patrick.

Nearby the lilies postured, their glorious mouths spotted red and their stamens sticking out like tongues.

'No. Every night I used to wish my father dead. I concentrated on his heart stopping. I used to imagine his heart valve – then I'd tighten it shut in my mind.'

'You should go and see him,' said Patrick.

'Why?' she said. 'What's he got to do with it? I want you to help me.'

'And tell me, what exactly do you want me to do?'

She smiled.

'You can guess, can't you?'

She looked tired, her make-up slightly wrecked, off centre. There was a pollen mark on her shoulder where she must have brushed by the lilies.

'You know the right people. Please, Patrick, I told you. I'm afraid of him. I'm tired of this life. I want it all finished with.'

Her face was very pale. She had a high, white forehead.

'I'll just assume you're joking,' he said, putting on his coat. She was leaning against the wall, even whiter now, the palms of her hands touching the white panelling.

'Victoria, tell me, have you had me followed?' he said more softly.

'No. Maybe it was Charles. Not me.'

Patrick caught sight of the maid bringing more glasses. She glanced anxiously at her mistress, then Patrick.

Victoria's eyes were too bright and glittery.

Maria put down the glasses and came over to her mistress and took her arm. She gave a quick glance at Patrick.

'Madam hasn't been well recently – but she won't rest,' she said. 'She never sleeps. I'll get her to bed – tell her guests she's ill. She'll be okay.'

CHAPTER 36

Mary Elgin,
Constantinople,
September 1, 1801

The plague here continues, and the Turkish authorities carry away the dead bodies during the night, which is so far lucky for us, as we have less chance of meeting them.

How the Turks love us now, since we defeated Napoleon in Egypt this March, chasing the French out of the area. Elgin is quite sure this will help him take away what he pleases from Athens. I shall never forget the celebrations here. It was the most beautiful night. Both sides of the Bosphorus illuminated, rockets, guns, cannon going off at all corners, all sorts of music, and a sort of masquerade. The Turks were as merry as Christians. I think they might have conquered Egypt over and over again had they but fired half the number of cannons in earnest they are now firing in joke.

The climax was the Sultan showing himself to all his people as he lay on a silver sofa. While Elgin was at a conference, I was rowed for a while and, not realising it was forbidden to pass near the Sultan, I asked the sailors to row past him. He seemed to nod good naturedly at me though I heard it was considered degrading for him to meet the eyes of a foreigner. After I had gone by, I glanced back and saw he had picked up a telescope to watch me!

Elgin has become quite the most important foreign representative, as the ambassador of the nation who had brought about this victory. They cannot do enough for us and, as all Elgin really wants is Athens, he is going to use his influence.

He's drawing close to what he wants now. He doesn't sleep at night. He prods me all over, every night, poring over my skin.

I intend to sleep apart from him.

CHAPTER 37

'You have to consider your relationship with Paolo may never have lasted,' Elizabeth said to her, but she hadn't wanted to listen.

'I think,' Elizabeth had said, 'that you feel you've got romantic love ticked off, that you needn't bother with it again.'

'I'm not sure that I do,' said Anne.

'It was a romantic idyll, a holiday romance.'

'You may be right but why are you saying this?' she had asked Elizabeth, who sat at the pine kitchen table with a tiny portion of salad, and it seemed to Anne that she had never seen anyone make so much effort merely to stay upright at the table. Elizabeth's body seemed to shrink each day, as though the limbs wanted to reduce down to their smallest volume. There were marks on the table; biro marks, crayon marks.

Elizabeth had hung her head. 'I just want . . . if you're looking after Lily I want you to know who you are and be that person. You can't be so afraid of losing people if you don't let yourself love anyone.'

Elizabeth looked up, and the eyes were still bright, as though all her personality were poured into the eyes, while she had abandoned the rest of her; even her lips no longer looked like hers, they were thinner, and seemed to hover in her face. Her long-sleeved checked shirt billowed over her arms and her hands were horribly thin.

'You see, there isn't time,' she said urgently. 'There really isn't time. You think there's time but you're wrong. Some people hide behind their faces, disappear, far back, let their eyes, noses, faces, assume the bother of communication with people. It's the people who truly inhabit their faces who seem alive; so many of us are never quite present during our own lives. For the rest of my life I want to be present, that's all, to do what I want to do, to be me. And I know I may not have much time but maybe time isn't important. A year is a lifetime, if that's all you have, and one hour can hold the crux of your life. I know I've said it before – but there is only now.'

Anne slowly cut up a tomato.

Elizabeth caught her breath.

'Let's not talk now,' said Anne.

'No,' said Elizabeth, taking a sip of water. 'I want to. It won't get easier. And I know you. I remember you, so beautiful, that first day at Edinburgh.'

Elizabeth coughed. Her shoulders seemed to sag together.

'Let's go and sit next door,' said Anne.

'You should realise,' said Elizabeth, taking a breath, 'that Paolo loved danger. He would have got killed sooner or later. You know there wasn't a war he didn't attend. It wasn't your fault in any way.'

'That's not quite so. I could have stopped him flying that day. I could have insisted he didn't.'

'That's absurd.' Elizabeth sighed. 'Maybe I do need a bit of rest now,' she had said, and coughed again.

Anne had offered to stay permanently but Elizabeth refused. 'I want the time alone with Lily while I can.'

CHAPTER 38

Mary Elgin,
Constantinople,
September 19, 1801

I am lonely for Scotland, and think of the seabirds and moors and cool breezes. My little girl is just over two weeks old. She is a fat little thing with black hair and blue eyes. When she was just seven days old I had her vaccinated against the smallpox. I am working hard with Doctor Scott, who has fresh vaccine sent over from Vienna, and I hope we shall completely establish the vaccine here in Turkey; it is dreadfully fatal.

The sicker Elgin gets, the more he talks of the beauty of the Parthenon. It is as though the beauty of it is all there in his head and as he grows more and more unwell he wants to possess the beauty even more. He wants to have it to himself. His disfigured face disgusts me.

CHAPTER 39

At the library Patrick looked around for Anne. She hadn't been there for a few days now, and he'd heard nothing from her. That morning, he had leant against the heavy Edwardian wardrobe, pushing it a little to the left. He lifted the carpet, from the edge, and then the black floorboard. There were what was left of the diaries, neatly bound in a light blue ribbon, the colour of Cambridge, protected in a cellophane bag. He had continued deciphering them.

As he left the building Patrick saw Anne in the distance, swirling along in the wind, her velvet coat sweeping behind her, like some blackbird.

He called after her but she didn't appear to hear him, and she climbed into a cab, and he ran to the middle of the road and hailed one too.

'Please follow the girl in that cab,' he said.

A pain throbbed at the centre of his head.

Her cab stopped outside the warehouse conversion and she hurried in just as his cab drew up. He buzzed the name Fitzgerald on the list outside. The wind stabbed at his face.

'It's Patrick Browning,' he said.

He moved restlessly from foot to foot.

'I'm so sorry. I'm busy,' she said. 'Another time.'

He waited until a woman in a raincoat came to the door, opened it with a key and he slipped in. Patrick ran up the stairs two at a time and knocked on the door of her flat.

Anne flung the door open, her brow low, her lips not nearly as severe as the rest of her face. They seemed to be half smiling, as though warmth were trying to escape but couldn't quite make it. The room behind her was awash with light from the wall of glass doors.

'You do like to get your way, don't you?' she said.

'Why yes,' he said, standing at the glass doors. 'What a view. I needed to talk to you. You know what it's about.'

'I assume you're an only child,' she said.

'That's right,' he said.

'I find it gives some people a radiant confidence, others arrogance. I put you in the latter category,' she said.

'The latter category!' he said, smiling. 'How English and academic you sound.' He loosened his collar, which was hot where it touched his neck. Anne was watching his neck where the frayed collar touched his skin.

'I'm Scottish in fact,' she said stiffly. 'Born in Scotland. How is your work going?'

'Fine. Except when people steal things from me.

You waited till I'd deciphered some of it then stole it. Well, it won't astonish you. You only have the early parts.'

'Alexander told me you thought I'd stolen something. I didn't.'

'You called me. To arrange to meet me. Last Thursday.'

'I didn't,' she said, her arms crossed.

There was that strange stillness about her, a kind of self-protective calm. He found it hard not to believe her and walked over to the wide windows overlooking the silvery-grey river which shivered in the wind. Some music was playing.

'You should go now,' she said. 'Alexander will be back soon. He's in a strange mood. You shouldn't be here when he gets back. And why did you go to my mother's? That was outrageous. Don't you think about what you do? Or do you just do whatever you like?'

He plunged his hands into the pockets of his jeans.

'I was curious about you. You and I, we're alike. I sort of recognised what she said about your childhood. Your father and mine, they were alike.'

She raised her eyebrows.

'I spend my time,' he continued, 'in the library in another world, you know, Elgin fighting the authorities, Elgin ordering the statues down. And when I talk to other people we don't communicate because I'm in the past and they're in the present.

We're in different time zones. It makes me angry. Most people don't know what I'm talking about.'

'I don't know either,' she said fiercely.

'Of course you do,' he said.

'I didn't take anything.'

'Then Alexander did.'

'I don't think so,' she said.

'I don't care who took them. I would just like them back. Mary Elgin was treated unfairly when she was alive. I want to set the record straight. You're the same. I know it. Why do you stay with that man?' he said.

'Maybe I like him.'

'Why?'

'Why what?'

'Why do you like him?'

'Did I say I did? And you have a relationship?' she said.

'Here and there,' said Patrick.

'I heard a married woman.'

Patrick shrugged.

'You love her?' she said.

'It's an affair.'

'Just another affair,' said Anne. She put a pastille in her mouth.

'No. I'm fond of her.'

'And the others?'

'What?'

'You have other girlfriends?'

'Not really. So who told you about the married woman?'

'Alexander. He knows everything.'

'I don't like him.'

'He's not really likeable. That's not his point.' Her eyes were full of amusement. 'What does your married woman do?'

'Nothing.'

'Ah. She's rich. Or poor.'

'Rich. She collects paintings, but is selling them at the moment.'

'She's in love with you, is she?'

'I don't know.'

'Does her husband know?'

'I don't know. Poor guy.'

'So you don't hate him?'

'Not at all.'

'If you don't hate him, you don't love her.'

'You live with Alexander?'

'On and off. It's his flat,' she said.

'So he's not married?'

'Yes, he's married.'

Patrick frowned disapprovingly then, realising what he was doing, laughed at himself, and she laughed too, a peal of laughter, fresh and clear like a stream in a mountain.

They regarded each other with warmth.

'Pity,' she said.

'What?' he said.

The front door swung open, and Alexander entered carrying his cashmere coat. Patrick wondered if he'd been listening at the door.

'Ah! A visitor!' said Alexander.

'Hello,' he said.

'Ah! It's my friend the thug! Come to pick the clever Anne's brains, have you?'

In spite of his roundness, Alexander looked nimble compared to Patrick, who was unrealistically solid. Yet when Patrick moved he had a kind of delicacy, solid and fluid at the same time.

Alexander sauntered to the bookshelf and, with a quick unpleasant glance at Patrick, began chucking books down on to the sofa.

'The late-eighteenth and early-nineteenth century is her period. Nelson! Napoleon! She knows about them all,' he said.

Anne began to pick the books up from the sofa, and put them in a pile on the coffee table. The shiny faces of Nelson, Napoleon, Tolstoy, Beethoven, all piled up, one on top of the other. Anne stooped to straighten a dustjacket which had come off as Alexander had flung it, and her look was of intense affection for the biography of Nelson. The hair held back on either side of her forehead by her cheap butterfly hairslides stayed where it was, but the rest of her rich red hair fell forward as she bent down. There was a patience and distance in her behaviour as if she were incapable of being angered or hurt by Alexander, however much he tried. Her manner wasn't subservient but calm and Patrick wished for a moment he had her inner quietness. Patrick moved towards Alexander with an air of menace, his jaw and shoulders seeming to move before the rest of him.

'You and your attacks on Elgin. Without Elgin the Turks would probably have destroyed them,' asserted Alexander, his body and voice expanding to almost fill the room. 'Greek, English, what does it matter? He saved them for the future and that's what owns everything, anyway, the future.'

Anne's skin was bone-white and he decided she was more affected by Alexander's behaviour than she seemed to be at first. But then she moved quickly towards Alexander, her lips suddenly wavy with emotion, and smiled at him, and put her hand on Alexander's arm as if sensing his sorrow and fear of time passing. He looked into Anne's lovely face then turned his head away, and took a deep breath.

'I'm hungry. I need some food,' said Alexander. He brushed by Patrick. 'Thank you for coming but I'd be grateful if you didn't pop by again. We like our privacy – unless, of course, Anne, you arranged to see this young man?'

She shook her head, and opened the French door on to the balcony, where she leant on the rail. Patrick walked out on to the balcony. In the cold air the snaking river was a gossamer scarf dropped from a height.

Anne stood at a distance from him and stroked her bare white forearm, then she looked at Patrick, opened her lips slightly. She moistened them with her tongue, in a quick, scarcely noticeable movement. She turned her head and continued to stare at the river, where a few desultory boats continued to trail past and the seagulls swooped and soared. He wanted to stroke her arm.

'Bye now,' she said.

She crossed her arms and held them close to her, as a tourist boat drifted by, leaving an elegant wake behind in the glistening water.

Alexander called out, 'Anne!'

'You should go now,' she said.

When he got home somehow everything looked different, as though it had all been moved over half an inch and the colours just slightly altered. A red vase which sat on the television set now looked an acceptable shade, an interesting maroon, whereas the last time he'd seen it he was sure it had been irritatingly red. The few twigs Victoria had placed in it, which previously had looked ridiculous to him, now looked charming, a tribute to nature. The old striped rug on the floor of the main room, spread out before the television like an offering, now seemed much less frayed. The whole flat looked better, he thought, a little brighter, as though it had all been cleaned.

For the next two days Patrick had a high temperature. The headache had begun with a light colouring in of pain on one side of his forehead, then it had spread and his limbs had begun to feel strange, like heavy blocks.

He lay in the low bed on the floor, from where he stared out on the grey wall and the skirting board with its scuff marks.

It reminded him of being a child, this helplessness, and he kept thinking of Mrs Morgan, and sometimes he thought of Victoria.

As he fell asleep that night he could see Mary Nisbet stooping down and stroking the head of a broken Greek god.

During the dark blanket of that night he dreamt of Mary Elgin again, with her slightly sloping shoulders, slightly too long nose, her dark merry eyes. He was at a ball with her, and fireworks went off, startling her, and she grabbed his arm and he led her through servants dressed in Chinese costumes, over an artificial pond, passed the King and Queen of Naples, he obese and she delicate and fine boned, up on a throne. Patrick and Mary bowed as they passed the King and Queen. Mary wore her pink and silver dress for the dream, and pearls round her neck.

They made love on a raised platform in front of all the people dining on fragments of fried meat. She raised her skirts as he thrust into her and everyone clapped. He could see Emma Hamilton, her breasts nearly bare, clapping with special delight, with her aged husband and shrivelled hero Nelson.

Suddenly Mary seemed to realise what she'd done and began to cry.

'But it was so nice,' he whispered to her, stroking the tears from her eyes.

The two people on the table closest to them were Anne and Victoria; both seemed relaxed, Victoria with her arm around Anne's shoulder.

He awoke, sweat pouring off him, soaking the sheets, in the uneasy shadows of the morning. For a moment, he wondered where he was.

As he began to sense the present take over his body and mind again – the skin come back on his body, the brain reform into some semblance of the person he had learnt he was – the objects positioned in the sides, the heavy table light, the dark wood desk, the floor, scattered with his possessions, mirroring the chaos in his mind.

He moved restlessly, not looking at the clock, hoping it was not yet morning.

He kissed Mary's white face, which suddenly faded into mere bones, and he cried out.

Later, Victoria came round, again without calling. She wet a flannel, squeezed it and put it on his burning forehead. Victoria wore a crimson shirt and crimson lipstick and her hands were cool and capable. She talked a lot and he hardly listened to what she said.

Her pearl earrings seemed too bright for his dour room, the floor of which was strewn with newspapers and magazines. His mouth felt dry.

'Could I have a glass of water?'

She gave him one and the water felt gorgeous on his throat as if he were diving into it. The next morning Victoria was back, bathing his forehead.

She acted strangely that day, jumping like some animal hearing a predator every time there was a noise outside.

Her hair was ink black, now carved into a precise geometric form, angled at the nape.

There was sweat all over his forehead, and under his arms and on his back. He walked over and flung open a window and she was behind him, her arms round his waist, her head resting on his back.

'He beat me up again last night. You should help me,' she said.

When he was better, he called Charles up.

'I should like to meet up with you,' said Patrick.

'Sure. I'd love to meet for lunch. Have a talk. You know, about Victoria too. She hasn't been herself recently, with her father being ill . . . and, oh yes, I have some important news for you. About your publisher. I bumped into him yesterday. You really will want to know this. We were at school together, Stewart Edwards and I.'

'L'Azzurro, Greek Street, around one?' said Patrick.

'Well,' said Charles, squinting behind his glasses.

Patrick realised he was staring at the man's mouth and imagining, with some disgust, him kissing Victoria. Probably the perfume she wore Charles had bought for her, maybe at an airport on the way home from covering some story. He thought of the bruises on her body.

Patrick's chair jutted out into the middle of the restaurant, making waiters have to go round him, while Charles sat securely with his back to the wall. For a moment, Patrick considered how easy it would be to have him killed.

'You should stop beating her up, you know,' said Patrick loudly. 'Or I'll do something about it.'

The whole restaurant seemed to pause. There was a swirl inside Patrick, and an emptiness somehow, and he realised he wanted to turn over the table, then wring this man's neck.

A waiter glanced down at Patrick nervously, as if afraid a fight might break out. Patrick sat too wide and too tall, and stiff, as if made of muscle, and glowered down at the urban journalist holding his napkin on his lap, his hands a little too close together, a little nervous.

For a moment Patrick was aware of everything, of Victoria at home sitting on the sofa, flicking through a copy of *Country Life* wondering whether that was the answer, the country mansion, another life, of the waiter hovering behind him, helpless, a plate of plaice with aubergine spreading out from his hand like some heavy weight, of the weather outside, docile, thoughtful, in that in-between state in which London passed so much of its days, and most of all he was aware of Anne, at a distant corner of his mind, and her quiet concentration, her quiet certainty, her separateness.

'What are you talking about?' said Charles in a falsely cheerful voice, his eyes flicking to Patrick's clenched fists.

Charles tidied his napkin, on the table, with his square fumbling hands.

219

Patrick glanced at the menu, which had been handed to him with an ingratiating sort of bow by the waiter, who then drew back with a miniature leap.

'Plaice and fries,' said Patrick. He wasn't sure if he could sit through a meal with this guy.

'Fish and chips! Why it's years since I saw anyone order that,' said Charles.

Patrick paused, his hands still, his shoulders still, his chin tilted slightly, inquiringly. Patrick thought he saw Charles's ears twitch a little.

Patrick took a roll of bread and ripped it apart.

Charles took a sip of the Evian water.

Patrick drank some wine. He wiped his mouth. He was aware of the door a little way away and kept imagining walking towards it, and out.

Charles cleared his throat. He sipped some more Evian. On his marriage finger was a gold wedding ring.

'And, Patrick,' said Charles, 'what do you like to do, when you're not working?'

He shrugged.

Patrick took another swig of white wine.

'I work most of the time.'

Charles watched him bleakly. 'Oh, by the way, Stewart Edwards told me that he isn't going to publish your book. I thought it would be worth you knowing.'

The waiters fluttered anxiously around, weaving through the tables and chairs as if performing some dull folk dance.

On the walls there were paintings of the Mediterranean Sea, bright blue.

'Said you were late with some chapters.'

'What?'

'Probably some minor bit of your contract. Victoria really is too old for you.'

'You should leave her alone,' said Patrick, trying to take in what Charles had said about his book.

'She's no fool. That's why I fell in love with her in the first place. She's very calculating you know. Sometimes I get angry with her. She likes to taunt me.'

'So you *do* hit her?'

Charles leant forward.

'So would you if you lived with her. I can see that from the way you're sitting right now. And at the moment she's very odd. Jumpy and peculiar. You have no idea how strange she is.'

'If you go on beating her up – if I hear of it – I'll do the same to you.'

Patrick pushed away his food and stood up.

'I'll pay the bill on the way out,' he said.

The following morning Patrick opened a letter from his publishers which told him his contract was cancelled because of late delivery.

Outside the sky was a bruised blue and grey.

'We have acquired another book on the subject,' read the letter.

He thought of his publisher, whose gums were a

soft pink, delicate as the petals of a rose, and how his face hung with slack ugly folds.

Once he had lunched with him and watched the publisher eat lobster, little bits of flesh left all around his mouth. His tongue had come out of his mouth like some immense fish and flapped around his lips, scooping up the bits of dead lobster.

Let him do as he pleases, thought Patrick. I shall simply make sure my book's better, the best. I can take my time.

That evening, on returning home, as he opened the front door, he noticed someone bent over the dustbins in the semi-darkness. He assumed it was a tramp.

He approached the frizzy-haired figure, who turned round, startled.

'You?' said Patrick. 'What the hell?'

It was Joseph Fairley, the bookseller he'd met at Victoria's.

'Oh,' said Fairley. 'Good Lord. What a coincidence!'

'Coincidence?' said Patrick, and took Fairley's arm, dragging him into the hallway and closing the door. 'What are you doing?' He shoved him against the wall.

'What's the matter with you? I just dropped my paper in your dustbin.'

Patrick pushed the light switch, and the bare bulb revealed a frightened-looking Fairley, in leather gloves.

'What are you looking for?' said Patrick.

'Just my newspaper. I dropped my paper.'

'Did Victoria send you?' Patrick pushed Fairley again.

'Stop that,' said Fairley.

'You know,' said Patrick. 'I'm tired of being nice and courteous and civilised while everyone else behaves like thugs. Beating me up. Creeping round my house at night. Breaking into my flat. Was that you, Fairley?'

'No,' he said, straightening his collar.

'You know,' said Patrick slowly, 'I think I might smash your head against that wall unless you start telling me the truth.'

Fairley glanced round anxiously at the grey wall behind him.

'This is to do with Victoria, isn't it?' said Patrick.

Fairley didn't say anything.

Patrick pulled Fairley's shoulders forward ready to throw him back against the wall.

'Yes,' whispered Fairley. His face was very pale.

Patrick swallowed. He realised he's suspected for some while. He remembered that odd look on Victoria's face when she came out of his study one day. He'd thought he'd only been asleep for a moment, but maybe it had been longer and she had read some of the diaries, enough to interest her.

'It's to do with Victoria and Charles,' said Fairley.

'The first time I was attacked. Do you know about that?' said Patrick.

'No,' said Fairley.

Patrick put his arms round Fairley as if hugging him, then got a grip on his right arm and forced it behind his back so Fairley winced.

'Yes. I know. I heard from Victoria. It was Charles who arranged that.'

'Why?'

'Jealousy.'

'And the second. For the documents?'

'As you know, the rumour is they contain something amazing.'

'Well? You've read them.'

'There's another section isn't there?'

'Nothing you're ever going to see,' said Patrick. Patrick let him go.

'Get out,' Patrick said.

'You realise I may have to report this assault to the police?'

'I said get out,' said Patrick.

Patrick told himself it was Charles who was to blame.

'What are you doing here?' said Charles, and looked Patrick up and down as Patrick towered over him at Charles's newspaper office. Patrick hadn't been able to get hold of Victoria on the phone, and when he called at her house there was no reply to the doorbell, though he sensed someone was there.

Charles was sitting at a row of computers, surrounded by papers. One hand fumbled with a white handkerchief.

'Can we talk?' said Patrick in a clear, American drawl, leaning both hands on the desk, as though the whole of him was at an angle, the voice, the body.

Charles Napier twitched his nose again and slightly adjusted his bow tie, a suggestion of old-fashioned British eccentricity, out of place in this stark modern building where rows of journalists sat glaring at computers and stabbing letters into them as the light eased through the tall windows. His back was dead straight, as if it had metal in it, only the outskirts of his being twitched; the nose, the hands, the little feet which moved anxiously beneath the table.

Charles squinted at him and made an attempt at tidying his desk, his hands fluttering like disorientated birds.

The other journalists were all so intent on whatever they were doing that no one seemed to notice the American standing over Charles, or if they did, they didn't seem to care. A round-faced blonde female, her hair fluffy as a baby chick, gave Patrick a quick smile as if trying to subdue some much larger and more wicked smile.

'I'll talk here if you like,' said Patrick. 'I can be very patient. But I do have a loud voice. It really can carry and . . .' Patrick bent lower, and lowered his voice too. 'I just am not sure if you want everyone in the room to hear what I have to say.'

As Patrick stood over him he could smell pot pourri and saw that there was a brass bowl full of it on his desk, lying there like ashes.

Outside, the clouds sped through the darkening sky and Patrick could sense this white stone building hoarding all the winter light, taking it away from the other people walking far below.

The television news was on, talking about high seas and waves whipping the coast.

'Charles,' said Patrick, still soft. 'You work on a respectable broadsheet. If I were you, I'm not sure I'd want people to know I organised thugs to beat people up. You might get sacked immediately, don't you think?'

Charles neatened the papers on his desk, straightening the corners of a pile, boxing it in, turning all the angles to right angles, the sides of his mouth flickering.

'You know nothing about me,' flashed Charles. 'Nothing.'

'One look at you and, on the contrary, I know everything.' Patrick's voice was insistent, and seemed to turn in Charles's half open mouth like a screwdriver.

Charles stood up, pushing back his chair. His little waistcoat had the top two buttons undone and his bony hands did them up, as if the waistcoat were armour. Charles quickly examined his nails, as if that was somehow essential to their discussion.

'I really have nothing to say to you,' Charles muttered, fiddling with his papers.

'Charles Napier,' began Patrick in a loud, clear voice. 'I have reason to believe . . .'

A few journalists turned to listen and Charles snapped, 'Okay, I'll talk to you.'

Charles examined his nails again, then collected his tweed jacket from the back of his chair and walked grandly out. It occurred to Patrick how hard it must be for him to sit with all the much younger journalists, all equal, on these tables.

Charles took each step carefully, as if walking through treacle. One bearded journalist watched him with raised eyebrows.

Patrick followed Charles to the marble hall. A lift arrived and some people got out but Charles and Patrick remained where they were, Charles leaning against the marble as if he were too hot, although the air conditioning was blasting down his neck.

He looked down at the marble floor, then smiled at Patrick. It wasn't an agreeable smile. It spliced through his face and showed his teeth. He had thinning hair and looked too uncovered somehow, too naked.

'This is nothing to do with Anne Fitzgerald, is it?'

'I have no idea what you're talking about,' said Charles.

'You had me beaten up. Twice.'

A ginger-haired girl bounced, chatting to her friend, to the lift, and glanced at the two still men, one of them so tall, both looking exhausted.

'You got someone to take my documents, didn't you? Who was it? I'd be amazed if that creep

Fairley had the courage. It was someone else, wasn't it? The guy who's been following me?'

Patrick noticed Charles had soft grey hush-puppies, very scuffed, and found himself sorry for him.

'Fairley said he knows the auctioneer who sold me them,' said Patrick.

Charles slowly lifted his arm a little, pulled back his gleaming white cuff and examined his watch.

'Victoria's scared of you, isn't she? Have you put her up to this?'

'I have some work to finish, if you don't mind.' Charles forced himself to stand straight, without the support of the cold marble wall, and bit his lip slightly.

'You must have been disappointed with the diaries. You only got a few pages.'

Charles seemed enormously weary.

'She knew about your work, you know,' said Charles.

'Who?' said Patrick.

'Victoria of course.'

Of course, it would have been so easy for Victoria to speak to Fairley, who knew there was a dramatic revelation in the diaries. But so far Patrick hadn't read anything momentous of the kind which these people were after.

'She has imagination,' continued Charles. 'And of course she wants me to do well. I need a story. I've had a bit of a problem recently. She may have mentioned it. A misunderstanding about some papers which could cause a nasty scandal. With her father dying, she's very difficult. That's why we have our little disturbances. You should leave her alone. She shouldn't mix with thugs. She adores me. You probably don't realise it, but she does.'

'I doubt that,' said Patrick.

Charles's lower lip moved, trembling slightly. The two men stood there, in the hallway, as the lifts came and went.

'Who is this Fairley?' demanded Patrick.

'An old boyfriend of hers; you weren't the first, you know.' Charles looked round.

'But you should remember that I work for a respectable broadsheet. I would hardly be involved in anything of the kind you describe. It's just not my world. No doubt it is yours.'

Patrick gathered Charles up by his collar.

He dropped him, and walked into the lift. The doors closed behind him.

It was nothing to do with Anne. Patrick felt a great relief.

Outside, the sky had curdled from a deep grey to a lighter, duller shade.

In the club that night a ginger-haired man in his early thirties pushed open the door, which hit Patrick. Patrick looked at him, waiting for an apology.

'You've just knocked the fucking door into me,' said Patrick.

'Well, you're a doorman aren't you?'

Patrick shoved the man against the wall with one hand.

'Apologise.'

'What for? Calling you a doorman?'

'Knocking the fucking door into me.'

There was a little snot in the man's nose and his lips were wet. He had small green eyes which were far too close together.

'You shouldn't be in here anyway,' said Patrick, and threw him out.

CHAPTER 40

Mary Elgin,
Athens,
April 15, 1802

I walked over the Parthenon with Elgin. There were white stones scattered with red poppies here and there. Lusieri was there to draw the monuments and help arrange their dismantling.

Elgin and I walked towards Lusieri, who was sketching under an umbrella along the west side of the Parthenon. A high scaffold rested against the wall on which stood two men, one was a humpback. He seemed very agile on the scaffold and was not afraid to climb to its highest point. The draughtsmen were busy inside the sanctuary.

The heat was oppressive.

A Greek with deeply set brown eyes, a full black moustache, Lusieri has a short pointed black beard. His drawing is detailed, meticulous.

Elgin has been given permission to take away some of the stones by the Turkish authorities: 'if the said painters wish to take away any pieces of stone with old inscriptions, or sculptures therein, no opposition shall be made.'

Elgin wrenched some of the statues down from where they stood high over the city, above the Turkish soldiers, above the tents pitched at random, above the dirty narrow streets, below an enamel blue sky. A workman beside me said he thought he could hear them cry out.

CHAPTER 41

Anne received a call from the little, en-amoured bookseller from Edinburgh, Jimmy.

'Hello, Anne. I don't know if you remember me,' he said.

'Of course. How could I forget you?'

'I . . . er . . . found out some information.'

'That's very kind.'

'Other people have been asking around, incident-ally. I've told them nothing. I have managed to find and speak to the man who bought the diaries, then sold them on. He's in Spain now, very sick, and may be dying.'

Jimmy coughed nervously. 'Yes, it was rather fortuitous. Well, not really fortuitous. The man dying.' He stammered. 'I'd . . . I'd . . . I'd been trying to trace Robert in Spain but with no luck – my partner knew he had something to do with some shady Elgin sale. Then Robert called to sell what remains of his books. We pay some of the best prices in Edinburgh.

'Robert said he was on morphine now and he rambled rather. He told me the man he'd bought

233

them from was a Mr Nick Field, in his eighties now in the Golden Retirement Home, just south of Edinburgh. He sold the diaries to a Patrick Browning, an American. You are the only other person, as far as I know, who knows about Nick Field. Robert Frank is a drunk, but an honourable man in some ways. He'd promised not to tell anyone who'd sold them to him.'

'So why did he tell you?'

'He's very ill. Maybe he even thought someone should know. He told me about the old guy saying there was a revelation about the Elgin Marbles, something about buried treasure!'

She thought of Alexander. So that was his interest. Robert Frank must have gossiped about the content of the diaries. Her heart began to beat very fast.

'Robert said they were passed down through this Nick Field's family. Some great great grandmother had been a maid of Mary's and had apparently loved her dearly. When she died she didn't want Mary's horrible children to get hold of her documents so she kept the most secret ones. But she couldn't bring herself to destroy them, though Mary had in fact told her she should. I think the diaries spent the last couple of hundred years in a Field family chest, along with a Bible and old wills.'

'I'm coming up to see Mr Field.'

'I'd love to come too, drive you over, if that would be all right with you.'

'Of course. I'd be grateful.'

Anne took the early plane to Edinburgh.

She checked in at her hotel and took a cab to the bookshop, where Jimmy half leapt from his seat when he saw her. He grabbed his glasses, and tidied his desk.

'Hi, Jimmy,' said Anne.

'Hi,' murmured Jimmy.

'I called Nick Field at the Golden Retirement Home. He seemed grumpy and sleepy – but still – after a while he agreed to see me. He says he has the important diary items, and says they're the ones I *really* want to read.'

'Wonderful!'

It was raining in Edinburgh too, the streets drowning in water, mushrooming with umbrellas.

'Shall we go now?' she said.

'Okay,' he said shyly.

He moved stiffly, shyly, towards Anne, looking down at the wooden floor covered with old rugs.

'I'll close the shop early!' he exclaimed, and pushed his shoulders forward to express determination. He jingled some change in his pocket.

His car was parked, badly, some way away. They drove off, through the countryside around Edinburgh, as the rain quietened down.

'It's very good of you to help me like this.'

'Oh, it's nothing. Nothing at all!'

She found herself telling him about her brother who'd gone missing.

And then she told him about Paolo, and she hardly ever mentioned Paolo to anyone. As she talked she felt knots were being untied inside her, a whole macramé of trouble. All the air of tension and unease was maybe a way of keeping it all from fraying, coming apart, but sometimes it felt so tight inside her. It was good to talk about it, looking out over the wide countryside, with the rain opening out smells, sensations.

Then she heard herself talk about Patrick and part of her wanted to leap on the words, grapple them to the ground, as they left her mouth. The other part thought – this is good – keep talking – sometimes it's good to hide things, keep them buried, but there's a time to take them out. If they lie inside too long they can become malignant, creep into other cells, take away joy.

She heard herself say that she was living with a man she intended to leave.

'I fear he's involved in various criminal activities,' she heard her voice say.

'Really?' said Jimmy's startled voice.

'Borderline. Deals. You know. I never quite know where he is when or who he sells what to and where he gets the stuff from.'

'My! Stolen goods!'

'I don't know,' she said, thinking how green the countryside was in the rain. 'I'm probably wrong. I shouldn't be talking about it.'

'Why stay with him?'

'I've got used to him. He's familiar – in some

ways my father was the same type of person. God, am I boring you?'

'Of course not . . .'

'I couldn't sleep last night. The thought of seeing this old man, too.'

'Yes.'

The Golden Retirement Home was a granite building set among soft green lawns. It had a Victorian conservatory to one side and to the other a few of the elderly people were sitting out in the gardens on wicker chairs.

The car, an old mini with boxes of books piled up in the back, pulled up on the gravel drive and the books shuddered forward as he stopped abruptly.

The sky was a thick grey but the light was clear, as if shimmering of steel. It was as though the sun were somewhere, pressing through the clouds. The square retirement home, with its dark stone bricks, looked anything but golden.

Anne rang the bell and through the glass door could see the receptionist, in a grey suit and grey hair, look up. She came to the door, and Anne and Jimmy entered, with Jimmy standing bashfully a little way back.

'I've come to visit Mr Field,' said Anne.

'Ah yes,' said the receptionist, and took them to sign the visitors' book and take a security pass each.

She led them along a corridor and up a lift to the second floor and as they passed various rooms the residents looked anxiously out. A little old lady was in her dressing gown, another putting on her slippers. Anne felt like an intruder.

And then they knocked on a door and a sharp voice commanded 'Come in!'

Nick Field was sitting in his armchair with his stick, a huge threadbare black cardigan wrapped around him. He looked cold, although the room was warm; his long thin nose was slightly blue at the end. Behind them, the window showed the countryside falling away.

'Miss Fitzgerald!' he said. 'Delighted.'

'Hello, Mr Field,' she said. 'It's kind of you to see me.'

'Who's this?' he said.

'My name's Jimmy . . .'

'I'll talk just to the young lady, thank you,' he said.

'Fine, fine. I need a walk,' he said, and left.

'Oh,' said Anne.

'He your boyfriend?'

'No,' said Anne. 'Just a friend.'

'Sorry I can't get up,' said Nick Field. 'But I'm *old*. Damned nuisance. What can I do for you? Sit on the bed, my dear. You're quite safe. My legs are wobbly.'

It was a spartan room, with an old television, the bed covered with a beige candlewick cover, and a few pictures, one of an owl, another of a valley, a third of a mountain range, none hung straight.

The veins of his hands stood up and little red

veins covered his face. His grey eyes seemed a little cross, as though age had crept up and pounced on him unexpectedly.

Anne sat down.

'I've come to ask you about the diary I believe you sold to Adam and Turner.'

'Yes?'

'You did sell some diaries?'

'That's correct. To that old drunk at the auction house. Paid me a fortune. Apparently some American had been phoning him up day after day asking him for *anything* on the Elgins so when I came along he got straight on the phone to him.'

Mr Field lit up an unfiltered cigarette and took a puff.

'I had a fall and had to be admitted to a nursing home. There was a place here. I had to sell off everything quickly. I could have waited for the diaries to be auctioned but I wanted it all cleared up.'

'Yes. What I should love to know,' said Anne, leaning forward, hands on her lap, her skin luminous as the light from the window fell on her, 'is what was in them?'

Mr Field took a puff.

'Why?' he said.

'Why do I want to know? I'm writing a book on Mary Elgin.'

'Ah,' said Mr Field, his eyes glittering and a thin smile slicing through his weathered skin.

'Did you read them?'

'What I could. I'm an electrician by profession. My eyesight isn't good and the writing is difficult.'

'I see.'

'My great great grandmother worked for Mary Elgin over at Dirleton. They were close. In her last years Mary lived a very quiet life, improving buildings, helping the poor, that kind of thing. She was a great benefactress. One or two people said it was a penance because of her wild life. But my ancestor said she was just a good woman, who suffered a great deal, and was greatly mistreated.' The smile crept on to the face again. He took another puff, then tapped the ash into a glass ashtray. He seemed to be enjoying her visit.

'It was why she hid the diaries,' he said.

'Yes?'

'There were things in the diaries and letters.' He smiled again. 'Certain revelations.'

'You read them all?'

He looked at her sharply. 'Maybe I did. Maybe I didn't.'

'What was in them? He's going to have worked it out, the American Patrick Browning who has them. There's no point in keeping the secrets now,' she insisted.

'Oh, but it's nice to have secrets,' he said. 'It's a warm feeling.'

He chuckled.

It was beginning to rain again, and rain lightly dashed against the window. He looked round.

'It gets dull here.'

'Do you have a wife?'

'She died a couple of years ago,' he said.

Anne looked down.

'Other people have come to try to see me. But I wouldn't see them. And when they came here they weren't let in. But you sounded nice on the phone.'

He smiled again, sunlight in his grey eyes.

He made himself more comfortable on his chair. 'I liked having the old paper in my chest at home. I miss it now. I liked her diaries. You know. The ink. I felt I knew her. That she was with me. She had a strong presence. I don't feel it any more. Once or twice I went to her house – Archerfield, in Dirleton – it's a ruin now, and I imagined her writing her diary up in one of the windows quite near the sea. They're redeveloping it all, going to turn it into a golf course.'

'Yes, I've been there,' she said.

The eyes brightened again.

'Those Marbles ruined her life. Because of them Elgin was imprisoned in France and she met her beau and fell in love and that was that. But she had her secrets too.'

'Sometimes it's better to give up your secrets,' she said.

'Is it? Your secrets make you different.'

There was a knock on the door and a woman in a white overall popped her head through the doorway.

'Any coffee or tea and biscuits?'

'Please,' said Nick Field. 'Lovely. Tea.'

'Two sugars, darling?' said the lady.

'Coffee . . . black,' said Anne.

She served them. Anne longed for the woman to leave.

Nick Field crossed his ankles, showing his threadbare grey socks.

'But Patrick Browning has the secrets anyway. He'll publish them. And my book will seem irrelevant. I couldn't bear that,' she said.

Nick Field chuckled.

'If you would like . . .' she began.

'To be paid! Oh I've been paid once already. I'll tell you for free if you keep me in touch with it all. Keep me in touch with Mary.'

'Yes,' said Anne.

'And I'll give you something,' he said, with a smile. 'It's the other diary sections.' He pointed over to a dark wooden chest of drawers. 'The ones you really want. They all really want. Top drawer at the back, behind the socks. They are more important than any of the others. They are the key!'

She opened the drawer and searched with her hand at the back of the drawer, and came to a plastic folder, which she took out. In it were a few pages on yellowy paper, written in curly writing, and tied with a blue ribbon.

The old man laughed. 'Take it out then!'

Her chest corkscrewed, her pulse speeded up, her breath shallowed out. She could see the metal

242

nib moving over the paper, making words out of brown ink.

'It's Mary's writing,' said Nick Field, chuckling. 'The diary items written in tiny writing. It took me weeks and weeks to work them out. Weeks. And I'm good at that kind of thing. There are one or two letters to Robert as well, and secret letters she apparently never sent.'

'Diaries and some letters?'

'Mostly it's diaries.'

As Anne studied the manuscripts her whole body felt strange – her toes, her knees, her fingers, her skin, which felt raw. For a long time she sat, him watching her, as if it were part of a test. For a moment, she wished Paolo were there with her. He would have loved all this. But he would have taken it all over. He always had to be the central one.

'You wait till you decipher it all! It's short but extraordinary. Extraordinary!'

Anne was shivering as she stroked the paper. 'But I thought Patrick Browning had the diaries.'

'He might have diaries. But not these ones! The ones I sold reveal much about Mary's mind – her unhappiness, her growing dislike of Elgin, but they are only the prelude to what you hold there.'

'But . . . this is amazing,' she said, staring at the words before her.

'That's right! That's it!' said Nick. 'You wait though!'

He chuckled again.

'You told Robert Frank the first set contained a revelation about the Elgin Marbles,' she said.

'No, I told him the *diaries* did!'

'You misled him.'

'Yes. I misled him. I needed the money to pay for here.'

'I don't think he ever told anyone about you – except one bookseller friend just recently.'

'Maybe he was quite decent. I wanted my privacy.'

He took a handkerchief from his pocket to blow his nose, which was tipped with red at the end. He stubbed out his cigarette. The film of smoke clouded the room.

She felt wildly excited.

'You have them, dear. I got them all dancing then, did I?' he said. 'Even the little hints I gave. But it scares me a bit. You have them, dear.'

'Yes,' she replied, 'you did get them dancing. But what is in them?'

'Oh, you'll have to read it for yourself. You may say I should have alerted the authorities, or even tried to find the treasure myself.'

'What treasure?' said Anne.

He laughed.

'The head.'

'I'm sorry?'

'You were clever to find me. You charm people.'

There was a silence.

'It's the head of Hermes! Messenger of the gods. Bringing us messages from the past.'

'What?' Anne stared him.

'It's a missing part of the Elgin Marbles that the diaries tell you all about. Tell you where it is. Where she hid it. And that it's the head of Hermes. Or so Mary thought.'

'My God.' Anne could feel her heart thumping furiously inside her. She had a sense of great freedom and lightness as though the messenger was something travelling through her.

'That's incredible. Hermes. It would complete the statue. It would be so beautiful.'

'Oh yes,' said Mr Field brightly.

It was preposterous, she told herself, it couldn't be true. It was too wonderful to be true, like a window suddenly opening.

She could see the torso in her mind, heavy marble, waiting for the head to give it real movement, to give it wings.

'And what exactly do the diaries say?' she said softly.

'Oh, my dear.' He leant forward. 'That she hid it in a safe place. Kept it from Elgin.'

Anne remembered how Alexander had kept talking about what parts of the Marbles were missing. No doubt it was his sixth sense for money which made him land on Hermes. She remembered him standing there, in the British Museum, his skin shiny: 'So when Elgin was around the head of Hermes had only fairly recently gone missing? Maybe it could even have been lying around there somewhere,' Alexander had said.

She wanted to know how involved Alexander was in it all.

'That's astounding,' said Anne.

'Yes.'

'The head had disappeared by 1749 – Elgin just took the battered torso. But why haven't you told anyone about it?'

The small, dull room was transformed. The small black-framed picture of Edinbrugh castle seemed to be beautiful. It was hung lopsidedly and that too seemed part of the harmony of the whole room, presided over by this glowing old gnome of a man, with the drab curtains and the lacy cover neatly spread over the top of the chest of drawers. Patrick: there was somehow not the heaviness now when she thought of him. But of course, she reminded herself, even if Mary had buried it somewhere it didn't mean it was still there.

'To be honest, I liked the secret, and I liked knowing I had it.' He coughed. 'I felt close to her. You know, when all the family stories are passed down about Mary, you feel close to her. The years have gone, but you feel loyalty. She wanted it secret. She was afraid of what she'd done. Her intention was not to be any more notorious than she already was.'

Her feet, she was surprised to note, began to tap.

Mr Field's hands sat in his lap and his whispers of grey hair covered his head. He suddenly looked quieter.

'You have a lovely smile. There,' he said. 'I knew I'd feel sad when I told someone the story.'

'Oh, but you mustn't,' she said, finding herself on her knees by him, holding his forlorn grey hands.

'You've done the right thing,' she said. 'Absolutely. And I promise I'll tell you everything that happens, in detail.'

'It probably isn't there, you know,' said Nick Field with a smile.

She stood up, on tiptoes.

'What?'

He looked up, with a quirky smile. 'She tells us precisely where she hid it. In Athens. I wish I could come with you.'

'In spirit you shall,' said Anne.

CHAPTER 42

Anne called Patrick and they went to a restaurant where he sat very close to her and
it was dark. To his surprise, she ordered a
steak. 'I like meat,' she said. When a tiny morsel
of spinach, ended up at the corner of her mouth
he longed to reach out, wipe it from her, then put
his finger in her mouth.

He kept watching her tiny hands.

Her tongue reached out and quickly licked her
lips.

Her face was delicate and when she spoke of her
mother all the wariness drained away and there was
only a certain sadness and warmth.

Patrick reached for the salt and knocked his red
wine over the white tablecloth. When he stood up
to stop it getting all over his clothes, he knocked
over the chair. The whole restaurant turned and
stared.

'Never mind,' said Anne, her voice warm, even
a little affectionate, and then he noticed she was
watching his hands. 'I'm sorry your publishers
cancelled your contract.'

'Yes, and signed you up instead,' he said.

'I told you. My publishers have folded. I had no choice. Besides, we're in competition.'

'Except for tonight.'

She smiled, and leant forward. 'Except for tonight.'

'Why did you want to see me tonight?'

'I thought it might be my last chance. You might not speak to me again.'

'Because of your taking my contract.'

'Not that . . .' She coughed. 'Just . . . as we both get further into the story.'

'Anyway, what else have you found out?'

'We're competitors, Patrick. Why should I tell you?'

'I suspect this whole thing is getting . . . I feel that there's money involved. It could make this a little . . . dangerous. In a way, it might be a time to work together.'

She smiled.

'Ah – you think I have information you want?'

'No, that's not it. Genuinely, I think it's getting out of hand. These people – this girlfriend of mine – I don't know. I'm getting a bad feeling about it all. I've been beaten up twice, my place has been ransacked.'

'So you don't still think it was me.'

'No, I don't,' he said, and he put his hand over hers, and looked around.

'You are jumpy tonight.'

'I told you.'

'Yes, you told me.'

'There might be more to it.'

'I see,' she said, nodding seriously. She straightened her napkin on her lap. There was some high, plaintive madrigal music playing and he thought how strange his state of mind was becoming, and how the music affected him, and how he should loathe this enemy of his sitting there, with her auburn hair and green eyes and the gentleness in her smile, and the mockery.

'Would you like coffee at my place?' he said.

'I've just had coffee,' she pointed out.

'*More* coffee?'

'Yes, maybe I could do with some more coffee,' she said, and again there was a sadness in her manner, as she stood up, tucking her hair behind her ears, her face slightly pale.

They arrived at the flat. 'I can't stay long,' she said. He liked the funny little way she screwed up her nose. There were freckles on the bridge of her nose he hadn't noticed before. She stroked her right eyebrow. For a moment he felt wrapped up in Anne's delicate form and the exact way she stood, leaning slightly to her right and it was as if were she to lean in a different way, he wouldn't be drawn to her quite so much.

Her eyes blinked at him, in a kind of surprise, as if she'd just recognised him. He liked the particular way her hair flowed down to her neck with its silly butterfly hairslides, the way her swan's neck skimmed down towards her shoulders, the precise way her arms fitted into the sockets of her torso. The long legs too, they drifted up to her dark centre, and he wanted that too, all the swirling centre of her. He needed to touch her, as if that would ground him. He found he didn't want her to be unapproachable. He was tired of idealising her.

Her skin was white and her thin bones would break easily and his arms wanted to protect her yet he was acutely aware that by holding her close he would be protecting himself. He stroked her hair and it felt so soft he thought he had never touched anything so soft. Maybe this was love.

As he kissed her he thought, distantly, how extraordinary it is the way sexual desire allows you such liberties so suddenly. One minute you're shyly playing with the salt and pepper pot, next moment your hand is pulling up her skirt.

He was aware he took up a disproportionately large amount of space. 'See, I told you the flat was small.'

'Mm,' she said.

Her mouth looked quivery and her eyes as lovely as ever, green and startled, as if he had barged into some private room behind them. Her mouth was a little apart and he could see the slight sweat on her skin. He'd observed that before she spoke she sometimes looked fragile but that was replaced so instantaneously by confidence that he'd decided the delicacy was an illusion.

It was warm in the room and the walls moved towards him. Outside, he was aware of the traffic, blaring, pushing, shoving, limping lumps of metal shoving past each other in the fume-filled streets.

He was aware of every centimetre of his body – the skin under his armpits, the flesh on the palms of his hand, his broad shoulders. Sometimes he almost envied the gods of the Parthenon made of cool marble, surveying the centuries without heat or despair or pain. Her lips were still a little open.

He put both his arms round her waist and kissed the lips. The kiss was extraordinary, like falling backwards off a cliff. It was partly the warmth of the lips, partly the proximity of her body, partly the way her mouth invited him in while her tongue teased him, lightly touching his, and partly something unpredictable he couldn't give a name to. Whatever it was amazed him, destroyed his insides and threw them away, replacing them instead with a dark, intense tornado pleasure which was both very precise, to do with these lips and this body, and very imprecise, as it seemed to gather everything up that was important in the world – from plagues and pestilence to the scent of roses.

And then he held her close, and her tiny body seemed to him like some lush body of sensual delight, some Ottoman courtesan's, especially the way she moved, like a cat purring when stroked. Her whole skin seemed to purr as he took off her shirt and her white skin – marble skin – was hot under his hands.

'Mmmm,' she murmured. There were no curtains on the window, only the black sky out there and the one or two stars, half smothered by city smoke, which watched them.

She undid his tie with her tiny hands and he took off his shirt and she ran her hands over his shoulders, his arms.

They drew close again and he ran his tongue to the corners of her mouth. Her body purred more. His hands ran over her leg to the inside of her thigh. He stroked the back of her knee, kissed her elbow, then trailed kisses up her forearm, kissed the side and back of her neck and licked her ear and circled his fingers over her face. In her face there was still the play between hardness and softness, the hardness of desire and the softness of something else he saw in her he liked just as much. She took off his trouserbelt.

The window was slightly open at the top and the night air crept in, like a third person here in the darkness, twining itself round them as they stood close, pressing their flesh together.

She wasn't like anyone else he'd ever made love to. She was passive one moment, assertive the next, as though never allowing him quite to know what she was like.

He fell asleep with his large arm lying over her shoulder. In the morning they would discuss things – he'd tell her what he knew.

Patrick dreamt of his mother.

'When I leave this room do you disappear? Do you?' he asked her.

She looked slowly up, pushing her fair hair from her face and frowned.

'No, darling, I just stay where I am.'

'And when one day you die will I ever see you again? Will you disappear then?'

'Yes,' said his mother softly, holding her sharpened pencil in her hand. 'I'll disappear then. But maybe I'll come back to you in dreams.'

When he woke up, Anne had gone.

'I'm sorry,' said her note. 'Forgive me.'

CHAPTER 43

Lily sat crosslegged, crossarmed, on the floor, seeing how many different shapes she could make with her mouth as she watched cartoons on the television. Her goldfish mouth worked well; the cheery smile flung up one side of her face lacked a certain authenticity; the baby mouth, in which she thrust out the bottom lip, she enjoyed doing but then it made her feel a little sad, as though something had just gone wrong. A fly buzzed around the room, a pilot out of control. Her mother read a newspaper, clasping it as if she were drowning, huddled at one end of a sofa.

Her mother looked thinner and thinner. Lily wondered if her mother was just going to disappear one day. It seemed that might be happening.

It would be frightening to be left all alone in the house.

Her mother had been crying a great deal the last few days and Lily had to keep getting her tissues and putting her arm round her.

Sometimes her mother frightened her, her arms were so gaunt, like something from a horror movie,

255

and the skin was loose around her wrists, as if designed for another person.

Lily looked out of the window, waiting for someone to come and save them, as someone always did in the movies, but no one came.

She remembered guiltily her attempts in the past to stop her mother leaving her for even a couple of evenings. 'I can't sleep without you being in the house and I cough and my foot itches,' she had said. She had got out of bed to show her mother her itchy skin under her foot, and her mother had had to get some cream for it, and by the time she had rubbed it in, and got her another glass of water, and hugged her some more, it was too late to go out.

In the last few weeks Lily had overheard conversations between her mother and Anne which she hadn't wanted to hear.

'I feel so angry,' her mother had said. 'When I asked the doctor what caused it he said he didn't know, and as he said it I could suddenly remember being in a pram, and the daylight reaching me there, in all its glory, and I thought, why doesn't he know what caused it? How dare the world contain and understand computers, the Internet, all these dazzlingly complex inventions and yet not have worked out how we ourselves work and fail to work?'

Lily had rubbed her nose. She hadn't liked hearing this but thought she should listen, just to try to see if she could work out what was happening.

'They're so casual, doctors, sprinkling death around the place. I wish I'd spat in his face, thrown a knife at his dull paintings of cornfields. I was thinking of that pram, and the light, you know, Annie,' her mother had continued.

Lily felt there was a metal weight in her stomach, like one of the metal cannon balls she had seen in the Tower of London.

'And I thought,' went on her mother, 'How dare he? The rubber plant beside him, in his office, had the squashy quality of his skin. Perhaps people choose their plants to match their faces, do you think they do? Just as people choose pets that look like them? He tapped his desk with his biro. He wore a white coat. These men, Annie, they choose uniforms and disappear into their jobs.'

Lily touched her stomach, wondering if the weight really was there, if maybe all the heavy bits inside you collected together when you felt sad.

'I wanted to say to him,' said her mother, even more softly, with a voice which seemed very strained, as if it might just come apart, 'can't you promise me more? More than just one year? Just to tidy the photographs and write a book for Lily. Just one year isn't quite enough. You see, I had the time before, I just didn't know it.'

'It's a great idea,' said Anne, in a cheerful voice which somehow started off cheerful but as it hung in the air didn't sound cheerful at all, like some of the songs on the radio which sound happy on the top but underneath seem sad.

'Yes,' said Lily's mother, a bit brighter now, 'I want to write a book telling her all the things I would have told her during the course of her life – to check on the back of the bathroom door when you leave a hotel room, always to get a full survey on any property you buy, to look at people when you speak to them, all that kind of thing.'

Lily went up the stairs to her bedroom, and it seemed a long way up and when she was there it seemed a long way from the two women talking downstairs.

She got into bed and put her head on the pillow and there seemed too much space all around her, in her room. Her black pig, with the white ruffle round her neck and pretty checked dress, lay with her in the bed.

Tomorrow I'll ask mummy if I can have a smaller room, she thought.

The next day, Anne took her to school, and talked all the way about the woman she was writing about, called Mary, and when she talked her eyes were bright as marbles.

'I have to tell someone,' she said, 'I have this secret. Even this man – someone I really like – I haven't told him. I nearly did. Then I ran off, and haven't collected any messages.'

She talked about a chapel up on a mountainside, and as she talked Lily could imagine herself up on the mountainside finding the buried god Anne spoke about.

'Do you think my mother will be okay?' said Lily.

'Oh,' said Anne, 'the mind can move mountains.'

CHAPTER 44

The music pounded through Patrick as he leant against the wall, wearing a black suit. He watched a guy whose body overflowed over his chair like a cake in an oven overflowing its tin. A pretty young girl put a hand on the man's immense knee. It was a continent of a knee. Patrick wondered if the man – a rap star – could feel her touch. The rap star's face enlarged into a smile. The smile rose horribly into his face, making his eyebrows rise too, his nose enlarge, and even more sweat shine from his skin. The pretty young girl caressed the rap star's knee.

People clustered round the bar, girls pretending to chat nonchalantly with each other, men drinking rapidly. Everyone wore black. It was supposed to be a cool place but everyone was quickly glancing at everyone else and no one in it seemed especially cool apart from the rap star who was in fact gross.

Patrick scratched his face. He'd been phoning Anne all day but the answering machine was on. His skin clung to his suit as if his body were trying to get out. Patrick stood with his legs apart, arms crossed, the list on the table beside him.

He could feel the sweat spiking his forehead.

Someone slipped her arms round his waist and breathed into his neck.

'Darling,' she said, with her voice like chocolate truffles, soft and warm and somewhat sickly. She took his hand and led him outside. She laughed gaily, and for a moment he was reminded of something fresh and exciting, a rustle like the rustle of paper on Christmas morning. Her tongue was in his ear.

'Patrick,' she breathed, and the beat from the club continued to throb. 'I thought I'd come to see you.'

The streets were dark and wet, cobbled like the back of a dragon.

Her hand slipped up the sleeve of his shirt.

'Leave me alone,' he snapped. He could feel that old fury building up in him.

'Angel,' she said, raising her eyebrows like birds, off and away. 'Why?'

'I saw Joseph Fairley. He told me.'

'Told you what?' said Victoria.

Patrick wanted to hit her, to shake her.

'That you and Charles had me followed, beaten up, robbed.'

'What?' she said.

She pressed herself close to him. He remained tense. He found he wanted to tear her apart.

'Look, the first time I knew nothing about it,' she said. The second time I agreed to pay some men to waylay you – I admit it – we wanted to get the diaries. For Charles's story. It was his idea. His idea. He always has terrible ideas. Do you love me at all?'

'Do you know Alexander Stephan?'

'Who?'

'He's not using you to try and get the diaries?'

'Of course not. I don't even know him. You look good in black.' She laughed and again there was freshness somewhere, but he wasn't sure where.

Her small mouth puckered up in front of him, and for a moment he wanted to kiss it, like picking a plum.

'I wouldn't have done it but my father was ill in hospital. Very ill – I was in a state. Take me home with you, Patrick. Take me back now. Come with me,' she said, her head on his arm. 'Please. I'll explain.' Her face looked up into his. He knew her mouth was a little sauna, hot and wet, and her teeth were small, milky-marble, but all he could feel was a sense of the darkness and coldness which lead up to a new year, the sudden dip, the fear, as the roller coaster begins to climb.

'I was offered money for the diaries,' she said.

'By whom?'

'My father's dead you know. He died. It was quite a painful death.'

'I'm sorry.'

'I didn't care.'

'Who offered you money?'

'I'm not serious.'

'You should tell me.'

'No one offered me money.'

She stood looking at him, with a kind of desperation in her face, and her little teeth chewed at her lip. Then her teeth started chattering and her eyes looked raw.

'Come home with me,' she said. 'Now. I need you.' Her hands were trembling. 'We could rent a Palazzo in Venice where you could write. Or buy somewhere in the States, maybe Long Island. You miss America sometimes. I've found out about a few places. New Orleans would suit us too – one of those gorgeous ante-bellum houses with immense porches and plenty of antiques. We could try to infiltrate society there. Or what about some rambling house outside of Rome? We could rent for a while then when we were bored we could move on. We won't be stuck like flies in amber, our wings out but unable to move, like I am here. Charles has stopped hitting me but he can't move. He's been in amber all his life. But you and I . . .'

He shook his head.

'Go away, Victoria,' he said. 'Your husband is standing over there. You have a husband. You have a marriage.'

'And would you come away with me if I had neither of those things?'

After a moment she said, 'I don't have any of those things.'

'Victoria, it's all over,' he said.

'Patrick,' she said, after a moment.

Her features tightened and he saw that her nose

was too sharp, her eyes too small, her chin too narrow, and she knew that he saw all that and she turned and walked stiffly back to the club, to the cloakroom, brushing her hands against her tight black dress, where she picked up her coat and left, into the dark night, the door swinging shut behind her. Charles followed.

Patrick stepped outside a minute later and thought he saw the shaven-headed ape he'd noticed behind him on a number of occasions. The guy was lurching in the same direction as Victoria and Charles, but at a distance. Patrick felt weary, a kind of sickness in his stomach. He turned away, walking by the river for a while as the music from the club boomed in his ears.

That night he couldn't sleep. He kept thinking of the way the shaven-headed guy had moved through the darkness.

The following day he called Anne, and got no reply. Next he called her mother and asked if she knew where Anne was.

'I believe she was planning to go to Athens,' she said.

CHAPTER 45

Mary Elgin,
Athens,
April 17, 1802

High up on the Parthenon, travellers take bits of the stones, chopping off a bit here and a bit there – a nose, a hand. Other parts have been sold for lime mortar. I wish I could save it all.

I had two letters from my mother today and one from Robert Ferguson.

CHAPTER 46

A few days after Anne had talked to Lily about the chapel on the mountainside, there was a message on the answering machine from Anne, saying that she was going to Athens, to a hotel called the Grande Bretagne.

'Athens,' said her mother in a small voice, standing by the answer phone, still holding Lily's rucksack in her hand.

'Shall we go?' she said, a smile breaking out over her thin face.

'Really? But what about school?' said Lily.

'Hang school!' said her mother. She threw the rucksack on to the dingy pink sofa. 'It would be fun.'

There was a little colour in her cheeks.

'Are you really serious?' said Lily, looking up at her mother. 'Just to leave school?' She gave a sunbeam smile.

'It'll be lovely this time of year, it'll do us good, and it would be nice to spend time together without school and the rain and cold. Just be lazy.'

Her mother went to sit down, next to the brown rucksack. She began to check through for Lily's homework; the spelling list, the russet maths exercise book, the reading book.

'When are we going?' said Lily, moving from foot to foot. Her school uniform was a dingy dark green skirt and blouse. Her local church primary school was only about five minutes' walk away but the cost for the good schooling was a certain formality. Lily, however, never managed to look tidy in her uniform. The skirt was always at an angle, at least one of the buttons undone, and the tie loose.

'Soon,' Elizabeth said. 'If I can get a flight and a room.'

After a while she stood slowly up and walked up the stairs to her study on the first floor, overlooking the garden, and began to phone.

Every now and again Lily entered and her mother was still talking to airlines, on and on and on. Lily's heart was beating very fast. Finally Lily got fed up with hovering and went downstairs to watch cartoons. And then she heard her mother's heavy footsteps on the stairs. They had changed since a few weeks ago; they were heavier and slower now, although her body was much lighter.

'Lily!' she called.

Lily jumped up. 'Yes?' she said, at the bottom of the stairs, looking up.

Her mother looked down at her and for a moment her face seemed to crumble as she saw Lily.

'Can't you get one?'

'I *can* get one. We're going. Tomorrow morning!'

'Yesss!' said Lily, making an imaginary high five.

'We won't tell Anne,' said her mother, as she reached the bottom of the stairs, holding with one hand on to the bannister, the light from the glass in the front door lighting up her grey face. 'It'll be a surprise. Besides, she might try to dissuade me.'

'Would she?' said Lily, a little anxiously, raising herself slightly on tiptoes to see into her mother's face more clearly. She was sure there was a little pinkness on the cheeks. That was a good sign, thought Lily.

Her mother shrugged.

'Let's have tea,' she said. 'Then pack.'

For tea, they each ate a large round ham soft roll dusted with flour, and Lily ate with enormous interest and enthusiasm, especially enjoying the dusty flour on her hands, and the way parts of it broke off as she ate.

'I'm looking forward to the blue sky, white stones and sunshine, and the air on my arms and face,' said Lily's mother.

'Me too,' said Lily.

For once, Elizabeth managed to eat nearly all of the roll.

'You've had me followed too, haven't you?' said Anne to Alexander, flipping to a popular TV show.

Alexander stopped chopping for a moment.

'No,' he said.

'I hate this show,' said Anne.

'You think you've been followed?' said Alexander.

'Sure of it. Every time I watch this it gets worse. Come to think of it, it gets worse even as I watch it. Why are you spending so much time with me, Alexander?'

'I think you could be in danger.'

'This show! Do you think everyone thinks it's stupid but still watches it? I suppose that's it. At least it's something everyone can feel superior to. All over the world. I don't suppose there's a single person who feels humbled by this show.'

'Anne, what is the matter with you?'

Anne leant forward and got her drink in her hand, and liked the cold of it.

She turned and smiled. 'Nothing.'

'You're not listening. What I said was that I'm spending so much time with you because I think you're in danger.'

'From whom? Or what? Emotional danger? Financial danger?' She turned back to the television then got up, switched off the show, and tossed the remote down. The curtains weren't drawn and she could see the lights on the other side of the river.

She thought of the body she once saw floating down the river in Hong Kong. Paolo was beginning to seem a long way away.

Alexander tipped the vegetables into a frying pan which sizzled with olive oil.

'Not from me. I'm not a danger to you.'

Alexander's back was to her, and she could see his wide neck redden a little. He stirred the vegetables.

'Patrick is involved with a married woman. I hear . . . she hates you.'

'I don't know what this has to do with me,' said Anne. 'Or you.'

'I'm doing some business with her. I bought a study of a cocker spaniel from her. Victoria Napier is her name.'

'Well, good for you. I'm sorry,' she said, running her finger over the dust. 'It's just tonight. I feel sad.'

'I think you ought to take care,' said Alexander. She could feel him breathing behind her.

'Thanks. Have you had an affair with her?'

'Would you care?'

'I'd be interested,' she said.

Anne opened the French doors and walked out into the cool of the evening, the lights on the water.

'If I thought you'd care, I'd be happy,' he said.

Alexander followed her. She didn't look at him as she leant on the balcony.

'I'm tired, Alexander. You have your wife. Your child. You know we can't last,' she told him.

She thought of Paolo. He would have left her in the end, like he'd left all of his other women, as he only liked life when it was intense. He didn't want ordinary life.

★　　★　　★

270

Anne quietly got out of bed with Alexander still asleep. During the last days she'd managed to decipher the three diary items – from April 30, May 3, May 4, 1802. Through a gap in the curtains she could see the lights on the boats out on the river. He slept deeply, on his side, his plump face different in sleep, softer. It had been hard to leave Patrick a few days back, knowing what she was going to do, that after this he wouldn't want to see her again.

It was curious how different the air was in a room when people slept; it smelt of slumber, warmth, sheets.

Anne pulled on grey trousers, a grey sweater. Holding her sandals in one hand, she walked quietly to the bathroom where she brushed her teeth and packed her make-up and wash bag. Her eyes were beginning to get used to the darkness, and she could still hear Alexander's rhythmic breathing. As she emerged from the bathroom he stirred and she stood still for a moment, wondering what she would say if he woke.

Anne opened the wardrobe door and took out her small black leather suitcase. The wardrobe door creaked and she stopped, holding her breath. Alexander merely turned over.

She pushed back her hair and secured it with a rubber band. She'd arranged a car in Athens to take her up to the chapel of Agia Triada for Wednesday evening, when there were no services so the place would be empty for her to have a good look round.

She packed a dress, changes of underwear, another pair of trousers, some strong shoes, put in her wash bag and make-up and locked the case, taking it out of the room and into the shadows of the main living room next door. The walls and furniture were so light-coloured that the room, even at night, wasn't dark, and the curtains were open so the lights from the buildings on the opposite bank glittered like Christmas tree lights.

Anne called a cab, telling it to wait outside and not ring the bell, and made herself coffee while leaving Alexander a note saying she was going up to Scotland.

The airport was cold and bare and Anne could see the Parthenon in her mind, under a blue sky. She shivered, feeling small and frail. But if she found what she was looking for she'd feel huge, strong, able to confront anything.

Anne was angry at herself for feeling nervous. There was nothing to be nervous about. She found herself checking out the people all around her, and her heart thumped.

She stretched out her legs. 'If only someone would reach their hands down and free us,' wrote Mary to Robert. 'You and I, we are captives, in our way, caught in our time, unable to break out.'

Her flight flashed up on the board.

She kept expecting to see Alexander coming up to her with a fat smile on his face.

I shan't let him stop this, she thought, as the

plane darted up into the sky and she looked down on the lights of London trailing below her.

What she had read in the diaries Nick Field had given to her really was extraordinary.

She thought of Lily and Elizabeth. 'You see,' Elizabeth had said recently to Anne, 'I feel grateful in a way. I realise how wonderful life is. I might have more, but I might have a whole year, a year. A lifetime, if that's all you have. We throw away our time, hurl weeks and days and hours out of the window, lose our time, mislay our lives, spend years waiting to live.'

The world, she thought, is transformed over and over by love. Elizabeth's eyes were so full of love for her daughter. None of it had dispersed, in spite of her unhappiness. If anything it had grown more. It seemed she was giving Lily enough love for a lifetime.

In some way Anne felt that this head of Hermes was something to do with love.

CHAPTER 47

Mary Elgin,
Athens,
April 30, 1802

I am still in Athens helping to organise the shipping of some of the stones. Last night as I fell asleep I kept seeing the marble figures. On the east pediment, a river god drew himself up and a piece of drapery hung wet, over his arm. Next to him a girl in a short tunic rippled, every fold showing the movement of the wind.

Although hoisted up on a pediment, many feet above the ground, when this statue was taken down the back was nearly as carefully worked as the front, although it hadn't been visible for over two thousand years. The folds at the back were beautifully finished.

I could imagine the west pediment's missing head of Hermes, which had been drawn so well by Jacques Carrey in 1674. The chunk left behind, the torso, needed that head turning back.

I thought of the horse pulling the chariot of the moon god – the jaw gaping open, the eyes bulging, the veins standing out.

Of course I knew all the arguments for removing

the stones. That travellers were stripping off all the treasures anyway, that the Turks had used some for lime mortar, that if we did not take them the French, under Napoleon's directive, most certainly would.

Still, it seemed wrong to be pulling down whole stone carvings from high up on a building that had been standing since five hundred years before the birth of Christ.

As I stood among the stones today, shaken by the beauty of the statues high above, one of the men working there asked me to come to see something he had just found during an excavation. I walked over the rubble.

The man stopped, and pointed, and there in the ground, lying down, face staring up into the sky, covered in dust, was a magnificent head of a man, unimaginably beautiful. I knew at once it was the head of Hermes.

I had no desire to take it away. The lips were half open, as if crying out. Elgin did not know about the find. I knelt and dusted this fallen god.

Mary Elgin,
May 3, 1802

Lusieri sat nearby, under his perpetual sun umbrella, drawing. He did not notice anything, of course. When I first met him I was impressed by him: his height, his drawing, his presence. He is an achingly slow drawer. It is said that he is so slow that by the time he is halfway through drawing a building, the building had either been knocked down or extended.

And as I knelt down, moving the earth and rubble from the lovely face, I thought: I do not want to give E this. I do not want this displayed like a trophy in his mansion Broomhall. His aim is to remove the stones for himself, not for the nation, though he says otherwise.

As I knelt in the dust, I thought how beautiful the sculpture was and I thought, I cannot give this to him. This young god here must somehow escape. This Greek god carved with the dignity in his lips and in his dead eyes and in the tilt of his chin. I do not want him made captive. I felt it was I who was lying under rubble, unable to breathe.

The man who had found the head stood before me. I shielded my eyes from the brightness. His shoulders were broad. And it seemed to me how broken we all were, with our poor bodies, staggering under the weight of our lives. E. with his headaches and pains, with his disintegrating nose, his gaunt features, me with my sickness at sea, in childbirth, even poor skinny Lusieri and his helper the dwarf who can climb to the top of monuments with such agility. But this Greek seemed perfect, without physical faults, like the statue would have been once.

I told the Greek to take the head, hide it, then tell me where he had put it.

Mary Elgin,
May 4, 1802

The Greek returned to see me today and told me he buried the head near a little chapel on the hillside above

276

Athens, Agia Triada, on Mount Parnitha. He says it is very beautiful, a tiny white chapel surrounded by pine trees and will protect the Greek god.

It is buried about five feet deep about three yards from the back of the chapel, to the left, by a little fir tree.

God in heaven bless and preserve us all.

CHAPTER 48

Patrick had a call from Victoria's Spanish maid Maria. She asked him to come round at once. The pretty, dark girl answered the door.

'Hello,' she said shyly. 'Come in.'

The Pugin wallpaper emblazoned the hallway and the lilies in the huge vase on the hall table were dying.

'I'm sorry to trouble you,' said Maria in her tight voice, with a bow of the head.

There were grey rectangles on the wall marking where the paintings had hung. The paintings used to crowd in on him; the flower painting with the wasp on the rhododendron, the picnic in the garden, the young girl in a dense white frock. His mouth was dry. The heating was up too high and even in her absence Victoria's voice hung hot in the air.

'It's like this in every room,' said Maria. 'She's sold all the paintings and the antiques. A man came to get them this morning. You want a coffee?'

'No thanks,' said Patrick.

'He had a van. And all the documentation. They are both away. Mr and Mrs Napier. I didn't know what to do. He came round with his men – two big men. The two men stood on either side of the little round fat man,' continued Maria. 'They weren't nice, Mr Browning. They were big. He kept smiling but I was afraid. There was a letter from her with the documents telling me to give the paintings and all the antiques to the man. So I let them take it all. Did I do a bad thing?'

Maria's forehead creased into tiny furrows.

'Her father died a few days ago. She went crazy. Really crazy. She screamed and screamed and cried and broke things and shouted at Charles. Said he was stopping her relationship with you. Said she hated him. Said she knew he wanted to find the Elgin treasure just for a newspaper story but she wanted the money. She wanted freedom.'

'The what?'

'The treasure. The Elgin treasure, she said.'

Patrick's tongue was dry, his whole mouth was dry so he could hardly speak. His mind was running back and forth

along everything that had been said. So that's what they were all after.

'And where did she find out about this treasure?'

'I don't know, Mr Browning. She was very excited about it all.'

279

'The man who came for the paintings – what was his name?' Patrick could feel the sweat on his back.

'I don't remember.'

'Try.'

She looked away, then rubbed a hand on her apron. 'Alexander,' she said. 'I've seen him before. He's done business with Victoria you know.' Maria frowned again. She held her hands closely in front of her.

'Where did Victoria say she was going?'

'Did I do the right thing – in letting the Alexander man take things? There was the letter.'

'I expect it was what Victoria wanted. Do you know where she went?'

'I heard her talking on the phone about Athens,' said Maria.

'Athens?'

Maria blinked, trying not to cry.

'Yes, and,' said Maria, glancing up, frightened suddenly, her hands resting palms down on her apron, 'Mr Napier hasn't been back for a couple of days. But,' she coughed, 'his passport is here . . .'

'Yes?' said Patrick, keen to leave. The house felt uncomfortable to him now, a sort of ghost house. It even seemed to smell damp. The curtains which had looked so overwhelmingly tasteful and British, heavy silk swathes, their sheer weight and glamour suggesting a confidence and sense of tradition, now looked as if they'd been bought for a different house.

What was left of the furniture reared up, dark and heavy, while all the expensive pieces which had artfully been scattered around, swathed in cloths or vases, had been taken.

'I am worried, Mr Browning,' she said.

'He's a grown man, Maria, I shouldn't worry,' he said, bending his head down, smiling, and gently touching her on the arm.

'You don't like Victoria, do you?'

'I can't say that, Mr Browning.'

'Are you afraid of Victoria?'

Maria nodded.

'It's lonely here at night,' she said. 'I'm afraid. I tell myself they're coming back but I don't know. I gather up the post and I've kept all the newspapers. Suppose they don't come back? Of course I keep the house neat but if they don't come back I'll just leave.'

'Not yet, Maria. Stay a few more days. Where do you think she's gone exactly?'

She looked down at her hands. 'She wrote down the name of a place by her bed while she was talking on the phone a few days before. It's still there.'

'Can you get it for me?'

Maria scurried up the stairs and brought down a scrap of paper.

In Victoria's writing was scrawled the words 'The chapel of Agia Triada – Mount Parnitha, Athens.'

Victoria and Anne. Both in Athens. Both maybe

281

looking for the same thing. His mind kept churning over.

'Take my number, Maria, and phone me if you have any problems.'

Patrick flung a few things into a bag and called the airlines to book the next flight to Athens.

Bits of Mary's trial for adultery kept coming into Patrick's mind as he tried to sleep. 'That the said Mary Countess of Elgin and Kincardine has been guilty of the crime of adultery.'

The maid admitted that, 'when they rose early she had observed the Sofa in the drawing room tumbled and out of order, and so marked that she believed Mr Ferguson and Lady Elgin to be engaged in criminal intercourse.'

Mary spent her last years at Archerfield and died in 1855, nine years after Robert. She was set to rest 'in a tomb not only unkempt and forlorn, but nameless too. It was not until 1916 that her name was finally inscribed on the hideous stone,' wrote her great-grandson. So much for her loving children. It would be good to restore her name. He was startled to find he cared about this as much, if not rather more, than the glorification of his own name.

He found himself thinking of the first time he had seen Anne Fitzgerald, her head tilted, watching the frozen stone bodies in the British Museum while her black velvet coat seemed to spread all around her like water. It was hard to know what had so arrested him about her. She was beautiful, certainly, with her crinkling mass of red hair and her pale face, but many women were beautiful. As she'd stood there it seemed she, like the statues themselves, was more than human, somehow gathering up time and hope and loss in the arrangement of her features, in the arrangement of her limbs. Maybe this was what love was, he thought, why love was such a very great emotion, maybe you love people for the qualities they have which can withstand time and tragedy; hope, passion, a way of confronting the world, and the details which don't change, the manner in which she raises her right eyebrow when very interested in something, her way of tilting her chin. These things will remain the same all her life, even when she's old.

It is the ordinary things about her I like best. The way she squints when thinking, rubs her nose, the way her hands are too small for her body.

The phone rang.

'There is something I didn't tell you,' said Maria's voice.

'Yes?'

'There was a phone call. Mrs Napier took it in the bedroom. But the answering machine in the hall went on recording the conversation.'

'Yes?'

'I listened. I was worried about Mr Napier. A

man was telling Mrs Napier about how, after she and Mr Napier left the club . . .'

'Yes?'

'I didn't want to tell you. I didn't want to get involved.'

'Go on.'

'The man said he'd done what she asked him to, and he wanted the money.' Her voice faltered.

'Did the man say anything else?'

'He said, "You wouldn't know him." There was a pause then Mrs Napier said, "Good. That's over then."'

'You're serious?' said Patrick.

'I don't know anything. But he hasn't come home. He was kind to me.'

'You must go to the police . . .'

'I can't.'

'You must.'

But before he could call the police himself, his phone rang again.

'Patrick?'

'Yes.'

'It's Phil from the club. I thought you ought to know. The police have been here trying to interview everyone about a body found in the river last night.'

'A body?'

'Yes. The face was slashed.'

'I don't believe this.'

'Do you know something about this? What shall I do?'

'Tell them to speak to Maria, who works for Mrs Napier. And Phil, find out about the shaven-headed guy who was hanging round there that night.'

Patrick carried his bag down the creaking steps, the walls spotted with fingerprints and scratches, and he felt too large for the house. When he flung open the front door the stale air of the street crept in and he strode out.

CHAPTER 49

Mary Elgin,
Paris,
May 30, 1805

My adored child William died of a fever a few weeks ago. I shall never get over it, never. Nothing can be the same again, this child was an angel.

He was such a passionate little mortal. The fever which took him took my life with Elgin too. I fear this huge affection I had for William will destroy me. I am turning to Robert for support.

CHAPTER 50

'Have you any idea where one of your guests might be – her name's Anne Fitzgerald?' asked Elizabeth, in the foyer of the Hotel Grand Bretagne. It was a large room clad in oppressive dark green marble scattered with clusters of uneasy people. Outside the cars and fumes of Athens bustled by in Constitution Square. With blue trousers billowing round her legs, a scarf round her thin neck, Elizabeth didn't command attention. People treated her as if she were invisible. Lily, who in her own home was an empress, with sofas for glittering coaches, was just a skinny, frightened little girl here. She found herself wishing Anne were around. Anne always made people take notice of her. Even when she waited patiently her presence was overwhelming somehow.

'She's staying here,' piped up Lily fiercely and the dark-haired man behind the desk scanned her with mild interest.

'I'm sorry?'

The receptionist stared at the nervous woman grimly.

'One of your guests, Anne Fitzgerald?' continued Elizabeth. 'We were hoping to see her.'

'No,' he said, more gently, checking her room number. 'She's in room sixty-seven. But she's out. The key's here. Sorry. Shall I take a message?' He smiled at the little girl, who glared back.

They went to sit down, disappointed. Elizabeth's wrists were very thin. Lily felt there were butterflies beating their wings inside her.

A heavy-jowled man with shiny black hair like Marmite lurched up to them. He had been sitting by the desk in the foyer, and was one of the drivers of the two taxis retained by the hotel. The hotel was proud of this special facility and ensured that its drivers spoke enough English for tourists.

'The woman you mentioned, my friend, another driver, called for her earlier – he was taking her to Mount Parnitha. You want to come?'

Lily didn't think they should go anywhere. When they first arrived her mother had insisted on walking up on the Acropolis, a great jumble of white stones on a flat mountain above Athens and while they were walking her mother had become very exhausted and had to sit down and looked as though she were about to cry. When Lily had asked why her mother was like that her mother had just said: 'It's so – so amazing.'

It really hadn't been. There were just lots of tourists and rubble and some old stones. Lily had liked the temple with the stone ladies holding it up instead of pillars but they weren't really old, her mother had said. They were replicas. Much of it was old though, from 500 years before Christ was even born. But Lily had no sense of time. She only knew eight years anyway, 2500 meant nothing. She could hardly count up that far. She was far more interested in a cat that sped over the stones and the way a little Japanese girl walked over the stones, picking up her feet daintily. It wasn't big things which interested her but little things.

'If you see the frieze up close,' said her mother, 'you'd like it. You can see muscles.'

'Mmm,' she'd said, thinking about getting back to the room and opening the little sewing set left in the bathroom.

But now her mother seemed to want to chase after Anne.

'Why not wait till she gets back?' said Lily.

Her mother's face was very bright and excited and she didn't like to put her off.

'Oh, it'd be fun just to bump into her! She'll be amazed!'

'It is getting late,' said Lily – one of her mother's phrases.

'Oh never mind,' her mother said. 'I want to see her. Give her a surprise.'

Her mother's eyes were very shiny. Everything else about her looked dry but the eyes were shiny. The ceiling towered high above them.

'She was going to the chapel of Agia Triada,' said the driver. 'On Mount Parnitha.'

Lily thought about the centaurs – half man, half

horse – in the ironwork of their bedroom balcony, and how they made soft mysterious shadows.

'The chapel!' said her mother, still sitting down, hands on her lap, the veins showing.

'An ancient chapel, very interesting,' said the driver, jutting out his square chin.

'Oh Lily!' said her mother excitedly.

If I were sick I wouldn't want to see an ancient chapel, thought Lily. I'd want something fresh and clean.

'Let's stay here. She'll find us,' said Lily.

'Come on,' said her mother, standing up wearily. 'How far is it away?'

'Not far,' said the driver. 'And there are deer and tortoises in the woods.'

Lily jumped up.

'Okay,' she said. At least my trainers bounce, she thought. They left the hotel with its dark atmosphere and went out into the unkempt streets where the man's car waited for them. It was dented in places and touched up here and there with what looked like tippex. The seats were torn.

'What a car!' said her mother as she struggled to open the door.

'I'm looking forward to seeing Anne,' said Lily brightly.

It was beginning to rain softly and the rain made it darker, as if curtains had been closed.

Lily shivered. Her mother was still sitting up straight.

'It was wonderful to see the Acropolis!' said

her mother. 'I still can't believe it. It made me feel quite extraordinary. Full of, I don't know, *energy*.'

Lily stared out of the window at the concrete shell of an empty apartment building. It was raining a little more now and the driver's windscreen wipers were flashing back and forth, back and forth.

It was about half an hour, through gruelling traffic and interminable low-slung buildings selling parts of cars, before they came to a more open road, then a little longer before they turned off along a small road. All the time her mother had talked about the Acropolis and the Parthenon, about Athene and how much more important wisdom was than power. 'Athene and Poseidon competed for the city and Athene won! Wisdom won! Not power but wisdom and kindness! She won by giving Athens the olive symbol of peace.'

'And olive oil I suppose,' said Lily, who was feeling bad-tempered.

'Look at all the olive trees, and the fig trees,' said her mother. Lily looked at about fifty plastic tables and chairs laid out on some rough grass for sale, as if waiting for a party which was never going to happen. She saw a house which was crushed on one side, with a bed pouring out of the window.

'Why's it like that?'

'The earthquake,' grumbled the driver.

Further on there was a factory that looked as though it had been stepped on by a giant. She sat close to the window. In London all the houses were in rows and most quite tall and squashed together, as if waiting in a queue for a bus. But here the houses and factories were strewn round untidily, and all squares or rectangles.

'Mount Parnitha must have been on the fault-line,' said Lily's mother.

They passed other houses, with cracks in them. Lily wished she'd been here during the earthquake.

They began to wind up the mountain and at each turn there was a little of the bend missing. Below them the little white houses were growing hazier.

'The road. It's not good,' said the driver. Lily could see dead trees, and trees covered with moss and then ahead of them there was something big covering the road. The driver slowly came to a halt.

It was a huge tree lying across the road.

'Oh no. It must have fallen,' said Elizabeth. 'Been damaged in the earthquake.'

'How are we going to get round it?' said Lily.

The driver was already reversing.

'We cannot go on,' he said.

'But we have to,' insisted Lily's mother. 'I want to get to the chapel, to Agia Triada.'

The windscreen wipers thudded from side to side.

'We'd better go back,' said Lily.

'No!' said her mother. 'It's not far up, is it?'

'No,' he said. His collar stuck into the flesh of his plump neck. 'Just up the hill.'

'There!' said her mother, climbing out of the car and paying the fare, standing so stiff and tall it hurt Lily: her mother wanted to curl up but she stood stiffly.

'Up there,' said the driver, nodding his head in the direction of the hill.

'Will my daughter be able to climb up there?'

'Yes. Yes of course.'

'Can you wait for us?' said Lily's mother.

'No. Not possible,' he said, winding up the window. He tapped his watch. 'Another appointment. But I come back in two hours.' He smiled, and began to reverse down the hill.

'Oh,' said Lily's mother, in a funny little voice. 'So here we are.'

The clouds were gathering as they began to walk up the wooded slope.

'Well, this seems a long way away from all the tests and injections in London, I must say,' said Elizabeth, striding up, in her sensible shoes, through rocks and trees.

'Yes!' said Lily.

'Difficult to believe I'm ill,' her mother continued, turning up the collar of her mac.

'Yes!' said Lily, noting that her trainers appeared to be losing some of their moonman bounce.

A faint metal glow seemed to fill the skies, from the sun trapped behind the clouds. It wasn't as solidly grey as in England. The sky was uncertain, as if it might do anything.

The slight drizzle made the ground underneath a

little slippery except where it was matted with pine needles.

'It's as though I've left the illness there,' continued her mother, 'among the ultra sounds and mammograms.'

Her mother was climbing more slowly now and was a little out of breath.

In parts the sky was a heavy white, as if filling up with snow, getting ready to tip down. It seemed to Lily they'd been travelling for a long time since leaving London and they'd come to somewhere else completely.

'Lovely fresh air,' said Lily, and stopped to pick a yellow daisy, while her mother panted beside her, and her thin legs looked as if they might cave in like old papier-mâché.

'Lovely,' said her mother. 'The fresh air.'

'Good to get a spot of exercise,' said Lily, echoing another of her mother's phrases. Sometimes it seemed to Lily that nothing was as beautiful as her mother's face, even when she was ill. It always contained such love. Although her mother's skin was chalky now, it still had a kind of radiance as it looked at Lily.

Lily grinned.

'Imagine – we're in Athens!' said Lily. Lily had no interest whatsoever in Athens. 'Just like that! Athens!'

'Yes!' said her mother, looking up at the fir trees ahead. It was the paleness of her mother's lips which concerned Lily most of all. They walked on.

'It'll be nice to see Anne, won't it? She'll be pleased to see us,' said Lily brightly. 'You'll feel so much better when you see her.'

'Oh, I don't feel unwell now. Just a bit – lacking in energy.'

Lily took a crushed Twix bar, which she had been hoarding for weeks, from her pocket. 'Look!' She waved it in front of her mother.

'Oh Lily,' said Elizabeth.

'Have it!' exclaimed Lily. 'It'll give you energy!'

Elizabeth stopped. Her hair was thin and dry on her head.

'Don't you want it?' said Elizabeth.

'Oh no, I'm not hungry at all.'

'Well, I suppose it might give me energy,' said Elizabeth. 'I'll have a bit.'

A spray of water fell from the trees above as a slight wind rustled through them. Elizabeth's skin was too white and shiny, like a stone.

'It must be nearly the top,' said Lily. 'The man said it wasn't far.'

Her mother's floppy hat suited her face thought Lily. It was strange the way her navy trousers almost billowed round her legs, they were so skinny.

'I think we should hurry,' Lily said, 'something's going to happen.'

'What?' said Elizabeth.

'The air's gone very peculiar,' said Lily, 'as if everything's holding its breath.'

Elizabeth stumbled on. Lily was tired and her

brain was blurred, as if stuffed with polystyrene, white and light and empty.

They stopped and rested for a while and Lily held her mother's hand and as they rested Lily closed her eyes and felt drowsy and thought she could hear a woman's voice calling her, and the voice sounded as if it were coming from a long, long way away yet from some place very near, just the other side of a breath or a smile, but somewhere real too. She rested her head on her mother's shoulder.

'The woman Anne's writing about, what's her name again?'

'Mary. Mary Elgin,' murmured Elizabeth.

'Oh yes. Anne told me,' said Lily, and looked round, through the fir trees.

CHAPTER 51

T he flight was bumpy and squashed and Patrick felt sick by the time he arrived in Athens. The sun was out and the sky blue above the ramshackle low buildings.

So Victoria had been behind everything.

With an uncomfortable lurch, he recalled just how public and how threatening his behaviour had been to Charles at that lunch and at his newspaper offices. He wondered if Victoria suspected that would take place when she encouraged him to do something about Charles's attacks.

He didn't want Victoria anywhere near Anne.

He took a cab to the Plaka district. It was hard to believe that the Victoria he had known could have done something like this. When he looked back, they had had good times together and the relationship had only begun to turn sour once he had met Anne and her father became seriously ill. But there had always been a kind of ruthlessness and desperation about her, a kind of panic about time passing. He repositioned himself on the torn cab seat as he was flung to the right by an especially imaginative and brave turn on the part of the driver.

Patrick threw his bag on to the bed of his hotel room. Outside his window a male pigeon leapt on to a female one and there was a flutter of wings on the flat roof, within the filigree of aerials. Patrick was sure that shaven-headed young man he'd seen the night Charles disappeared was the guy who'd been following him these last weeks.

As he rested for a few minutes he was aware of everything. The scratching of a beetle. The shifting of the floorboards. Every sneeze and creak and breath. The Acropolis, a risen loaf above the poorly built rectangles of modern buildings. And above it all the Parthenon temple looking so delicate, something carefully made of paper.

He tried to put Victoria out of his mind.

He could see them all up on the Acropolis – Mary Elgin, Elgin, Lusieri, everyone wary of everyone else, Mary with her long dress and parasol already hating Elgin, the labourers everywhere, and one with a kind of fervour in his face digging down into the rubble while the sun blazed down in a sky as blue as lapis lazuli.

There was something he couldn't quite see, couldn't quite understand, something in the whole pattern was blurred, incomprehensible. How did someone like Mary, from such a respectable family, ever have the nerve to reject her husband Elgin and go off with Robert? What gave her that courage, or foolhardiness, or was it there all along? Her spirit was there in the diaries but there was something missing, some piece in her character, in her life, that would explain it.

He guessed it was to do with Athens.

Curious how close Mary was, closer than Victoria with all her points and sharp angles, set squares and compasses, yet there was a chunk missing.

He listened to his breath. A fly buzzed around the room. He heard a lift open and close.

Wanting to be someone, yet with whole rooms of my life uninhabited. There's an empty attic, an empty side room.

His chest rose and fell. He thought of Victoria. She'd waited so long to be the wife of an editor and she'd begun to realise it would never happen even if Charles got this story. The person she wanted to impress, her father, was no longer alive. Patrick closed his eyes.

We all want that. Stature. To be a person of stature, one of the statues, to be a little like a god, and that desire brings out the best and the worst in people.

The shutters creaked. When he thought of Victoria she was another room inside him, painted an angry red, with empty rectangles on the wall.

CHAPTER 52

Mary Elgin,
Archerfield,
Scotland,
February 10, 1806

In all my torment, I see that moment when I made the Greek young man take away the head of the god. That is one good thing I have done in my life.

Although loving Robert feels good, I do not know if it really is good. Sometimes it seems just like madness.

The head of the god had a broken nose, like Elgin, but I saved it. It was the great thing I did in my life. It is not chained up now in a dark room off Park Lane. It is not being squabbled over by self-important politicians like the other great statues, huge figures striding the world, greater than me, greater than Elgin, the world made flesh, extraordinary monsters from a distant time. I am weak. But for that moment I was strong. Perhaps in a lifetime it is enough to do one good thing.

I think of going back there and finding it.

Then I think if I did that I might be tempted to give it to Elgin, and I must not do that, for he twists and turns all he has.

But he has suffered in prison in France, all those

years, and sometimes I feel sorry for him too. We both suffered. He is not an evil man.

Robert should leave me. He shouldn't pursue me. He should be strong, otherwise I will lose my children, my beloved parents, and I shall bring shame on everyone.

I have been strong once. But his letters make it so hard.

10 December, 1806

Dearest Mary,

I can boast of loving you with a passion never felt before; for with all the violence of our feelings which may be found, perhaps, in others, never, never was there at the same time such a perfect complete union in our souls. How every feeling, every wish, every thought is alike. Yes, my own beloved Mary, we were made for one another. Oh, Mary in my arms, with the friend you love and live in, what may we not do and say – all is then affection and love.

Robert

Dearest Mary,

Never, never was love true and sure like ours. More and more we love and adore one another – and at last free from all fetters we shall enjoy the most perfect bliss this world can bestow – oh God, we cannot live away from one another.

Robert

Mary Elgin,
Archerfield,
April 28, 1808

I have just been through a divorce court which has destroyed my reputation. The children have been taken away from me. I have nothing now, except Robert, and my dear parents, who have stayed kind to me throughout.

I shall be forgotten by history. I have stepped too far out into the limelight. I must now withdraw back into the shadows.

Archerfield,
November 9, 1836

My dear Robert,
I suspect I shall not send this letter, my dearest husband. It was all a long time ago, all that pain and rapture. There is something I wish to confess to you and although you and I are man and wife now and should have no secrets, there is this something I want to tell you and cannot.

When we were apart, when I was still married to Elgin, we wrote so much. You are away from me, in London, and I am up in my beloved Archerfield.

I did something once that helped separate me from Elgin. It is hard for me to say what it was. It was, I suppose, my first true act of rebellion. I find myself shivering now, although I am writing on the desk my father used to write on when he was alive, near the fire.

It would be wonderful, my darling, if you and I could say it was all worth it – the meetings in hotel rooms, the secret signs, the clandestine letters. But sometimes, at the end of a day like this when all the warmth has left the sky, I wonder.

From the minute I did what I did – hid something that Elgin felt belonged to him – I entered into a world of secrets. It was from the best of motives I assure you – a moment of vigour, of love for something apart from family and friends, love for the beauty of an object and what it meant. And our love, why that always seemed pure, the purest thing in all the world. Say that our love will live on, through the centuries, though we never had a child of our own. It is love that lasts, surely, through the uncertain years.

But now you leave me alone more and more with your work for Parliament and I spend my time in Archerfield growing old, without my children, still in a kind of disgrace, with only the servants whom I like to think love me. But how do I know? Maybe they despise me even without knowing my other outrageous action.

I did what I felt was right. It would have been impossible to do any different. Yes, I suppose in the end that is what is true. I had to do what I did, in Athens all those years ago, and I had to love you. You were so beautiful too, with your bright eyes. My darling, maybe I cannot send this letter.

I do love you, Robert. Help me believe love doesn't disappear into the vapour.

Your
Mary

CHAPTER 53

The miniature white chapel sat there, cracked in places from the recent earthquake, with broken tiles on the roof and a tiny wooden doorway. Anne thought it looked so frail, among its guard of fir trees, its silvery tiles, its scattering of browning fir needles on the roof, and above it the sky white and dense now, the dark green of the fir trees rising up all around. It looked as though it might be made of sugar, a cake made of sugar.

The cross had fallen from the top of the chapel and was propped up near the door.

Anne smiled. The chapel was as delicate as words on a page, the loop and curl of brown ink whispering secrets through the centuries, another kind of ghost. Mary's reputation may be trapped there under the rubble or the earth.

I shall have that head that Mary describes. I shall have it in my hands. I know that I shall have the head, she thought. I can feel it in my hands, the weight of the marble, the shape of the parted lips.

It was raining with a fine drizzle. She walked round the chapel, wondering where exactly the head could have been hidden. The area in front of the chapel and to the left was paved, and the area behind built up. Some of the paving was cracked and looked as if it had been taken up. A caretaker's house stood further back, apparently derelict, with a broom wedged over the path to stop anyone coming up. There was no one around.

In the little courtyard in front of the chapel wild dandelions and daisies grew through the stones.

That taxi driver should have told me I had to climb a great mountain before getting here. She picked up a fir cone.

The wooden arched door of the chapel was half open and she entered, having to bow low through the door and arriving first at a little smoke-stained vestibule with an oil lamp in the corner and icons on the wall. The next wooden door looked as if it had been forced open. She swallowed as she pushed it open and breathed in the drowning smell of old time and the religion of icons and darkness.

The walls and low dome of the tiny church were covered in frescos and at the far end, below a small window, there was a wooden carving of Christ on the cross above an altar.

There were cobwebs on the window ledges. The faded saints and apostles opened their hands in blessing, their fingers outstretched. Anne could almost taste the candles and oil lamps in her mouth.

A woman stood with her head bowed, back to Anne, in front of the crucifix, the tiny chapel tight around her. A fly buzzed in the corner and the woman turned round and smiled, as if in greeting.

The woman had black, chiselled hair and a dark raincoat.

'Why hello,' she said.

'Hi!' said Anne.

The haloes of the saints who encircled the walls shone out in gold like the crosses on their robes.

The woman had greeted Anne as if she knew her.

'A little gem, don't you think?' said the woman's honeyed, low voice.

'Yes,' said Anne.

'Very deserted round here, really. Considering.'

'Yes. Must be the rain,' said Anne, looking round. There were a few icons on the walls, one of Christ holding a golden bible in turquoise robes, with a gold leaf background.

'I think it's delightful that the authorities are so trusting,' said the woman. 'Not to lock it.'

A few rush-seated chairs sat in rows and in the middle of the chapel, below the small dome, hung a black iron chandelier. Further up, near the altar were stacked some paintings including one of a Madonna and child of extraordinary loveliness, their faces so still. By the altar there were two large brass candlesticks.

The woman moved closer to Anne. She had peculiarly small white teeth, thought Anne.

'Why did you come here?' said the woman.

'Oh, just curious. I heard it was a pretty chapel.'

'I lit the candles.'

'Lovely,' said Anne. 'You walked up?'

'Some of the way. I like a walk – I followed the stream up. I like candles, don't you? But I don't think I'm religious at all. My father died recently, and I thought, oh well, that's him gone. Trouble is, I keep thinking it. Every second of every day.' She laughed.

The woman was watching Anne intently. Her lashes had so many layers of mascara it surprised Anne that she could open her eyes.

The effigy of Christ's body drooped just behind the woman. There was a leaded window on either side, both with black bars, but very little light came through. Anne was wondering where the head could have been buried.

The woman kept smiling and her hands played restlessly with the belt of her raincoat.

There was a bare unlit electric light bulb hung above the crucifix.

'Would you say you were determined?' asked the woman.

'I'm sorry?' said Anne.

The woman drummed her fingers over the wooden back of a chair.

'Would you say you were a determined person?'

'Why?' said Anne, frowning. It was cold in the chapel. 'I should be going,' said Anne.

The woman took a step down.

'Don't go,' and her words sounded more like a command than a request.

CHAPTER 54

Patrick scrambled up the mountain towards the chapel as fast as he could.

The fir trees above darkened the ground, which was wet and slippery in places and dry in others, under the trees. Here and there were groups of nettles and branches and rocks.

There was an odd stillness in the air. The silence seemed to fill every space, between the trees, between the leaves, under the bushes here and there. There was an eiderdown of pine needles.

He couldn't hear any birds.

If Mary had ever come up here, she would probably have been taken up to the chapel by a horse or mule. The driver had told him the road was only built about thirty to forty years ago and before that had been a path.

The air was tense and heavy. A film of sweat covered his body and his mouth felt empty, as if it contained no tongue. He half expected to see Mary walk out from behind some tree as he hurried by, with those staring chestnut eyes.

'Excuse me!' called a shrill voice.

A skinny little girl in a white jumper, jeans and trainers stood in front of him.

'Excuse me,' the shrill voice insisted. 'Do you speak English?' she said, enunciating her words. The little girl had straight blonde hair and looked like something she had drawn herself – a funny little straight mouth, poorly depicted straw-like hair, and limbs which could have been created with a ruler. Her white trainers were scuffed and dirty from the climb.

'You don't have any water do you? We're thirsty.'

'Sure,' said Patrick, taking a plastic bottle of mineral water from the pocket of his coat. 'Take it. I haven't drunk from it.' He undid the blue cap and grinned. 'You okay? You shouldn't be alone here. Are you with anyone?'

'Oh yes,' said the child. 'I'm with my mother. We're fine.'

'Sure?' said Patrick. There was something uneasy about the child.

'Look, my name's Patrick Browning. You really shouldn't be alone here. It's going to get dark soon and there will be a storm. Why don't you come with me?' he said.

'No, no, we need to take our time,' said the little girl, her head to one side, carefully explaining. He liked her piercing blue eyes and careful manner.

He checked his watch.

'You're sure . . . ?'

'Certain,' said the child. 'We're meeting a friend,' she continued.

Patrick stopped, frowned.

'I can't stay chatting,' said the little girl, blinking at him.

Patrick walked after her, though the little girl marched haughtily forward. He saw a pale woman sitting on a rock, her head in her hands, by a stream. When she heard Patrick and the child she looked up, startled.

'Hello,' said Patrick cheerfully. 'I insist on accompanying you.'

'Are there wolves in the wood?' said Lily. Patrick shrugged. In fact his driver had said there were, and gazelle, but all the wild boar that used to roam here had been eaten.

'We could go back down. The car I came in is waiting there,' he said.

'I want to go on climbing up,' said Lily's mother.

CHAPTER 55

'I was praying before you came,' said Victoria. She turned back to the altar. The cold from the grey stone floor seemed to seep through Anne's bones. 'It's very serene here, don't you find?'

Anne smoothed back her hair, which was a little frizzy from the damp. The damp seemed to be getting into her chest, her skin, everywhere. She took a fruit pastille from her pocket and sucked it, then chewed into its soft sugar.

Victoria turned her back to Anne and Anne remembered the thin shoulders of Patrick's lover that day on the stairs of his house.

Anne felt sharp, alert, her nails long, aware of the folds of her coat, the cracks splitting up the walls. She could smell the damp, smell the fir needles, smell the time trapped in the walls. Anne put on her small red leather gloves. Her own legs felt thinner, sharper, capable of running fast. At the corners of the chapel were a few stray fir needles, as if they'd drifted in for a little spiritual consolation. Anne leant down and picked one up. It felt sad here, sad and dank, not somewhere that was hiding the beautiful head.

Victoria's face was exuberant. The eyes were too bright, the lips too red. Anne turned to leave. Her black leather boots were caked in mud from the climb.

Victoria tossed back her head.

'Oh, please stay, it's lonely here.' On the dome above the black candelabra Christ looked down, covered with gold crosses, with an expression of great compassion.

Anne coughed. Her face was white in the half gloom of the chapel. 'I'm sorry. Really, I just came up to see it – the road was closed – I climbed up – I'm a bit tired now. I think I'll walk on to the village, and maybe come back later.'

Victoria laughed, and as she laughed her features imploded, looked smaller, as though they could all be gathered up with one hand and thrown away. A black leather handbag with two silver buckles hung over one shoulder.

'Of course you're an expert on Mary Elgin?' she said to Anne.

'I'm sorry?'

'I said you're an expert on Mary Elgin.'

'I'm writing a book on her, yes.'

'Like Patrick Browning. He's my lover.'

A mosquito buzzed in front of her and Anne stretched out her hand and caught it.

'Aren't you angry?' inquired Victoria. Her eyebrows were high and arched.

Anne shrugged. 'No.' She checked her watch. 'It's getting late.'

'What do you think of Mary, really?' said Victoria, leaning against the raised stone area by the altar. Her black mac was tied with a belt.

'If you don't mind . . .'

'Stay,' said Victoria, sharply. Then more softly, she continued. 'I don't want to be alone. And I'm interested in Mary Elgin. Really. I maybe look like – I don't know – a Holland Park lady – but there is more to me.'

Anne could hear the cry of crows outside.

'She was an impressive person,' said Anne softly. 'We know a little too much about her to find her completely impressive. Women tend to reveal too much of themselves in their diaries and letters. Men are more cautious. They are better at presenting a composite image to the world.'

Victoria frowned. The staring faces of the saints were all around, as if holding hands tightly around them. The damp was in Anne's chest.

'You like her?' said Victoria. 'You'd have her as a friend?'

'She's dead,' said Anne.

'Don't be absurd,' said Victoria. 'You can feel her here now, can't you?'

Anne paused. 'No,' she said. 'We don't know she ever even came here.'

Victoria ran one hand over the other.

'Ah, but you can feel her presence. I can.'

Anne found this chapel smaller by the moment, the faces of the saints pressing closer to her like faces in a crowd. There was just one small dusty window at the far end.

'I feel more aware of things now, you know, Anne, since my father died,' said Victoria, with that little tuck of a smile which made her face smaller. 'More sensitive.'

Victoria opened her eyes wide and stared directly at Anne. For a second Victoria looked all of a piece; the smart black hair, the smart raincoat with the large pockets, the black bag. She was leaning against the wooden rail in front of the altar.

'Great to imagine her here,' said Victoria.

'I told you, we have no evidence she came here.'

Victoria was staring at one of the saints, and blinked.

'Creepy here, don't you think? All these saints. My father died recently.' She raised her eyebrows. 'Do you think he's with them?'

'I am very sorry,' said Anne. 'I know we have a mutual friend in Patrick and I know you're feeling a little lost this evening. But it's getting cold and dark. Why don't we both walk down the hill together. Or at least have coffee in the village?'

'She was very alive, wasn't she, Mary? I mean, she lived,' said Victoria. 'She was an ambassadress in Constantinople. She knew Emma Hamilton and Nelson. She met the Turkish Sultan. Yet she ruined it all, had an affair.'

It was growing cold and Anne wanted to leave.

'She did one great thing though,' said Victoria. 'She dared to hide a head from Elgin. It was an outrageous thing to do, wasn't it? Outrageous. The courage that took. But it made her too brave. It emboldened her to leave Elgin and that ruined her. Now she's referred to merely as "vivacious" Patrick says – and you know how damaging most such adjectives are when applied to women.'

'I am glad you appreciate Mary,' said Anne. Anne's features felt very still. 'But what do you know about a head?'

Victoria shivered. Anne didn't think she looked healthy; her hands trembled and there was darkness under her eyes.

Anne wanted Victoria to stay at this distance from her.

Victoria smiled again. 'All these dead people. You don't really *adore* them but you still would rather they were alive.'

'Of course,' said Anne levelly. 'I can understand that.'

'Even people you *dislike*, when they die you feel different.'

'Of course,' said Anne.

'Especially if they're family,' said Victoria, staring at the painting of Jesus.

'Yes. It's getting dark outside. We should go. You shouldn't stay here alone.'

Victoria shrugged. 'I don't care.'

'I should get back,' said Anne.

'You're looking for the head?'

'I'm sorry?' said Anne.

'The head of Hermes.'

'Tell me, what do you know of that?' said Anne.

Victoria tipped back her chin.

'Darling Alexander read those diaries. You do live with him you know. You didn't hide them well enough. He studied them all night. That tiny writing! He's very clever you know.'

Victoria's hand stroked the painted wall.

'He came to value some paintings of mine. We became friends.'

'I see.'

'Turned out we were looking for the same thing. We'd both heard interesting rumours. Some old drunk had talked too much, but not quite enough. We hoped you two would lead us to the diaries. No one would speak to us, but with his charm and yours . . .'

'But the head . . .'

'The guy I paid to follow you and Patrick wasn't much good at following, kept losing you at all the important times but it seems he has other talents. Did you ever notice him?'

'I think so. The head . . . ?'

'I've been here a couple of days. I've had a good look. Moved some stones around. Oh, and Alexander sent some men up here a week or so ago, after reading your precious diaries.'

'Yes . . . ?' said Anne.

'Would I tell you if I found it? I employed a few men. They pretended to passers-by that they were employed by the government!'

A fly buzzed by Anne and hit against the window at the far end.

'You didn't find anything,' said Anne.

'Oh I did. I found something,' said Victoria.

Victoria took a box of matches from her pocket and lit the two candles in the tall candlesticks in front of her. Her face was golden for a moment. Her eyes were bright.

All the liquid in Anne's body seemed to disappear and she felt quite dry.

'I fear Alexander could end up giving it to the Greek government. Doesn't think he would but he would. I found it myself, you see. But I have no reason to return to England. I did think maybe if I were fabulously rich Patrick would love me, or if I found him the head, but the way he looked at me, I don't think so now. Nothing would work. As for home, I really don't have much there. When my father died, I just lost interest in the house, lost interest in Charles, and by then Patrick had lost interest in me.

'But I wanted the head, if it existed, because that's beyond death and time. If I told him I had it, Alexander and I could sell it. He knows the right person. Some collector on the South China Seas who would never let anyone see it. Amusing really, don't you think?'

Anne began to move slowly towards the door.

'Oh, don't go,' said Victoria. 'You were being so nice. Was that your technique with Patrick? He liked me a lot – well, Mary then me. But then you came along and that was that.'

Victoria walked towards Anne. 'Don't go. I'm

enjoying your company.' Her hand lay over her black shoulder bag. 'You know, sometimes it's easy to do terrible things. Really terrible things. You just do them. It's the aftermath that's unpleasant. You're a clever young woman, I suppose you find that obvious.'

'No, not obvious. I think you should sit down,' said Anne. 'You're trembling. This has clearly been a very difficult time for you.'

Victoria nodded.

'You are right.' But she didn't sit down. There was a noise outside, and she unbuckled her bag and quickly took out a hunting knife with a brown handle.

'This is to protect us if we're attacked. It used to be Charles's. He was big on hunting.'

'Tell me, where's the head?' said Anne.

'How persistent you are. But you still don't really believe me, do you? You don't think I found it?'

'I don't know.'

Victoria laughed.

'You don't. You see. You don't really believe in her! You don't believe in the history you read! And I do. Foolish Holland Park wife. I'm the one who believes. Out of all of you. It was Patrick who made me believe in Mary. He seemed so enraptured. So when Alexander told me what the diaries said I came here at once.'

'I see,' said Anne.

'I hope someone doesn't try to get into this

chapel,' Victoria said. 'It must be exciting to attack someone with a knife. You go on to some other level. I don't much like the level I'm in now. Are you in love with Patrick?'

Anne's tongue was enormous in her mouth.

'Patrick? I don't know,' she said.

'I think you do,' said Victoria. She looked down. 'From the tone of your voice I think you do. It's the way you say his name – Patrick – as if it's something separate.'

'If you stay here I'll see if I can go to the village and get you a coffee.'

'I don't want you to leave this chapel,' said Victoria. She pushed her hair from her face. 'Interesting you and I came here first. You need to seize what you want, don't you? Charles, you see, I mean, I ended up not liking him. Despising him. But I used just to accept him. After my father's death, I thought life is *short*. You need to get on with things, to do what you need to do to get the most out of your life. Besides, he was about to be the centre of a huge scandal. My lawyer sister would have been thrilled. She probably would have asked if she could help me in some way. She would have been *sympathetic*.'

She smiled.

Victoria's face in the candlelight seemed larger than that of the inquisitive saints who stood staring at them from the walls of the chapel.

CHAPTER 56

The big man wore a huge grey coat which seemed small on him. Even the pockets were big. His nose was large and his eyes brown and enormous. He had long eyelashes and a sweet smile which ran up the side of his face. As for his shoes, they could have contained about twenty of her feet. His presence made Lily feel very young and light. Although he was frowning, the brow lowering like some whale into the sea, there was still a kind of merriment about him, as if his whole presence here on earth was comic and unexpected but wholly serious at the same time. Lily's mother, by contrast, seemed ordinary; the stout shoes, the anxiety in her hands, the way her mac hung limply over her body, the way she kept stumbling, although the big man held her arm, and kept stooping, concerned, with such kind eyes, to see if she was okay.

'I'm fine,' her mother said, and she wasn't the beloved, loving mother of London but someone out of place. She wasn't even watching Lily, which she usually did, she was too intent on watching her own uncertain footsteps as the day gave

out its light and began to suck back the darkness.

The pine trees looked like soldiers all around,
interrupting their journey, and Lily wondered why
they had wanted to come here to the chapel. It had
seemed such a good idea, an adventure. Recently
her mother's life had been so limited. She'd been
shut up in the four walls of the house, visiting the
doctors, trying to eat. It had taken courage to come
here, and now all the courage seemed to have
deserted her and it was growing cold. Through
a gap in the trees Lily saw a flash of red, and for
a moment a small red deer looked at her, and its
face was gentle and inquisitive. Lily moved slowly
towards the deer and Lily's green anorak caught
on a branch of a tree and tore. The deer stared at
her in alarm then leapt off, even lighter than Lily.
Lily stopped and examined the tear. There was a
bit of fluff underneath and she took some out.

She leant against the grey-brown bark of a tree.
There was thunder in the distance. She'd heard
so much about 'Athens this' and 'Athens that' so
when she'd seen the pile of rubble lying on the
Acropolis she'd been disappointed. But at least,
she comforted herself, it was strange here on the
hillside. A magic mountainside, she told herself.
There'd been the giant springing from nowhere.
There'd been the thunder. The inquisitive deer.

Her trainers were scuffed and damp. She bent
down and wiped some grass off them.

Her mother had been told to imagine her body

was a soldier and that the soldier had to bayonet the cancer again and again.

Now that was magic. That wasn't scientific, and yet people believed it. Doctors had done studies, and found it worked. So what was magic and what was science? You had to believe in magic. She, Lily Richardson, believed in magic. There was religion too, and she didn't know where that fitted in, whether that was science, definitely true, or magic. So maybe there was magic here.

It was magic, Lily decided, picking off a piece of bark, that her mother had come to Athens when she was so ill. She had wanted to come so she had come. Anne said once that the mind can move mountains.

A stone lying near some mushrooms moved, and a grey head, and there was a tortoise.

'Lily!' called the giant's voice.

'Hello,' said Lily to the tortoise, and bent down. 'There!' she thought. 'A stone turned into a tortoise.' The tortoise trundled away on his fat little feet.

'Lily!' shouted the giant, and a bird flew frightened from the tree above.

Anne had told her how poor Mary Elgin had buried some god up a mountain. Lily half expected to see Mary walk out from behind a tree.

After all, the stone had turned into a tortoise.

Or maybe it was the Acropolis Mary went to, Lily wasn't quite sure. Lily rubbed her eyes. She was tired.

'Lily!' cried the giant's voice more urgently. 'Where are you?'

The voice seemed to echo a little. The voice was like the man, big and kind. Maybe he'd love her mother and marry her and save her. That would be magic. He'd rescued her once, after all.

She ran after the voice.

'Coming!' she said.

CHAPTER 57

Behind Victoria was an apostle, painted in grey, with silvery halo. The fly had landed on the halo and was cleaning itself.

'Will you marry Patrick?' said Victoria.

'I'm sorry?'

'Patrick. Are you going to marry him?'

Anne shrugged.

'I'm considering marrying him,' said Victoria, in a high, ragged voice. 'Because unfortunately my husband died.'

'Oh? I didn't know.'

'Yes.'

'When?'

'Oh recently. I was praying for his soul when you entered. And that of my father. He died too. Did I tell you?'

'Yes. I'm sorry. Shall we go and see the head now?'

The older woman had dark slanting eyes. She pushed at her face, as if pushing back hair, but her hair was in place, in its tailored position to the nape of the neck, with only one or two soft strands escaping here and there, responding to the damp which had seeped into the air, the wooden chairs, the alarmed, curious faces of the saints painted on the walls, peeling here and there, showing white patches beneath. Victoria kept pushing back her hair, as if troubled by cobwebs.

Although Victoria's shoes were filthy, the rest of her was neat: the narrow shoulders, the tightly belted waist, the arched eyebrows, the thin red lips. Her hands had rings all over them, lovely rings, one gold with opals, one with an amethyst. She frowned as she pushed back at the cobwebs.

'You're like her, are you?' she said. 'Is that it? Like Mary?' She squinted at Anne. 'Maybe that's why he fell for you.'

Victoria shivered.

'It's cold,' said Anne. 'Come on, let's get out of here.'

'You don't know my name. It's Victoria Napier. You didn't ask it.' Her voice sounded slightly querulous. She squinted again, and pushed again at her face. 'You stand there, so self-sufficient, all in your greys and your certain movements. You remind me of my sister. She's a lawyer. Very, very clever.' Victoria coughed, and moved her muddy shoes from side to side. 'She seemed always to be made from thought, you know, not flesh and bone.'

She smiled, but her smile took something out of the atmosphere rather than adding to it.

'My father was a lawyer,' she continued. 'A clever man. But difficult. He was always impressed

325

by my sister, her air of calm authority, while I was all emotion and urgency. I thought I hated him. All my life I thought I hated him. Silly, all that sad waste of time. Do you think the saints know about things like that?'

'Where's the head, Victoria?'

'I heard there was an earthquake here a few weeks ago. This chapel's on the fault line – that's why the cross is lying on the floor outside.'

Victoria moved her feet again, as if trying to keep warm. Her arms were crossed over her front, the knife still in her right hand.

'He was white after he died. Worse than nothing. All the life gone and his skin all dead white, sort of bluish and nobody there.'

'I am sorry,' said Anne.

'I suppose . . . this head of Hermes. The messenger. It's the same kind of thing. Gods and messages. The head turned, looking behind. That's what we're all like, hurrying forward but looking behind.' She sighed.

'I'd love to see it,' said Anne.

'So you do believe I have it?' said Victoria.

'I told you, I don't know.'

'You remind me so much of my sister,' said Victoria thoughtfully. 'So considerate, so intelligent, so reasonable.'

'Where did you find it?'

'One of the men found it, under a paving stone at the back, a few yards from the chapel. I think the earthquake must have cracked the stones, opened up the earth. So it was easy to find. It was the right time.'

She smiled. Anne frowned.

Victoria's face had an animal quality, thought Anne, but she wasn't sure which one. Maybe a ferret; fine boned, with beady eyes and a way of twitching the head, listening for sounds. When Anne had seen Victoria on the dark narrow stairs of Patrick's flat she had looked so sophisticated. Now there was a rawness about her as the saints swirled around them. The knife had string tied around the handle.

Anne continued to talk to her softly, to keep her calm, as Victoria kept blinking and darting her glance over to the door, then to the window.

'I'm pleased you have found it . . .' Anne continued calmly.

An icon of the Madonna meekly bowed her head, lit up by the flickering candles.

A fly had landed on Victoria's left arm, and she brushed it away. There were too many faces watching them from the greeny black walls, from which the light was slowly withdrawing.

Victoria moved up, back towards the altar, her head down before the golden cross and flickering candles, her back to Anne.

'My father screamed out when he died,' said Victoria. 'My sister was there. Standing over him like an angel of death, everything flowing from her, her children, her husband, her peacefulness all around her, so it's impossible to tell one thing from the other.' She shrugged. 'And afterwards my house felt like a ghost house. Like this place. The whole house suddenly seemed fragmentary. Made of bits from here and there. I got rid of the lot. I sold some to your friend Alexander. Not a bad man. But not a good man.'

Victoria moved her small feet up and down, like a cat pawing the ground.

'And,' she said, 'my husband, he seemed another fragment. Irrelevant.'

Anne could see the woman was shaking.

'I'm leaving now,' said Anne. 'I have to go now. You should leave too.'

'Go then,' said Victoria, not turning round.

'Come with me,' said Anne.

'Go away,' said Victoria.

Anne walked towards the woman's thin shoulders.

'You should come away now,' she said gently.

'I am meeting people here . . .' said Victoria. 'About the head.'

'There's no head here,' said Anne. 'You're not meeting anyone.'

'No. I found it.'

'You didn't find it,' said Anne.

'You know,' said Victoria, 'the police contacted my mother to ask where I was. I'm a suspect over the death of my husband. Something to do with my housekeeper's evidence. Terrible really, to contact my mother so soon after my father's death. I told you he died, didn't I? Do you know anything about this?

'Apparently Patrick encouraged Maria to talk to the police. It's one of the things that's depressed me rather, I want to tell you,' said Victoria. 'It makes me think there's no hope. He really doesn't love me at all. But of course I knew that. They think I had my husband murdered. I am, I have to say, becoming implicated in a murder. A murderer. If there was hope, you know. I want to tell you . . .' She took another breath. 'I want to tell you that if there was hope I'd, well,' she said seriously, 'I think I would probably have to kill you.' She shrugged. Her gold earrings glistened. She wore a gold bracelet round her left wrist. 'As it is, well, I'm so tired of it all. Really tired. My poor husband. Have you ever been this tired?'

'No. No I haven't,' said Anne levelly.

Anne tilted up her chin, tucked her hair behind her ears, and stepped carefully forward, her coat all around her, towards the woman, who was gripping the knife tightly, and smiling.

CHAPTER 58

Patrick kept talking to Elizabeth about Mary Elgin, to keep her spirits up as they clambered through nettles and brambles and logs covered with ivy until they came to a small stream.

His voice boomed out through the wet air as he supported the skinny woman who seemed light as balsa wood. He felt so burly, his bones and muscle heavy, while this woman was so light that he felt he needed to weigh her down to stop her floating off. The little girl kept wandering off and once seemed to disappear but returned after a while. Her face and her mother's were the same; thin, sharp, intelligent, but life filled the child's, overflowed into the hands and feet and face which couldn't stop moving, jumping, fidgeting. The woman, however, only had life in her eyes and her voice, which was full of humour and a warm Scottish twang.

'So you're Patrick?' she said.

'Yup! That's right.'

'The American Patrick.'

'Yes, I'm American.'

'You know Anne Fitzgerald?'

'Yes. Why?'

330

'She's my friend,' said Elizabeth.

'Extraordinary,' boomed Patrick. The little girl watched him intently.

They walked on. He thought of Athens, the trees sprouting up between the red roofs of the houses, and the dogs barking. The rain more or less stopped for a moment and he could hear the cry of turtle doves, a linnet, a goldfinch.

'You have a lot in common. She talks about history the same way as you do. She told me biography was all about ghosts. I sometimes thinks she prefers the past to the present,' said Elizabeth.

'Yes. I know. Sometimes she seems to.'

In his mind he could see the caryatids, the statues of maidens supporting the Erechtheion on the Acropolis. Elgin had taken the second from the right and she was in the British Museum still, languidly standing through the centuries; 2500 years now she'd been standing like that.

'But of course the present is confusing.' She stopped for a moment, panting, and brushed a leaf from her cheek. 'It has no sense of perspective,' said Elizabeth.

'Are you meeting her somewhere round here?'

'It's a surprise. I thought it would be a nice surprise.' She gave a little laugh then began to cough. But her eyes were a little brighter now.

'So you think she's at the chapel?'

'That's what a driver at the hotel said. Are you looking for her too?'

'Yes.'

'Is it something to do with Mary Elgin?'

'Sort of,' said Patrick.

'She was looking for something, wasn't she? She has been for months now. Something to do with Mary, she wouldn't say what; something to do with love, she said one day.'

They walked on. Patrick wanted to hurry, to get to Anne, but didn't want to leave Elizabeth, who kept stumbling in the slippery ground even as she talked, although her voice had begun to sound more certain somehow, as if something in the high mountain air were making her more comfortable and happier. Patrick was not really worried about the child, who clearly had boundless energy. She kept looking excitedly at Patrick then at her mother.

Elizabeth hung on to Patrick's arm.

'How long have you known her?' asked Patrick.

'Oh, I was her tutor at Edinburgh University.'

Lily was walking close to them, still looking brightly from one face to the other, hardly listening to what Patrick and her mother were saying.

His coat swept around him.

'You've been having some affair – with a woman in high heels and black tights?' she said.

Patrick laughed, and the laugh rang out loudly through the moist air.

'Oh, Victoria. That's all over, whatever it was.'

A fine rain drizzled down his face as if down a cliff as he looked up at the darkening sky.

'Maybe I am in love with Anne,' shouted Patrick through the rain to Elizabeth.

Lily stared up at Patrick.

'I saw a tortoise earlier!' said Lily suddenly. 'It was a stone then it turned into a tortoise!'

'How wonderful, darling,' said Elizabeth.

'And I saw a deer. And you know how usually they're afraid? Well this one wasn't at all! It came close and watched me. That's how I knew this was a magic place! Why don't you two come with me and we can find a tortoise together!'

Patrick grinned at Lily. The child's lips quivered. Elizabeth stretched her hand out and touched the child's blonde hair, and stroked it, and the child looked up.

'I think Anne's crazy about you,' said Elizabeth.

'Crazy?' he said.

Elizabeth paused, leaning against a tree, panting, the rain varnishing her pallid features, her floppy hat over her eyes. 'She doesn't show her emotions much.'

'Crazy about me?' he said.

He wanted to pick Elizabeth up in his arms and toss her with joy like a pancake.

'She's just afraid like the rest of us,' said Elizabeth. Her chest rose and fell. In her blue trousers, wet around the ankles, her floppy white hat which was now damp and grey, her limp beige raincoat, her sharp features pointing out of her face, she looked like some elderly tourist. But her blue Scottish eyes were still young, and her voice. 'Only I'm not afraid anymore.'

Elizabeth closed her eyes.

Lily was standing by them, her arms crossed, frowning.

'It's not true,' said Lily. 'She doesn't love you.'

Her mother blinked at Lily, then smiled.

'Oh Lily,' she said.

'It's true. She doesn't. She loves Paolo, who died. She hates you.'

Lily ran at Patrick and started to hit him, 'No, no, no.' He held on to the child's arms. He didn't quite understand why the child was behaving so strangely. In the distance Patrick caught sight of the little chapel waiting there, white, glinting, like a pearl.

CHAPTER 59

There wasn't really much blood at all. Just a little pool beneath the crucified Christ where the blood had come out of Victoria's wrist.

As Anne had rushed towards her, Victoria had swayed then slowly her legs began to crumple and she sprawled on the floor in what appeared to be a faint. The sound as she fell was hollow, like a hammer on a coconut. She lay very still, with an amazed expression and a froth of blood on her mouth.

Later, the coroners would say it was the blow to her head when she fell that killed her.

CHAPTER 60

It was a while before the ambulance arrived.

Elizabeth took Lily up to a tiny cafe up the road, where the vine above only just covered the area.

'I didn't see,' said Lily. 'What happened?'

A thin dog came up and dug his nose in Lily's knee and she smiled.

'He's hungry. I'll give him a sugar lump,' she said, and bent down, the sugar lump in the flat of her hand, and let the threadbare dog take the sugar.

'The ambulance has to get through the road-block,' Elizabeth said, and looked away. The dog growled softly. Lily gave him another sugar lump. Sunlight passed through the vine, making speckles of warm light.

'So what happened?' said Lily.

'An accident,' said Elizabeth.

CHAPTER 61

Anne and Patrick were outside the chapel, both leaning against the whitewashed wall. The doctor was with Victoria inside.

'So I suppose this is the end of it all,' said Patrick. His arms were around her holding her up.

'I doubt that,' she said.

He stroked back her hair and his eyes pillaged her face, seemed to take in every edge and curve.

That night Anne and Patrick stayed in separate rooms at the Grande Bretagne hotel, and were questioned by the police.

In the early morning, both of them unable to sleep, Anne and Patrick walked up to the Acropolis and were the first people there. Athens spread out, flat-roofed, below them. Little clouds daubed the blue sky and swallows swirled by.

Bits of pediment were strewn about under the olive trees, among the thistles and the stubs of cigarettes left by tourists.

A boy in jeans was pretending to look for something he'd mislaid but was clearly trying to take a little stone from the Acropolis.

The Parthenon rose up, balancing time in its mighty roof, a structure of beauty and energy.

All the emotion Anne had been dealing with so efficiently in the last years was back inside her now, and the ends of her fingertips tingled.

'Pity we didn't discover the head,' said Patrick.

A white butterfly landed on her hand and they watched it for a moment, before it flew off. At her feet the ants scurried around on their separate agenda around the nettles, the litter.

She thought of Paolo, but knew he'd have wanted her to let him go. There was no one who lived more in the present than he did. She thought of her brother too. Maybe he would turn up one day.

'Oh – if it had been there Alexander would have got there first. He's more ruthless than I am. But I don't think it was there,' she said. For a moment she thought of Nick Field's face the last time she saw him, a look that was amused and curious, as if wanting to know what she'd do next.

Athens was beginning to wake up, and the city murmur of traffic rose up. She looked at the houses below, some with red roofs, some with white, and felt again the warmth on her face. The TV aerials glinted on the flat rooftops. For once it seemed that she was nowhere but where she was, in no other time, and that this was what love was, this absolute pleasure in the present.

CHAPTER 62

Patrick and Anne drove out of Edinburgh towards the Golden Retirement Home.

'So Alexander's left the flat?'

'Yes,' said Anne, changing gear. 'He's agreed to sell it to me.'

'He accepts that there was no head?'

'Yes. He doesn't want to be connected with any of this.'

'I spoke to Joseph Fairley. He was terrified of the whole thing too – really scared,' said Patrick.

The sun shone on her hair. It was early spring now and the sky was blue between the small white clouds. Dozens of tiny birds billowed up from a grove of trees.

She turned to him and smiled. Her red hair framed her pale face, with its green eyes and scattering of freckles.

He glanced in front of them, his knees hunched up in the front of the small car, looking as though he were hiding in a cupboard during a game of sardines – the legs covered in corduroy trousers, the soft blue shirt, the wide shoulders. The hired car was a dull red, its finish worn down to the colour of a dull red school eraser.

The sun was bright today and the landscape spread out green and gorgeous.

'I saw Elizabeth in hospital yesterday,' Patrick continued. 'Lily is still determined I should marry her mother.'

'She wants you as a father.'

'Mmm. Elizabeth seemed better – very pink and funny.'

'The doctors say the operation went well,' said Anne, 'though it is early days. It's hard to be sure she'll be okay. Poor Lily. She thinks that somehow if you were to marry Elizabeth she'd be saved.'

'She's not the one I wish to marry,' he said.

Anne put her foot down and the fields flashed by. She could smell his skin, that warm smell, and sense the density of his body. The trees seemed to sparkle, spread out their branches, their leaves, whizz past her.

'Do you really think you're right, we're going to get some news here?' she said.

'We might. I know Mary. You forget. I was in love with her for a while. I know the kind of affection she would inspire. She treated people well. All her letters. All her girlish affection. All her diaries show that. And in turn she was loved by the people of Dirleton and by the people who worked for her.'

'I used to sleep with her, wake with her,' he said. 'I knew what she was like. I knew what kind of

340

person loved her and didn't love her. I knew what effect she made when she walked into the room. She was alive in my head.'

They drove up the road towards the Golden Retirement Home, which rested in the sunshine, its granite touched with a dusty golden light today, and the roof of the conservatory sparkled. The grounds were a brilliant green after the earlier rain. Here and there birds were trying to drag worms out of the moist lawn.

'I was thinking . . . perhaps we should do the book together,' said Patrick slowly.

Anne paused, and looked at him. 'Maybe.'

'I think the servants would have protected her. I think they'd have been protective. They'd have hated her foul kids. Hated Elgin. Not wanted them to have anything of her,' he said.

The car drew up in front of the retirement home and Anne switched off the engine. They paused for a moment. 'Come on,' he said.

Patrick and Anne walked up the main stairs and along a corridor, past lonely rooms, to Nick Field's door.

Anne knocked.

'Go away,' said Nick Field's imperious voice.

'It's Anne. I came to tell you what happened.'

'Go away. I'm not well. Too cold.'

'Please, Nick, just a few moments.'

'Go away,' he said.

'It would be in the newspapers. You'd be famous,' said Patrick.

Anne looked at Patrick sharply.

'Famous,' repeated Patrick.

'Go away,' said Nick Field.

'In *The Times. The Telegraph*,' said Patrick.

'I wish you'd all leave me in peace,' he muttered.

But there was the sound of him shuffling to the door. He opened it and couldn't help smiling at Anne.

'Oh come in,' he said, with a compact smile at Patrick. He shuffled to his armchair and sat in it, with pinched eyes and a grey stubble over his chin.

'Sit down,' he said, nodding at the bed.

'This is my friend Patrick Browning,' said Anne.

'Yes,' said Nick Field, adjusting a photograph of a woman on the side table.

Anne guessed it was his wife.

'You're a relative of Mary's maid, aren't you?' said Patrick. 'It's not many generations, is it? Your great great grandmother. And you come from Dirleton too.'

'So how can I help you?' Nick Field said.

The walls of the room were a pale yellow, with a border of pastel squares round the middle.

'It's a closed community, isn't it?' said Patrick. 'And I suppose at the time they must have felt bad about the way she was treated. Because Mary was a good woman, wasn't she? She gave the people of Dirleton new buildings, a new nave for the church, she was generous and kind, and much loved. Yet her children deserted her.'

'So?' Nick Field shifted around. 'It's nearly time for my tea and biscuits.'

Anne stood up, restlessly, and went to the window.

'So when your family inherited the diaries,' said Patrick, 'they read them, deciphered them, then one of them merely followed the instructions and found the head. The head of Hermes. That's right, isn't it?'

Nick Field's shoulders hunched together and he brought his cardigan more tightly round him. He had long fingers and the veins on the back of his hands stuck up like mountain ranges.

'Your family smuggled it back, did they? You had a great grandfather who was a sailor. Was it him? It was, wasn't it?'

'I want to go down for tea,' said Nick Field. He held on to the worn arms of the chair. 'I don't like to miss our morning break. Nobody does. We have it outside when it's sunny. They move the chairs out.'

Outside, Anne could see the old people moving slowly across the lawn towards a few wicker chairs.

'The head's been in the family ever since,' said Patrick. 'You sent Anne off on a wild goose chase.'

Nick Field shifted a little in his chair.

'I don't want to miss tea,' he said, with a twitch of a smile. He had bushy eyebrows, a little yellow at the edges. 'You can join me if you like. I think you both deserve a cup of tea after your long journey.'

'He's no fool is he, my dear?' said Nick to Anne. 'He has his theories! He at least tries to think. Nonsense of course. But still, he tries.'

'Mr Field,' said Patrick, leaning forward, his hands together, 'this head is priceless. It's not yours to keep. I know it's beautiful. I know all your family loved Mary. I know she was lovable. I know you maybe didn't want everyone to know what she did. But what she did was good. It was huge. It made sense of her whole life. We want to make her memory live forever. We want to restore her reputation. There's no shame in it. On the contrary. Besides, you can't hide it. She wanted it in Greece. She wanted to save it, not to keep it hidden somewhere in Scotland.'

'Who says it is hidden?' said Nick Field suddenly. 'I've always kept it for everyone to see.' He smiled.

Anne was still standing motionless at the window, her hands by her side. She could not believe what she was looking at.

'I'm sorry?' said Patrick.

'It's an outside ornament. I've always kept it for anyone to see. I used to keep it in my garden.' He chuckled. 'Quite a few people have asked where they can get one like that. One like that! I tell them it's unique. I tell them it's from the Parthenon in Athens. They laugh at my joke but they can't stop looking at it. They can't. It's so very beautiful you see. So very beautiful. Made of Pentelic marble by one of the greatest sculptors ever, Pheidias, in the fifth century before Christ!'

He chuckled.

'What you went on was a quest, not a wild goose chase. It was here all along. All along! It was made to be outside! Of course, as an electrician I was able to organise a good security system. And this is better than being eroded by all the pollution and sulphur in Athens and all that cleaning in the British Museum!'

Patrick stood, and joined Anne at the window. Anne had grown very pale. All the tension, the unease, the sense of treachery and distrust, had left her and her body was suddenly completely relaxed, the palm of her hand now resting against the window, as if touching the marble sculpture. Her other hand pushed back the waves of her hair, as if she were unable to cope with anything but what she was watching now. Then she took Patrick's hand, and everything seemed to come together, the past, the present and the future. And Patrick too felt something else, not just release, but a sense of having finally arrived at the place he wanted to be.

His body had never felt huger, more monolithic, as if it could do anything and be anyone. His head burned and he could feel sweat dripping off his forehead, off his back. His shirt stuck to him. But at the same time he felt cool, like the marble, as if he were the god out there on the lawn, looking over his shoulder as he had done for over two thousand five hundred years.

'Fuck,' said Patrick.

Even from there, they could see the wavy hair, the deep sockets for eyes, the strong tilt of the chin, all surrounded by a semi-circle of wicker chairs on which sat various old people sipping coffee and tea.

'They like it,' said Nick. 'It's given a lot of pleasure. And I've kept it safe, as she wanted. I've kept it safe.'

Some daisies grew nearby in the lawn.

Nick stood up, leaning on his stick.

'I can see it from the window. Of course it would look better on the Parthenon. But still. I kept it for her, didn't I? Until the time was right? Until someone finally loved her enough!'

A cloud had passed overhead and the only patch of sunlight shone on the pale head of Hermes in the middle of the lawn, displayed on a black plinth – the marble creamy, the head looking slightly behind, lips parted, crying out.

Patrick and Anne went down together, on to the lawn, where they stopped still for a moment, holding each others' hands, before hurrying forward.